Advance praise for Jim Knipfel's

The Buzzing

"Jim Knipfel has unassumingly been building a body of work which stands right up there with the best writing, comic or otherwise, ever done in America. His memoirs have had all of the virtues of memoir, and none of the sins; and his fiction, along the same line of virtue, is so abidingly confident that his first novel reads like it had been there all the time, waiting for you to pick it up."
—William Monahan, author of *Light House*, *A Trifle*

"*The Buzzing* is just the kind of wild-hair, wise-ass book this country needs right now. We may never see 'the Great American Novel,' but Knipfel's is a true American novel. Bravo!"   —James Taylor, editor of *Shocked and Amazed!*

ALSO BY JIM KNIPFEL

Slackjaw
Quitting the Nairobi Trio

THE BUZZING

A NOVEL

Jim Knipfel

VINTAGE CONTEMPORARIES

Vintage Books

A Division of Random House, Inc.

New York

Library of Congress Cataloging-in-Publication Data
Knipfel, Jim.
     The buzzing : a novel / Jim Knipfel.
       p. cm.
    "A Vintage original."
    ISBN 1-4000-3183-4 (trade paper)
     1. Journalists—Fiction. 2. Conspiracies—Fiction. 3. Paranoia—Patients—
Fiction. I. Title.
  PS3611.N57 B89 2002
  813'.6—dc21
      2002069024

Book design by Debbie Glasserman

www.vintagebooks.com

Printed in the United States of America
10 9 8 7 6 5 4 3 2 1

For Morgan, my muse, with love. She believed.

Never wise up a chump.

—W.C. FIELDS

The Buzzing

Chapter One

"Ya gotta help me out here!"

Oh, Jesus Christ, here we go, Baragon thought, rolling his eyes and fumbling into his limp shirt pocket for the already half-empty pack of cigarettes. *Why don't you people ever call anybody else?*

It was quarter after five on a Thursday afternoon in late February. The day had been a slow one in what was amounting to another slow week. Baragon had been thinking about getting himself together to head out, and he should've known better than to pick up the telephone when it rang. Old reflexes. Still, other old reflexes should have told him that phones that ring when you're about to split work never amount to any good.

Ruby, the receptionist, thought she was doing him a favor by putting these people through. She knew what his job entailed and, if only out of common courtesy, he'd never told her any different. Receptionists, especially in a place like this, had enough to deal with already.

"Uh-huh," Baragon sighed around the cigarette, which

he was trying to light without much success. "And, uh . . . what seems to be . . . y'know . . . the problem?"

The man's voice was ragged and wild, and after that opener, Baragon couldn't help but think this whole scene sounded like the beginning of some lost Hitchcock film. Two hours later, he'd be sitting on a plane to Honduras, to meet up with a man named "Jeb."

"*I* . . ." the voice declared, with a certain dramatic flair, "have been *kidnapped* . . . by the state of Alaska!"

Under most circumstances, Baragon would have hung up after hearing something like that. At least these days he would. But although he desperately needed the drink that was waiting for him at the bar, something in the strangled urgency of the man's voice made him want to hear more, if only out of twisted curiosity. That was an old reflex, too— the very same reflex that had landed him where he was today. Cigarette finally lit, he settled back in his chair and casually checked the tape recorder that was plugged into his phone. Just in case. This was, after all, what he did.

"Uh-huh," Baragon said. "So . . . uh, why would Alaska want to kidnap you?—Wait, before you answer that—why don't you take a deep breath and start from the very beginning?"

The man paused—Baragon could actually hear him inhale—then he started again. "First they raped my wife—"

"The state of *Alaska* did."

"Yeah. Yeah. Then they tried to blame me for it."

"Uh-huh."

"And then they blew up the rest of my family with a car bomb in Colorado. This was all back about seven years ago."

"Wow." Baragon looked around his desk for the ashtray, couldn't find it, and decided to use his coffee mug instead, hoping he would remember to wash it out first thing tomorrow morning.

"Then they arrested me for *that*, too."

"Alaska did."

"Uh-huh."

From the noises around him, it was obvious that the man was in some public place. Whether it was a madhouse, a prison, or a train station was unclear.

"So, tell me, uh, sir . . ." (always be formal and polite—he was usually tempted to call these people "bub" or "chum," but figured they had enough trouble as it was, without having to figure out how they'd ended up in a comic book) ". . . why, exactly, are you calling here to tell *me* all this?"

"Because you're the only one who can help me. My wife, after all this first happened, she wrote you a bunch of letters—"

"Wait—this all took place in Alaska and Colorado, but your wife wrote letters . . . to me?" Baragon began scrolling back through all the crazed, cramped, schizoid letters he'd received over the years but couldn't remember anything that sounded like this.

"No, Alaska only came in later."

"When they attacked your wife. That was in Alaska?"

"No, that was in California."

"So . . . Alaskans attacked your wife in California, blew up the rest of your family in Colorado, kidnapped you, and now you're calling me for help because your wife says she wrote me some letters."

"Yeah."

"Okay then." Baragon dropped the half-finished cigarette in the coffee mug and lit up another. It sounded like this was going to take a while. He reached over and turned on the tape recorder. The small red light glowed, and the tiny wheels began to rotate. It was illegal in New York to tape a phone call when one party was unaware they were being recorded, but there you have it. "So long as we're on the same page here. Why do you think she—your wife, that is—wrote, uh, to me?"

"Because she knew you had all the right political connections."

"Well, that much is true." Baragon shrugged his shoulders to no one in particular. For all the years he'd spent in this racket, he'd never once spoken to an actual politician. A few flunkies here and there, but that was all. It was a business he had no interest in.

"Yeah, well, see?" the man went on. "I need you guys to help me out. They're tryin' to pin all this shit on me—"

"When, all the while, it was Alaska that was doing it."

"Yeah, right, and then I heard that you were looking for me."

"You heard that *I* was looking for *you*?"

"Yeah."

"But this is the first I'm hearing of any of this—I don't even know what the hell your name is."

The man took another deep breath. "My name's Nick Carter, and I really don't have much time—"

"And where are you calling from, uh, Mr. Carter?"

"Last I knew I was in Barrow. It's . . . hard to tell, though—there are no windows in here. They could be moving me while I'm asleep and I'd never know it."

"Barrow . . ." Baragon racked his brain, if leisurely. "You mean Point Barrow? That in Alaska?"

"Yeah—way north. Look—you gotta get me outta here—They're—" Then Carter yelped—it sounded as if he were being dragged away from the phone by several men while one of them was stomping on his feet.

"Uuhhh . . . Mr. Carter?" Baragon asked pointlessly.

Suddenly there was another voice on the line, speaking in abrupt, indecipherable tones. It certainly wasn't English—or any other language Baragon recognized offhand. Too many rapid-fire vowels and syllables. Then the line went dead.

Baragon pulled the phone away from his ear, looked at it, shrugged again, then hung up.

Just as well, he thought, *that was starting to get boring*. He clicked off the tape recorder and hit the rewind button, then stopped it, hit play, and listened to the voice at the end once again. It sure wasn't English—but what was it? Inuit? Damned if Baragon knew. Gibberish of some sort.

He hit the stop button and set the tape recorder back where it had been, primed and ready for the next big scoop.

Roscoe Baragon had been losing his hair for the last fifteen years. In that same time period, he'd also put on about forty-five pounds. Way he liked to figure it, he actually had the same amount of hair he always had, but as his body expanded, he was simply growing out of it, the same way he grew out of most of his shirts.

For that same time period, he had been sitting at the same desk, with the same phone, in the same little *New York Sentinel* newsroom, surrounded by five other desks, with identical phones and identical computers. Baragon's desk was always the sloppiest of the lot, littered with stray piles of gray ash and teetering mountains of folders and papers he'd long since forgotten about. The beige keys on his computer keyboard had, over the years, greased over black.

The other desks in the office had been occupied by an ever-changing collection of eager, bright-eyed young hotshots, most with brand-spanking-new journalism degrees, and most about half his age. Few of them stayed at the *Sentinel* longer than a year. Some of them—the more greedily ambitious of the bunch—had been snatched up by the *Post* or the *Times* or one of the glossy newsweeklies. A couple of the particularly chirpy, stupid ones had moved on to local television. Others had been promoted to private offices. As each one left the small newsroom, his or her desk was refilled in a matter of days with someone else who fit the same description. Most of the time it didn't bother Baragon as much as it could have. He'd already had his glory years and was satisfied with where he'd ended up. He didn't care for all the headaches that came with a private office or a big-wig editorial position—the added responsibilities and all that extra money. Besides, these days, none of the other dailies or glossies were exactly going to any great lengths to steal him, the way they once had. *Fuck 'em.* Here he could come and go pretty much as he pleased, cover the stories he wanted to cover. He could dress the way he liked and be as cranky as he cared to be. There was nobody (well, almost nobody) he had to answer to. He was forty-two now, and no longer had the energy, the drive, or the cold viciousness it took to get ahead in this business.

The most important thing about the job, Baragon felt, was the fact that he was working in what he assumed was the last office space in New York City in which he would be allowed to smoke at his desk. To him, that meant more than money, prestige, respect, any of it.

He shut off his computer, pulled his stained and mildly rank trench coat on over his stained and mildly rank open-collared blue shirt (he'd never bothered much with ties), and stepped out of the newsroom without saying a word to the four other people who remained sitting in front of their terminals, frantically tapping away at their keyboards, all of them so deadly serious, all of them certain that this was it—*this* was the story that was going to snag them that Pulitzer and get them the hell out of this dump.

From the third office he passed on his way down the carpeted hallway, Baragon heard a high-pitched voice bellow: "Hey *you! Scoop! Get in here!*" It was too piercing to be considered either lighthearted or threatening.

Baragon stopped short, closed his eyes, then slowly turned around. There were clearly evil forces at work here—forces that were doing everything in their power to prevent him from reaching the bar that night. "What is it, Ed?" he sighed. He didn't need this right now, he was in no mood, but he stepped into the small office anyway.

"Baragon, what the hell am I reading here?"

Ed Montgomery was a living caricature of a major metropolitan newspaper's editor, and Baragon always thought that was how Ed wanted it to be. Sleeves rolled up, tie undone, a porcine face that grew a magnificent shade of magenta whenever he got angry—and he was almost always angry. Montgomery was ten years Baragon's junior, but no longer looked it. He had been one of those bright-eyed kids back in the newsroom, once. Baragon remembered how excited Montgomery became the first time he got an actual interview with an actual city official. It was, as it turned out, the sanitation commissioner, concerning the burning issue of "dead animal pickup."

As a result, Baragon had a hard time taking his act too seriously. He'd been watching Montgomery practice and refine it from the moment he got the promotion.

"Not real sure, Ed—you, uh . . . you wanna give me a hint? Or you want me to read it aloud to you?"

"Cut the bullshit, Baragon—" Montgomery said, gesturing toward his computer screen. "I'm talking about this . . . *thing* you turned in to me this morning."

"Yeah?" To be honest, Baragon didn't really remember all that much about the story he'd turned in that morning. He leaned against the door frame and waited for Montgomery to fill him in.

"'Voodoo Curse Haunts Natural History Museum'? C'mon, Baragon—"

"So? What about it?" Baragon looked bored because he knew what was coming. He knew what was coming because it was the exact same thing that happened every time he turned in a story.

"*Shit*, Roscoe—why do you insist on doing this to me? Do you hate me?"

"Maybe, uh, Ed, if you explain what the problem is, I could try to help you out. Is it just the headline?" Baragon tried to put on his most innocent face, but he just ended up looking a little nauseous.

"First of all, there *is no* voodoo curse on the Museum of Natural Goddamn History."

"That's not what I heard."

"Yeah?" Ed's face was growing darker. One of these days, if he was lucky, Baragon would be on hand when it finally exploded. Now, *that* would be something to see. "And where'd you hear that?"

"Have you read anything beyond the headline?"

"Believe it or not, I have. I shouldn't have—I didn't really *need* to—but I have."

"So you see the sources are all laid out very clearly."

"*Sources*. Baragon, some homeless guy calling himself 'Chief Tokesalot,' who's camped out in the park across the street from the museum, is not a source. Christ, you've been in this business how long now?"

"Longer than you, Ed, which is kind of sad—but look— the museum's got a new show of Haitian artifacts—pots and crap like that. And this guy was from Haiti, and he was pretty pissed about it."

"That isn't a source."

"He was pretty pissed about it. Y'know, the whole 'stealing his heritage' business. And he knows there's a curse because he's the one who put it there. That's about as good a source as you're gonna get."

Montgomery closed his eyes and pinched the bridge of his nose, just like world-weary editors are supposed to in situations like this.

"Roscoe, look—in your next-to-last paragraph," he tapped the screen, "you say here that there were zombies wandering around loose in the museum."

"Well, I dunno—they sure looked like zombies to me."

"'Looked like.' But you don't say 'looked like' in the story, do you?—here you say they were zombies. Simple as that. There's no 'looked like' about it."

"I—"

"No. Just—please—no more. Don't say any more. We aren't going to discuss this any further. There's no point. First thing tomorrow, you can either give me a real story about the goddamned exhibit—"

"Which'll sound like the same press release stories you'll be reading in every other daily—" Baragon interrupted, "—except that it'll be a day later—"

"Roscoe, have a seat."

"Ed, look, I'd really love to chat—but my bartender's expecting me. If I'm not there by six, he tends to panic and call Central Booking. Then the hospitals."

"Well, I hope he's smart enough to try Bellevue first— that might save him a lot of time someday. Take a seat."

Baragon sighed again, looked at his watch, and sat down. He was too old for this kind of nonsense. Especially from a youngster.

Montgomery cleared his throat. "Baragon, number one, this paper isn't a tabloid, but sometimes—no, make that most of the time—I think you'd be much happier writing for one. Have you ever considered moving to Florida? I've been there. It's nice. Lantana's a real nice little town. Did you know that every year they put up the biggest Christmas tree in the world? Everybody comes to see it."

"Yeah . . . Yeah, Ed, I did know that. But you know, I've never been that big a fan of Christmas. Or Florida."

Montgomery glared at him. He'd about had it. "I don't know why I don't just fire you, Baragon. In fact, when I first moved into this office six years ago, I don't know why my first order of business wasn't to just can you right then. Before I even turned this goddamn computer on or sharpened any pencils or made sure the phone worked, I should've just set my boxes down, called you in here, and *fired* you."

"Yeah, I know that, Ed. You probably should have, for both our sakes. But here we are."

"I can't go through this with you every single week anymore."

"Yeah, Ed, well—I think you're gonna have to come to realize one of these days that this town is actually a lot weirder than you'd like to believe it is. That's what I write about. New York sure as hell ain't—where is it you're from again? Apple Creek?"

"Shut up, Roscoe," Montgomery groaned, exasperated. "—the thing *you're* going to have to come to realize is that this town isn't *nearly* as weird as *you'd* like to think it is. It's not crawling with monsters and curses and whatever."

"Beg to differ with you there, Ed."

Montgomery shook his head, almost sadly, mercifully silent for a bit. "What ever happened to you? I mean, what went wrong? Something, somewhere, went wrong with you."

"We've had this discussion before."

"Yeah, but I just like to check every once in a while, see if you've found an answer yet. I mean—when I first came here ten years ago, you were killer. You were everybody's hero, what we all wanted to be—covering Berlin, Beijing, the riots—"

"—And now I handle the Kook Beat."

"But the *Sentinel* never *had* a Kook Beat until you started it—"

"—No New York daily did. Way I see it, I'm filling a gap."

Montgomery closed his eyes again. "You know, Jameson thought you were setting up something really big when you started turning in these crazy fucking stories. He thought you were really onto something. But you weren't. They were just crazy fucking stories about insane people, that's all. And after a while, he was just afraid of you. I think you're the reason he had that heart attack—*and* that stroke."

"Just one of those things that happened, I guess. Got you your job, though, didn't it?" He glanced at his watch.

"Baragon, look—you're tired, I'm tired—"

"I'm not all that tired, really. Just bored. And late." He looked at his watch again. "Damn cops'll be there before I am."

"Then fine." Montgomery turned back to his computer. "Go. If I have a new story waiting for me when I get in tomorrow morning, I'll consider it. One with a few facts this time. And if I don't have a new story waiting, well—"

"Yeah, fine," Baragon said. He stood and left the office, knowing full well there would be no new story tomorrow morning. He also knew that the story he turned in that morning would run pretty much as it stood—minus that "zombie" paragraph—if only to fill the space set aside for it.

Baragon rode the elevator to the ground floor, then stepped outside into the chilly late-winter rain. Not one to believe in the value of umbrellas, he lowered his head in a defensive move—both against the rain as well as those people who did believe in umbrellas—and crossed Broadway with a pack of other grumbling, half-dead wage slaves just getting out of work, then slowly strolled half a block up the street toward the subway. The streetlights and the storefront neon reflected off the sidewalks, the asphalt, and the passing cars.

Despite his size, he had a loose-limbed, lanky walk, left over from when he was a skinny, loose-limbed youth. Nowadays, however, it left him looking like an uncomfortable alien trapped in a strange, oversized body—the arms and legs dangling off his thick torso as if they were simply along for the ride.

Other commuters, anxious to escape the rain and get home, streamed past him as he descended the steps toward the platform.

He was never a big fan of the Thirty-fourth Street station. First, given its location below Macy's, it was always crowded, and crowds made him nervous. More disturbing, though, was that after you got through the turnstiles, you had to maneuver through a maze of randomly placed mirrored pillars. He could never figure out why the pillars were mirrored. Probably to confuse the unwary, and him.

Another thing about that station—even though the upper level was brightly lit, clean and mirrored, once you got down to the train platforms themselves, it was filthy and dim and stank of piss. Having stood on that platform nearly every day for the past fifteen years, however, he barely noticed anymore.

Ten minutes later, he crammed himself, along with several dozen others, onto an already-packed downtown train. Most of his fellow passengers, as they could manage it, were paging through the *Times* or the *Daily News* or the *Post*. Rarely, if ever, did he see anyone reading the *Sentinel*. When he did, it always sent a small quiver of shame through his guts.

Thing'd sell better if it were a tabloid, he thought.

Chapter Two

Baragon, as much as he could, avoided those bars where journalists were known to hang out. After he left the office at night, journalism was the last thing he wanted to hear about.

Fact of the matter was, he tried to avoid bars where anyone at all hung out. That's why every night he met his friend Emily at Jack's, over off Second Avenue, on Tenth Street. It was a bit of a trip for him every night, but that was okay. There were several other bars in the mostly residential neighborhood—lively places full of young, happy people who enjoyed their popular music, their Jell-O shooters, and the company of others like themselves. But Jack's, with no sign out front, no clear indication that it was even a bar—just a darkened recessed doorway off a narrow sidewalk—was rarely anything more than empty, except for Emily, Baragon, and Jack. Sometimes Baragon wondered why the place was so empty—and how it stayed in business—but he never dared ask. If, for some reason, word ever got around and Jack's became popular—and given the nature of this town, it would, someday—they'd have to find another spot. It had happened before.

He was with bars the same way he was with jobs, and homes and people. He'd find one he was comfortable with, settle in, and stay there until something forced him to move on. It was easier that way. That's why he'd been at the *Sentinel*—and in his shabby Brooklyn apartment—for a decade and a half.

He walked down two steps and pushed the door open, brushed the rain off his coat, and took a quick look around in the smoky gloom. Even when the place was empty, it was smoke-filled—something Baragon couldn't quite understand but appreciated nonetheless.

Jack's was a small, narrow tavern—with ten stools along the wooden bar and four small tables shoved up along the opposite wall. Bathroom in the back. There was no jukebox, no pool table, no darts, nothing by means of decoration much beyond the liquor license hanging on the wall above the cash register. Just glasses, alcohol, ashtrays, and a place to sit. Jack himself—a portly, bearded, quiet man with a ponytail—decided what his patrons would listen to (he was partial to visually impaired bluesmen—Blind Willie Johnson, Blind Willie McTell, Blind Lemon Jefferson, and the like) and kept the volume down.

It was all about as perfect as any bar Baragon had ever found. He glanced around for Emily—it was never that hard to find her in here—and hoisted himself onto the stool next to hers.

"Hey, doll."

"You're a little late," she said as Baragon caught Jack's eye. Jack knew what he wanted. "Jack hasn't started making calls yet, but I was getting worried. Everything go okay?"

"Ahh, I was on my way out when I got a call from some guy who'd been kidnapped by the state of Alaska."

"Now, *there's* one I haven't heard before."

"Yeah, but he got pretty dull pretty fast. Then Montgomery, well . . . he wanted to have a little chat."

"Another one?"

"Well, more like the same one, again."

"What'd you do this time?"

"What do I ever do? Gave him a story. He didn't care much for it."

"This was Chief Tokesalot?"

"Mm-hmm."

"Aww, Rosk," she said, with something in her voice that wasn't frustration so much as mild concern. "You know I'm on your side here—but sometimes I gotta wonder if you aren't just trying—just a little bit—to get yourself fired. You know how he's going to respond to things like that."

Jack brought Baragon's beer and picked up the bill that was lying on the bar. Jack never said too much, which was another reason he liked it here. Brings you the beer, takes your money, knows when to knock you, and that was pretty much it. By the time Baragon's change arrived, his beer was already half gone.

"I'm not trying to get myself fired."

"Maybe not consciously—*but*—have you ever considered, maybe, giving Montgomery something that's not, you know, unbelievable and nuts? You might give him a heart attack if you did that. Think about it."

"Aww, Em," Roscoe said, smiling sadly, not feeling the alcohol yet. "Everything's unbelievable and nuts if you think about it. Most journalists these days just get the news they report from, y'know, other journalists. In the end, what we call 'the news' has become a kind of magical realism—stop me if you've heard this lecture before—"

(She had, so often that she could recite it herself by now, but she let him go on anyway, figuring it was what he needed to do.)

"—presented in this format that people have been told to accept as true. Man in Wyoming kidnaps little boys, see, and dangles them from his kitchen ceiling while he jacks off, then he eats a couple of them. Or the stock market crashes. Or some war breaks out in some country that no one's ever heard of. Or, in today's case, there's a voodoo spell cast on the Museum of Natural History. It's all the same damn thing."

"Yeah, but people believe in the stock market. Nobody believes in voodoo curses. At least not here."

"Chief Tokesalot does. And I can take you to a little shop around the block from my place where they do, too. Sell roots and powders and shit. Maybe more people should believe."

"Difference is, though, that *you* don't believe it. Not really. But you still pretend that you do. At least around the office, and in your stories."

"Oh, I never say that I do—"

"I know that, and you know that, but—"

"Yeah, well." Baragon saw that Emily's glass was empty, drained his own, caught Jack's eye, and raised two fingers.

"It's just the way things work," he continued. "Hollywood makes a movie about some historical event—Battle of the Bulge, whatever—and to a huge majority of people, that becomes history, see? The movie—shit, this is such old news—becomes reality. In the end, there's no real difference between *Destroy All Monsters* and some drought in California."

Baragon had heard himself pontificate on these matters too many times. He wanted to talk about something else. "So how was your day?" he asked. Baragon had long been under the impression that Ms. Emily Roschen was far too good-looking to work at the morgue. He could never tell her that, of course—that would make things weird. Emily was his best friend and had been so for the past three years. One of his only friends, actually. His closest confidante. Baragon, not being very good at the whole "romance" thing—having actually tried it a few times when he was younger, with disastrous results—didn't want to blow it here. She was too important to him.

"Oh, it was fine, no major traumas. Pretty slow, actually."

"Ahh, a slow day for death," Baragon mused.

"There's a title for something," she said.

Emily looked younger than her thirty-six years, with long, thick black hair she usually kept up, and luminous, pale blue eyes that would stop most men dead in their tracks. Her smile was bright, though her job gave her little reason to smile.

She'd started working as a pathologist at New York's Medical Examiner's Office straight out of med school, five years earlier. In those years, she'd been witness to the aftereffects of nearly every inconceivably dreadful thing that could happen to the human body—from gunshot wounds to strangled babies to people who had been floating in the Hudson River for three weeks. Virtually everyone in the city who died from unnatural causes eventually appeared on her gurney.

He had met Emily on Christmas Eve three years ago at an otherwise-empty Jack's. Normally he didn't like talking to strangers in bars, but hell, it was Christmas Eve. He had no big plans, no parties he'd been invited to. His parents were both long gone, so he had no family obligations to worry about anymore. She didn't seem to be in any big rush to get anyplace, either, so without making a big deal out of it, hoping it would be clear that he wasn't trying to pick her up, he'd said hello. Under normal circumstances, he'd never bother speaking to someone who looked like she did, slob that he was, but these weren't normal circumstances, and he felt it would seem strange—even rude—not to.

Ms. Roschen, he discovered an hour and three beers after saying hello, had spent her entire life in New York. She was born in the Bronx but grew up on the Lower East Side. Her mother had taught biology at NYU, and her father had worked for the Transit Authority until he died of a heart attack when she was sixteen. Baragon also discovered that she preferred jazz standards from the twenties and thirties, accordion music, Hitchcock, and lowbrow comedy films.

Well, that's all a good sign, he thought. He knew he couldn't well expect her to be able to recite every line of dialogue from every film Klaus Kinski ever appeared in (even those dreadful Czechoslovakian Westerns), but at least she knew how to laugh. Better still, she hadn't laughed at him when he'd first said hello.

His eyes widened when he first found out where she worked, but he thought he played it cool. Still, it took him a few weeks, after running into her at Jack's a few more times, to learn that it would be easier on everyone if he kept his morbid curiosity in check around her. That he could usually do that was one of the reasons she liked him. Whenever he tried to pry for too many details about the goings-on at the morgue, she'd change the subject.

She never talked about her work much—like Baragon, she preferred to leave it behind her at the end of the day—but with him, she knew she could if she wanted to. He'd listen, he'd get it, and he could usually make her laugh about it in the end. As he explained on a couple of occasions, they were pretty much in the same business, analyzing the rotten things that can happen to people.

She did worry occasionally when she saw that strange light flicker in his eyes when he was looking at her—it was almost a leer—but she was relieved that he'd never tried to go any further. She was comfortable with things the way they were. No need to complicate them.

.   .   .

"But anyway," she continued, "how'd things end up with Montgomery? He threaten to fire you again?"

"Same as every day," Baragon said. "But I'll be going back in tomorrow."

"And doing a story about some guy who says he was kidnapped by the state of Alaska?"

"I doubt it. I wasn't really able to get too much out of him before we were disconnected."

"You hung up on him?"

"Naah, we just got cut off. No big loss. Story wasn't going much of anywhere. But I'm sure there'll be another one tomorrow."

She took a drink and shook her head. She knew he was right. "How the hell do all these people find you?"

It was a question he'd asked himself at least once a week for the past few years. "Sometimes I wonder that myself. When I was a kid and it happened—when the crazies latched on to me—you know, I thought it was because my dentist had implanted some sort of transmitter in my jaw when he removed my wisdom teeth."

"Mm-hmm. Now you're sounding like one of them."

"But now, I guess it just makes sense. You put your name on enough stories about enough insane people over the years, you don't make fun of them too much—at least not in any obvious way—just let them talk without editorializing, and I guess word gets around." He reached for a cigarette, surprised at himself for not having done that already since he sat down. Or maybe he had. He looked at the ashtray. Nope. Empty. He stuck the cigarette in his mouth, lit it, and inhaled. "Bully for me."

"Rosk—?" she began, which is how she always began when she was trying to be gentle but firm, "—you ever miss being, you know, a real journalist?"

He felt his mood—not exactly jovial to begin with—slip a

notch. He'd been through this conversation, too, with Emily, as well as a few dozen other people. He knew she wasn't trying to be mean. Still, it was the Nice Version of his run-in with Montgomery.

"I mean," she went on, "you used to travel, get out there, really see these things as they happened. It must've been exciting."

"Oh, I suppose, for a young man, sure. But now—" he said. "Nobody really does that too much anymore. No budget for it. Besides—who needs to go flying down to Paraguay to cover some, y'know, coup or something when you can find out everything you need on that fabulous Internet business?"

"I know you're joking."

"Yeah, well, these fucking kids in the office don't. Did I tell you that last week the server went down and I had to show one how to use a phone book? A goddamn *phone book*. He'd never used one of those before. Then I had to explain to another one that yes, indeed, we didn't just fight Nazis during World War II. There were a few other folks involved as well. Fuckin' incredible."

"Back to the point, though—you know what I mean."

He tapped the smoke in the ashtray and looked at his beer, his mood continuing to slip. "Yeah, I know what you mean. I try not to think about it. I'm just too damn tired, Em. That's all. I get my check, and I got my health insurance. I get by. I don't need much. Really. You know me well enough to know that."

She gave his knee a sad squeeze, and he ground his cigarette out.

"Hey, what more do I really need now? I got you," he said, "and I got the bar—"

"And you got your movies."

He dropped his head, embarrassed. "Yeah . . . I got the movies," he said quietly.

"Now stop that," she told him. "There's nothing to feel bad about if they make you happy."

His parents had taken him to see his first movie (a revival of *Pickup on South Street*) when he was seven years old, and in a way, he'd never left the theater since, except to go to the bathroom.

When he was younger, the theaters were his cathedrals. Ornate ceilings, heavy velvet curtains rippling down the walls, the reverent hush as the lights began to dim. That first electric crackle of the sound system kicking in became his call to service, the warm smell of buttered popcorn his incense, the closing credits his benediction.

He'd gone to the movies as often as possible after that first one. At first, his father would take him, but after he turned twelve, he usually went alone. You get someone else there sitting next to you, they'll want to make comments, or ask questions, or share the popcorn. It was almost blasphemous to him. Roscoe was there to worship. Of course, other people had never been that much of an issue. Given that he spent all his free time at the movies, he never really had any close friends.

This concerned his parents some. There was, after all, a question of his social development. Roscoe wasn't interested in team sports, or school clubs, or in playing with the neighborhood kids. All he ever wanted to do was go to the movies. When he wasn't actually at the movies, he was talking about what he'd seen most recently or deciding what he wanted to see next.

They tried making quiet suggestions now and again that he invite someone from school along, or perhaps that he might try doing something outdoors for once, but it seemed futile. When it was clear that his grades weren't suffering because of it, that he was still doing his chores around the house and that he wasn't running with a tough crowd, they decided that things could be worse and stopped bugging him about it. He knew they would.

There weren't many theaters in the small northern Minnesota town where he grew up—but they satisfied him. As he got older, a trip to the Cities on a Saturday afternoon for the daylong triple bills at the Orpheum became a regular part of his schedule. With the arrival of the megacineplexes and the ensuing death of the cathedral theaters, he took to gathering videotapes and staying home. Going to a megacineplex was like trying to watch a movie on a crowded bus in a traffic jam. He could've done it in an emergency—he'd just rather not.

He sometimes thought it was silly and childish for a man in his forties to spend so much time, still, watching movies—but he preferred the reality of gangsters and murderers and monsters to the insipid, banal one he had to deal with at the office.

Maybe that explained why he had gravitated toward the Kook Beat. Paranoid schizophrenics were living in their own personal horror films. They existed every day in a world filled with a menace the rest of us never saw. Until, of course, it was too late. He sometimes thought these people might be on to something.

"So what are you watching this week?" Emily asked, sensing his growing melancholy, thinking it might be best to change the subject.

He sighed, looked up, took another drink, then reached for another smoke. "*H-Man*," he confessed, almost apologetically.

"I'm afraid I don't know it."

"Ehh. Not too many people do. Odd little Japanese

gangster-monster picture. The monster's a kind of radioactive slime that liquefies people."

"Ahh."

"Man, I need another drink. How are you doing?"

"Little dry."

Roscoe raised two fingers Jack's way again.

Three hours later, he unlocked the door to his small Brooklyn apartment. He hung his coat on the wooden hook by the
door and checked his answering machine to discover, much
to his relief, that there were no messages. Messages at home
always made him nervous. Even though it was unlisted, too
many people had gotten hold of his number.

Baragon lived on the third floor of a brownstone on the
raggedy western edges of Park Slope. It was considered an
upscale neighborhood by Brooklyn standards, and he supposed most of it was, but the gentrification that had started
creeping into the area a decade earlier had yet to touch his
block. Where he was, the park across the street was still
home to dealers and two-buck chippies every night, the
local bars still home to thugs, and the shop owners weren't
very nice to you if you didn't speak Spanish. He could
understand that. He'd probably feel the same way if his family had been there for generations, only to see the small
bodegas and fish stores forced out by espresso bars and holis-
tic pet supply shops.

His apartment was a narrow one-bedroom affair, with tile
floors and not a single piece of comfortable furniture. The
walls were mostly bare, except for a small black-and-white
photograph of Emily he'd taken down at Coney two years ago.

His fat, six-toed tabby, Hedora, clicked into the kitchen
and meeped at him. Roscoe patted the tabletop, and the cat
leaped up with a grunt. Roscoe scratched behind the cat's

ears and down his back. He poured some food in Hedora's bowl and wondered what he might want to eat himself.

There wasn't that much to choose from—so, as usual, he made a cheese sandwich, opened another beer, and carried them into the living room on a cutting board. He sat down on the battered, well-worn couch in front of the television. He flipped through all the channels but found nothing. He refused to watch the television news anymore.

Instead, as he did nearly every night, he picked up a videotape and slid it into the machine. He was getting tired of *H-Man*, so he grabbed an unmarked tape. He had hundreds of movies piled on the bookshelves and on the floor, and he'd seen all of them several times. The unmarked ones at least had the element of surprise going for them.

He sat back down on the couch and took a swallow from the beer while he waited for the opening credits to come up.

What appeared on the screen instead was an image of a dwarf on a talk show stage, singing her little heart out. Some sort of nondenominational inspirational song.

Why is it, he wondered, *that dwarfs nowadays never sing anything but inspirational songs?*

With a thick sigh, he stood again, stopped the tape, popped it out, and replaced it with the next unlabeled cassette on the stack.

Just not in the mood for singing dwarfs tonight.

He waited by the machine, finger poised on the eject button, but when it became clear it was a real movie, he relaxed. Whatever it was, it would be fine. A damn sight better than dwarfs.

The logo at the beginning was a good sign. After another thirty seconds, he realized he was watching *War of the Gargantuas*. A cheap, shaky bootleg he'd paid far too much money for, embarrassingly enough, at a horror movie convention at a Midtown hotel seven years ago.

War of the Gargantuas had been released in 1966 by Toho Company, Ltd., ostensibly as the sequel to the deceptively titled *Frankenstein Conquers the World*. Since the mid-fifties, while Japan was still rebuilding after the war, Toho was the production outfit responsible for giving the world Godzilla, Mothra, Rodan, King Ghidorah, Gamerah—most every giant radioactive Japanese monster you could name. You think "Japanese monster movies" (or, in Japanese, *kaiju eiga*), you think "Toho." The Gargantuas in question here were two enormous apelike creatures, one brown, one green, who, as the title implied, beat the crap out of each other.

Good, he thought. *This one always cheers me up. Especially that nightclub scene.* He always hummed along with the song.

Chapter Three

Baragon was sitting in a molded plastic chair at a cafeteria table on the ground floor of a solid, innocuous four-story redbrick building on West Fifty-second Street. There was one window in the room, small, clouded with grime and covered with a thick iron mesh that allowed some light in, but not much.

Across from him sat a thin black man with closely cropped gray hair. His name was Abraham Campbell. He was fifty-three years old, and as he spoke, his eyes never stopped darting around the otherwise empty room. Campbell was on his third cigarette already and the interview had barely begun.

"So, uh, Mr. Campbell," Baragon ventured—slowly and simply, as was usually best in cases like this. "Why don't you tell me how you ended up here?"

There was a brief pause, eyes roving, then the man said, "From the military experiences." The words came out in tones that were clipped and precise. Confident teetering on arrogant. It sounded to Baragon like Campbell was dropping his voice an octave or two in an effort to be taken more seriously. "When I got out of the service five years ago, I went to an old soldiers' home in Orange County because the wife didn't want me to come home."

"Okay."

"But I *did* come home anyway. We had an argument, and one of her boyfriends attempted to kill me. And I got in trouble for it, as I defended myself."

Oh, here we go. "Yes?"

"Then I was told by the military—or so they tell me—I never received a communication. I wrote a letter to Cincinnati, Ohio—Disabled American Veterans. I'm one-*hundred*-percent disabled because of an injury I received while serving the government, even though it happened in Manhattan, see?"

"I'm, uh—I'm not really sure that I do, uhh," Baragon admitted. "What happened?"

"I got shot in the head."

Bingo, if it's true, Baragon thought, though what he actually said in response to that was "Oh."

"It was done by a police officer—or someone wearing a blue uniform—and the only excuse that I could render was that it was a robbery. I had cash money on me at the time. Some. It didn't seem to be much for an officer to waste his time or his job or risk his neck that he was gonna get *caught*, see? But he wasn't *gonna* get caught."

Shit, and there it went. Back up and try again . . . Keep it simple. "So tell me, Mr. Campbell—you—you say this happened after you got out of the military. . . . What branch were you in?"

"Marine Corps and Navy," he said, sitting up a little straighter. "The Navy-Marine Corps. Marine Corps's a branch of the Navy, see? So I retired, but Disabled American Veterans said they weren't going to retire me because I was having family troubles. The family claimed to be Soviet on one side and *also* claimed to be Seatopian on the other side—"

Oh, Christ.

"—This was supposed to be a Catholic town, right? The name was *Abraham*. It's a biblical term. And they were disrespecting the *Bible*. I did contact the pope of Rome and I asked him, 'May I?' I never received a communication from him."

Well, there's a surprise, Baragon thought. *Jesus, this is going to be one long fucking afternoon.* He tried to sneak a glance at his watch. Campbell went for another cigarette. Baragon ached for one of his own—but Campbell had asked him not to smoke.

"Okay—" Baragon said, tempted to simply gather his things together at that point and leave, but knowing that frustrating as this was, it would keep him out of the office for a few hours—and there was something to be said for that. "Let's back up one more time—you still haven't explained to me how you ended up here. In this place. This place right here." Baragon gestured at the walls to try to drive the point home to a man who was either clearly out of his skull or doing a damn fine job of faking it.

Campbell went on, and Baragon had the impression that he would've received the same answer had he asked what was on the lunch menu.

"I can't afford a cooperative apartment or a condominium," he said. "And don't need to be housed as a mental patient or a roomer in a place where they have what you call SRO."

"Single Room Occupancy."

"Yeahyeahyeah—bad things happen in those places. But I *can* afford an apartment, you see. And they should have never placed me on medication as a disabled veteran because

I complained about it so many times. *Now*, it's a criminal offense if you ask me."

"A lot of people would agree with you there," Baragon offered, attempting to be friendly, though he wasn't exactly sure what the hell Campbell was talking about.

"Who says you're a mental patient? The *psychiatrist* does. Well, that's bad news. Okay then. I'm on the right track. Even if I'm on the *wrong* track I'm on the right track."

That you are, chief. "Are you on some medication now, uh, Mr. Campbell?"

"I'm also a licensed private investigator. I have my identification."

Guess that answers that. With some difficulty, Campbell began tugging at the thin chain around his neck. At the end of the chain was a wallet, which he opened to display a badge—the kind of shiny plastic "private investigator" badge you used to be able to buy at most of the souvenir stands around Times Square. That is, until they were declared illegal, as a result of people like Mr. Campbell.

"Well, I'll be," Baragon said, wondering why they let him hang on to a wallet, let alone one complete with a long chain and a fake badge. "Look at that."

"I registered with the Department of Mental Hygiene at one time or another. In Albany. I have an English masters . . . a bachelor in English. And then I became a state psychologist *and* psychiatrist for the city of New York. Even though the state didn't employ me as a psychiatrist, I was employed as a state police captain. Sing Sing prison, you know? I wasn't employed as a doctor, even though by the city Department of Mental Hygiene I was qualified. *And* I went to the New York City Board of Health, back after I retired from the military service. A technical adviser, because there was a tuberculosis epidemic going on. See what I'm sayin'?"

This is absolutely pointless. There was a time, back in the first months after he started working the Kook Beat for the *Sentinel,* when Baragon firmly believed that there was always a kernel of truth to be found in what these nutjobs were saying. They were talking about something real, something they had seen or experienced, but the language got in the way. Still, he thought, if you listened carefully enough, if you sifted through all the rubbish, you could uncover what that truth was. He didn't believe that anymore. Most of the time, it was just rubbish.

". . . but any—*any*—how would you say?—deterrent that the psychiatrist might have placed in mind to keep me from attacking another patient, to keep me from attacking his staff?—he could be considered correct in doing it. Even if there's *candy* as a constant reminder"—Campbell's voice cracked on the word *candy*—"but there's nothing mentally wrong with me."

Yeah, buddy, you're right as rain. "Have you ever, uh, tried to attack anyone while you've been here?" *Might as well ask.*

"No I don't."

"Well that's good." *Maybe the office would be better after all.* "So, tell me again," Baragon attempted, for what he prayed would be the last time, to get something straight out of him. "How long were you in the military?"

"Twenty years," Campbell announced. "Actually, more than twenty years. Thirty years."

"And you were doing all these other things at the same time you were in the military? Getting all those degrees and licenses and such?"

Campbell stared at him, hard—and for the first time, Baragon began to wonder whether the cuffs would hold. It was time to dump the pleasantries, to come out and ask him straight, try to wrap this thing up. Where in the hell were the guards, anyway?

"Why did you set that church on fire, Mr. Campbell? I mean, you knew it was full of people. You must've heard them singing."

Campbell never paused, never showed the slightest sign of recognition. "Because I came home and my wife was no longer interested in me. She pulled a trick to get rid of me with her boyfriend. A *conspiracy*, okay? I can't blame her for that. She was shacking with him for so long. But at least she could have *warned* me."

Won't hold up in court, but it's good enough for me, Baragon thought before Campbell made the mistake of going on.

". . . Even once her father said I was *crazy*, and ended up pleading for insanity against my will. But rather than fight it, I went along with it and served my time. The doctor reviewed my case and everything and said, 'I find this person to be satisfactory,' you know? 'No longer a threat to himself or others,' whatever it was. So the doctor released me to my own custody. See what I'm sayin'? I got at least three of those in my favor."

Well, there's something else. Campbell began looking for another cigarette, but the pack on the table was empty. Baragon reached for his own pack, shook one loose and handed it to him, then set the rest of the pack on the table, within easy reach. He could spare it—he had two more in his bag. Sometimes a little bribe never hurts, especially in a place like this.

The door to the room opened and the guard stuck his head in. "Ten more minutes," he announced. Baragon waved his understanding. *C'mon, Abe, let's pick up the pace.*

". . . Creedmoor was one," Campbell was saying as he lit the cigarette. "They released me twice. There was a self-admission at Montrose once. They committed me, and they held me for five or six years."

"What was that for?" Baragon asked. Maybe another fire, maybe something better.

"It was a VA hospital, because there was a secret war going on—a secret war between the Soviets and SVA."

Baragon thought about the initials for a moment before guessing, "The . . . South Vietnamese Army?" It would've made sense—he was the right age.

Campbell stared at him as if he were the most unbelievably idiotic man on earth.

"*No*—the *Seatopians*. Seatopian Vigilante Action. Quiet as it was kept, there was a war going on. They attacked the federal government. *Secretly* attacked the federal government three years ago. I was held in custody. So they claimed me to be a Know About It."

Baragon began to perk up a little bit. "Well, you obviously do know about it, don't you?" he countered. "So, tell me more about this secret war. But we don't have much time—so, y'know, quickly."

"Well, I know just enough to know that there was a war going on. But I didn't expect to find that sort of activity in my own *family*. Abraham came back home from the military—he's federal government. But knowing that there had been several members of my family who had turned enemy, who had also served the federal government distinguishedly during the Korean conflict. And *now* they had joined enemy activity. They were *sore*." He was growing more agitated as he talked about it. "That's what I heard about it."

"Uh-huh. So they were pissed at you for working for the government."

"Yeah—plus I'm what they call a . . . what's the term they use? Starts with a 'p.' A 'p' or a 'd.' Opposed, or . . . possible. Princited? Uhhh . . . What's the term they use when it's possible to be something that someone claims you to be and you're not?"

"You mean potential?"

"*That's* it. Okay. Now I'm *not* a potential. I *might* join the enemy. Really I wouldn't—but now I'm potential. You see? So I've become a threat. Not my fault though, it's the *government's!*"

"Do you think that helps explain the fire at the church? Could that have something to do with why you did that, do you think?" He knew he was putting words in Campbell's mouth, but Christ, he needed more than he had at this point.

"I can understand that," he nodded vigorously. "I know the difference. You expect it sometimes. I expect it *most* of the time. I wonder why, because you stop and think about it—"

There was a knock on the door, and the guard stuck his head in again. "Time's up, Baragon."

Baragon turned and shot him a look but knew it was pointless.

The air outside smelled of diesel and sulfur as he walked through the damp Midtown streets, through the foot traffic and the honking horns, the delivery trucks, yellow cabs, street vendors selling fruit, belts, watches, bootleg CDs, hot dogs, crab juice, underwear. Hundreds of storefronts peddling the same crap but for more money. Sewing machine and vacuum cleaner repair shops. Bicyclists dodging down the streets and sidewalks, sad old men handing out flyers for discount clothing stores, the noise growing louder the closer he got to the office. The gray and beige towers loomed over him, but he never bothered to look up, keeping his eyes on whatever might, in an instant, fill his path. He always forgot why he had vowed to stay out of the heart of Midtown until it was too late. Time was he loved it there, he felt at home, but not anymore now that the Selwyn and the other grind-houses were gone. Still, he decided to walk back to the *Sen-*

tinel building today, and as he did, he tried to figure out just how in the hell he was going to present this Campbell interview. He knew he didn't really have anything on that tape except an hour's worth of useless twaddle, but he didn't dare admit that to anyone.

"Arsonist Was Police Commissioner"? That wouldn't fly.

"NYPD Murder Attempt Created Firebug"? No, not that, either.

"Arsonist Crazy as a Loon." Maybe. He could tell he was getting closer. Sure, he could easily go with "Campbell Released from Madhouse—Three Times!" but that would be far too simple.

By the time he reached the front doors to the *Sentinel* building near Broadway and Thirty-fourth, he'd just about decided to run the interview verbatim, simply calling it "That Wacky Abe Campbell!"

When the elevator doors opened on the fifth floor, however, he had a better idea. He walked into the newsroom, removed his coat and threw it across the desk, retrieved the tape recorder from his bag, sat down, plugged in his earphone, and began typing.

Then he stopped, picked up the phone, and called Emily at the morgue.

"Hey, Em," he said when she finally came to the phone. "Sorry if I caught you in the middle of everything."

"Not really—that guy who jumped in front of the A train yesterday morning. Real mess—it'll take a while, but he's not going anywhere. At least cause of death doesn't seem to be much in question."

"Well, good—I mean, not good for *you*, but . . . I was just calling to let you know I'd probably be tied up here later than usual tonight."

"Oh." She sounded worried. "It's not Ed again, is it?"

"Not yet. Just that story."

"Oh my God, that's right—I'm so sorry, I forgot that was today—how'd the interview go?"

"Oh, fine, I guess. He's out of his goddamned mind."

"You don't need to tell me that," Emily said. "After they dragged everyone out of that church, they all came here. I *saw* all those people, remember?"

"I know you did. Look—I hate to run like this, but I should get to work. Hopefully I won't be too terribly late tonight."

"That's fine—it's gonna take me a while to untangle this guy, anyway."

"Good luck with that, Jesus."

"Yeah, you too."

After hanging up the phone, Baragon continued typing.

Taped to the smoke-stained white wall next to his computer was a small hand-lettered sign Baragon had made for himself many years earlier. Black Magic Marker on typing paper.

THE FIRST TWO RULES OF JOURNALISM

1) There are some stories that, for whatever reason, simply cannot be told.

2) Everyone's a liar.

He'd never learned those things in journalism school. Fact is, he never went to journalism school—and, for the life of him, couldn't name a single journalist worth a damn who had.

As it was, Baragon had never bothered with college, period. At first it had been a blow to his folks, who ran a couple of Laundromats in Rochester. Neither one of them had been to college, and, as a result, they had high hopes for Roscoe.

In the end, though, they knew they couldn't force him into it. They only hoped he knew what he was doing.

When he was in the eleventh grade, he'd been asked to write movie reviews for the school newspaper. He'd never tried any such thing before, but as it turned out he had a bit of a knack for it. The words—and the bile—just seemed to come naturally to him. After a few months, he also (under the pseudonym Woozy Winks) started writing angry, vicious letters to the editor of that same paper, complaining bitterly about the piss-poor quality of the movie reviews. After graduation, he'd typed up a fictional résumé and got himself a job writing the crime blotter for the *Rochester Roundup*, a weekly neighborhood shopper. Two years later, after his editor decided that headlines like "Idiot Leaves Window Open, Loses Everything" and "Jackass on Skateboard Pummeled by Lummox"—together with young Baragon's flagrant overuse of exclamation points—were too mean-spirited, Baragon took a job as a cub crime reporter in Minneapolis. He made such a name for himself in Minneapolis that within four years, he'd moved south, to become chief investigative reporter at the *Chicago Banner*. Three years after that, he moved east and settled at the *Sentinel*.

Those two simple rules on his wall were conclusions of his own—things he'd come to realize after being in the business for as long as he had. Whether you were dealing with metropolitan police commissioners, captains of industry, immigrant shopkeepers, or raving, drunken, homeless crackheads, those two rules always held. Sometimes one because of the other, sometimes one in spite of the other.

They also happened to be the two rules Baragon did his best to ignore on an almost daily—if not hourly—basis.

Chapter Four

"I don't know how you do it, Roscoe."

At first, Baragon thought Montgomery was smiling. It took him a moment to realize that it was just a wicked facial tic his editor seemed to have developed recently.

"What's that, Ed?" They were sitting in Montgomery's office again, the door closed. Baragon was feeling cocky, as he was under the mistaken impression that he had the upper hand here and was about to graciously receive a rare, glowing compliment—perhaps even a series of compliments—from his erstwhile boss.

"Where do I even begin anymore?" Montgomery threw his hands up in frustration, then leaned forward in his chair to stab his points home on the desktop with a meaty finger. "Okay, a man sets fire to a church in Flatbush on a Sunday morning and kills seventy-three innocent people."

If they were so innocent, what were they doing in church? Baragon thought, but he decided to keep that one to himself. For now.

"The arsonist turns himself into the cops, who are now

keeping him in a secret location somewhere in the city, out of fear that he'd be lynched before he could stand trial."

"I'm with you so far, chum." Baragon swallowed the final "p."

"Every goddamned reporter in New York is scrambling for this guy. They're pulling their hair out trying to find him—but you—*you*, of all people—*you*, Baragon—manage, not only to find out where he is, but to set up a fucking *interview* with him."

"Good thing for us he wants to act as his own lawyer—and hasn't bothered to place himself under a gag order yet."

"Yeah, that's real super—but I still can't believe that you're the one who found him."

"Maybe I still got a little of the old stuff left, huh, Ed? Who knows? I've been doing this for a long time—and, believe it or not, there are actually a few people out there who owe me a favor or two."

"This could be the biggest coup the *Sentinel*'s had in a very long time."

"Well, I—" Roscoe looked down at his hands and smiled modestly.

"I said *could be*, Baragon. Let me finish."

"Sure."

"You get the interview of the year, and what do you turn in?"

Montgomery spun the computer screen so Baragon could read the headline he had typed with his own two hands an hour earlier:

FIREBUG FRAMED FOR KNOWLEDGE OF SECRET WAR

"—and the story itself is just gibberish. A secret war between the Soviets and—what did you call them here?" he scanned the first paragraph "—the *Seatopians*?"

"That's what the man told me, yes."

"Roscoe—here's a simple question for you—what in the *fuck* are Seatopians?"

Baragon took a deep breath—the same sort of breath he took whenever he had to try to explain something very complicated (like the phone book) to someone he knew simply wouldn't understand.

"To be honest, Ed, you got me there. But remember, it was a *secret* war."

In his heart, Baragon knew that he had really blown it. He knew how important this interview had been. Unfortunately, Campbell hadn't exactly been cooperative. Baragon couldn't very well have gone into that room and said, "Okay, Abe, my whole career is riding on this—so give me something good," or "Face it, Campbell, you haven't got a rat's-ass chance in hell, you're gonna fry for this, so why not help me out here before that happens? Leave yourself one friend in this world."

No, instead he just sat back and let his subject do the talking. In most cases, that was fine, because the stories don't really matter in the end. But here, it would have been so simple to pick up the phone and check out a few elements of Campbell's story. His military record, all those hospitalizations. If Campbell really had been released on his own recognizance three times, that would've busted this thing wide open. Even if he had simply bothered to check out whether Campbell's wife attended that church.

While he was typing, he thought he was doing a damn fine job. Looking back on it now, he was just beginning to recognize the depth of his folly. He didn't know why he did it, and he didn't dare admit that to Ed.

Three minutes later (after some more yelling), Montgomery followed Baragon back to his desk, where he watched carefully as Baragon reluctantly removed the cassette from his tape recorder. Montgomery then carried the tape across the office and handed it to Livingston Biddle, a 23-year-old who'd recently arrived at the paper. Biddle had a journalism degree from Columbia, short hair, round glasses, and an unfortunate affinity for bow ties. Since his arrival at the *Sentinel*, he had not missed a single meeting of the zoning board.

"Biddle," Montgomery said, loud enough so that everyone in the office could hear, "this is an interview with Abraham Campbell conducted earlier today by Mr. Baragon over there."

Baragon gave Biddle a small wave but didn't smile.

"—And I want you to take this interview and turn it into a feature by tomorrow."

"Yes, sir!" Biddle replied. "But . . . who's Abraham Campbell?"

Montgomery ignored him and turned back to Baragon, who had just slapped himself (quite audibly) in the forehead. "Roscoe, in fairness, you will share the byline. You did, after all, get the interview."

"That's very generous of you there, Ed."

"And who knows? Maybe you can learn a little something from Biddle here. He has a degree from the finest journalism school in the country—can *you* say that?"

Baragon started to say something but held his tongue, afraid that if he tried to speak right then, he might vomit.

"I'm normally not one to say something like this," Emily said, "especially after a day like I've just had—but don't you think that maybe you've had enough?"

Baragon was leaning his forehead on the bar. The cigarette burned, untouched, in the ashtray next to him. He had a quarter inch to go on his seventh whiskey of the night. He usually avoided the whiskey these days, knowing what it did to him. When he was younger, he could put away a fifth a day if he chose to and not feel anything the next morning. Not anymore. He was sweating bad and just needed to catch his breath for a minute. Then he planned to order another.

"I'm fine," he told her, not lifting his head from the bar.

"It's just that the conversation has become a little one-sided. I'm getting tired of listening to the sound of my own voice."

"But . . . who knows?" he managed. ". . . That fat little fucker sure don't . . ."

Emily looked confused, then brushed the long black hair away from her left ear, put an arm across his shoulders and leaned down. "I'm not really sure what you're talking about, Rosk."

He took a breath and tried to focus his eyes on her. "I joined the Legion . . . to forget."

Her own day had been no picnic, but Christ, even though Roscoe was her best friend in the world, this most recent bout of maudlin, drunken self-pity was a touch over the top. Especially if it was going to become a nightly ordeal—which it gave every indication of becoming. She glanced at her small wristwatch. They'd been sitting at the bar for more than seven hours.

"C'mon," she said, sliding off the barstool and grabbing his arm. "Closing time. I'm taking you home."

She wrapped his arm around her shoulders and heaved. She was a small woman but strong, and Baragon, much to his amazement, found himself—if unsteadily—on his feet.

"Why do you do this to yourself, Rosk?" she asked, not really expecting much of an answer.

"Because," he slurred, maybe not as completely out of it as she thought he was, "sometimes . . . I'm afraid."

She half-led, half-carried him out the door, tossing an

apologetic smile over her shoulder at Jack, who saluted her in response. "Afraid of what, hon?"

"That someday . . . I might . . ." He was speaking slowly, choosing each word, then making certain his tongue could form it properly before speaking it aloud, "just . . . be . . . *right.*"

That was the last coherent thing she got out of him that night. He nodded off on the train, and after she got him upright again at the Union Street stop a few blocks away from his apartment, he belched all the way down the sidewalk.

By the time she wrestled him up the stairs and through the door and poured him into the bed, she realized she was far too exhausted (and drunk) herself to consider heading back to her place in Manhattan. Instead, she fed Hedora and washed up in the bathroom.

All the fixtures in Baragon's bathroom—hell, almost everything in his apartment, she'd noticed a long time ago— seemed to come from another era. The tub stood on four ceramic lion's feet. Hot and cold spigots were perched on opposite ends of the sink, an x-shaped handle atop each. If you wanted to wash your hands in warm water, you had to keep shifting them between a stream of freezing water and one that was near boiling. It usually took some time. The only thing he was missing, she thought, was a pull-chain toilet.

He had an ancient gas stove and a black rotary telephone connected to an old reel-to-reel answering machine. Two clanking and sputtering radiators heated the place. His only concession to modernity, it seemed, was the television and all those videotapes. Emily found it charming, in its way. Roscoe didn't seem to notice any of it.

After she'd cleaned herself up, she climbed into bed, fully clothed, where Roscoe was already snoring loudly.

As Emily lay there listening to the intermittent wheezing

and rumbling next to her, she remembered the last words he'd said that night and began to wonder if maybe he was perhaps slightly crazier than she originally thought he was—and if maybe she was a little crazy herself.

Baragon, still nursing the savage hangover—the older he got, he realized with some horror, the longer and more tenaciously they held on—had been at his desk for a little over an hour. He hadn't said a word to Montgomery, or Biddle, or anyone else for that matter. Just came in, sat down, and scanned the news wires, the way he did every morning.

There had been a bad earthquake centered about twenty miles off the coast of Hawaii. Registered over seven on the Richter scale, the report said. And there'd been another big one in the Ukraine not long afterward. Then another one in Alaska.

That's odd, he thought, but took it no further than that. There'd been a lot of earthquakes in recent weeks—India, Chile, Northern California, Central America, Japan. They'd become so common since the first of the year that he barely even noticed the headlines anymore.

The only interesting side note this time around was that there were also some sketchy reports that the Ukrainian quake might have done some serious damage to a nearby nuclear reactor. *That's never good news*, Baragon thought—especially since over there they seem to build their nuclear plants out of wood chips, staples, and spit. And plutonium.

Oh, well. His head was pounding too hard to worry about things like potential Ukrainian nuclear mishaps right now. After the humiliation of the previous day, he began to wonder if maybe he should try to cover his ass somehow. It was an idea that made him shudder, but one he'd at least have to consider.

He opened a file of phone numbers on his computer and began scanning his list of usual sources, trying to think of one he hadn't hit up in a while. None of them had really come through for him lately—stories about homeless musical prodigies and some woman who was convinced that her golden retriever was the reincarnation of Henry Gibson.

(Baragon had tried to explain to her, in patient, gentle terms, that Henry Gibson was still alive, but she was having none of it.)

Things didn't look promising at all. Marjoe Gorton would clue him in about corruption and kickbacks among community board members again. For the past year Babs Abkemeier had been obsessed with an oven fire that had broken out in the apartment next to hers and how rude the firemen had been to her. Every two weeks she called to see if he had looked into it yet.

No, no, no, he thought as he clicked through each name. He was about to get a glass of water so he could swallow the morning's seventh and eighth aspirins when some youngster from the fact-checking department came into the office carrying some papers.

"Hey, Kolchak," she said brightly, looking right at him. "Fax for you."

He squinted at her. She couldn't have been more than twenty but carried herself like she was thirteen. "*What* did you just call me?" he asked.

"Umm . . ." she said, smiling nervously, "Kolchak?"

"That's what I thought. Okay, my *name*," he said, making no effort to reach for the papers she was holding, "is Mr. *Baragon*. Mr. Roscoe Baragon. *Missy*."

She blushed and looked to the floor, absentmindedly cracking her gum. "I'm sorry. . . . I thought that was your name."

"Where the hell'd you get that idea?"

"Well, um . . . that's what Mr. Montgomery said—?"

He knew that already but just needed to hear her say it.

"Now, Missy—" Baragon said sharply. "*Remembering* that I've been in this business longer than you've been *alive*, I want you to answer me a question. . . . Could you do that? Do you think?"

"Umm, my name isn't—"

"Look at those faxes."

She did. By now the other people in the office had stopped typing to watch the proceedings.

"Now, on the cover page—the one on top—that's the one that says who's supposed to *get* the fax—whose name do you see there?"

"Umm . . . Baragon?"

"Right. Very good. And the first name?"

"Roscoe?" She looked up, eyes as empty and bright as a dog's, as if she expected Baragon to give her a treat for getting the answer right.

"Does it say 'Kolchak' *anywhere* on that piece of paper?"

She looked it over again, carefully. "No, um . . ."

"Never mind," he spat, and snatched the papers from her. *These damn kids with their hippity-hop and what-have-yous.* Two weeks ago, swear to God—nobody believed him, but it was true—he had to explain the concept of "alphabetical order" to one of them.

Missy—or whatever her name was—continued standing next to his desk, as if still waiting for her tip.

"Thanks," he said absently, without looking up. She didn't move. Finally, bewildered, he did look up to tell her, as simply as possible, "Go . . . away."

She turned and left the office.

Fucking kids. Baragon, who had a nearly bottomless reservoir of patience for the mentally ill, had virtually none whatsoever for people under thirty-five.

He flipped quickly through the four or five pages of tiny, almost indecipherable handwriting and pursed his lips. Same damn thing he'd heard a thousand times before.

Well, he thought, *this is the business we have chosen.*

> Mr. Baragon
>
> *Jun Fukuda and the Nakano Clan subsumes the NY-Japanese business Men's Association (Not Japanese-American) and the Management training center, prostitution etc. Have replaces my sink with a bidet (a female toilet urinal) second-hand and dirty with a brand new extra hot and cold water valve for heavy-duty use presumably for when I am forced out of my room #302 at the Greenwood Hotel. Being made sick and defenceless. The Greenwood hotel refuses to replace my Original Sink with another sink but have ulterior motivations. They use all the water. The police are negative to my complaints. This is the tip of the iceberg of the communist Japanese Trojan Horse Homicide. What we have here is part of a potential biological homicide when I receive dirty, soiled and used linen. For years we have a pattern of undisclosed homicides here to fore. The rooms are the prize in this closed controlled environment at the Greenwood hotel. I have the proof and witnesses. The communist Japanese have stolen our nuclear capability and technology. They buy our politicians and influence for elections to take us over. The U.S. fleet is there. But the threat is beneath them, not in the city. You are the steward of our liberty and freedom. Silence gives consent. I'm a 77 year-old combat vet of W.W.II. A volunteer enlisted but out now, besieged, disabled and impoverished but operational.*
>
> *Please God help before it is too late!*
>
> *Col. Hans Heg (Ret.)*

Beneath the signature, Col. Heg had written his phone number as well as the hotel's address.

"Wow, good luck to you there, buddy," Baragon muttered to himself. He'd liked that "steward of our liberty and freedom" shtick and briefly considered giving the colonel a phone call but changed his mind and filed the letter away into an already overstuffed drawer, thinking maybe it was time he started writing about lost pets instead.

Chapter Five

On his way into the office the next morning—same as every morning—Baragon stopped into the You Betcha Deli next to the *Sentinel* building to pick up a large coffee (black) and three packs of smokes. He usually didn't smoke three packs a day—but figured it was always best to be prepared in case of an emergency.

There were four people in line in front of him. That was fine; he was used to it. It was a bad corner at a bad hour, and he was in no particular hurry.

This morning the man at the head of the line was one of the neighborhood lunatics. Baragon had passed him on the sidewalk a thousand times before, muttering dark nothings to himself or an invisible friend. It was hard to guess his ethnicity exactly—it sounded like a cross between Puerto Rican and Irish and Slovenian—but he was always around and always talking. To the guy at the newsstand, to cops passing by, to anyone foolish enough to pause a moment, thinking he was actually speaking to them. Baragon always lent half an ear to his patter whenever he passed, in the hopes of

catching something good or useful, but to date, his eavesdropping had been fruitless.

This morning, the ranter had trapped the unfortunate,
confused Pakistani fellow at the cash register, poking a finger into the *Times* he was holding up in front of him like a
shield.

". . . and *Alaska*, man," he was telling the poor sap behind
the counter, ". . . up in *Alaska* bad things are happening,
man . . . *bad* things . . . they're *killing* people up in Alaska,
and you never read about it here," he said, tapping the paper
again for emphasis. "They got *concentration* camps, y'understand me?" The deli man smiled uncomfortably and nodded.

Baragon wanted to pause, to see if maybe this little
shaman knew anything about kidnappings or car bombs, but
figured it might take another hour or two before this guy
got around to it. He decided to get his coffee and smokes
from the Li'l Dumpling Deli on the other side of the *Sentinel* building.

You'd think that after going to one or the other of these
places nearly every day for fifteen years now, one of them
would recognize him, learn his name, acknowledge that he
was a regular—maybe even give him a discount or something—who knows what? A smile or a hello. But neither one
did. Never once. It was like Baragon was invisible.

There was, mercifully, only one person in front of him at
the Li'l Dumpling—a teenaged kid in a dirty white T-shirt
and crew cut, taking his own sweet time trying to decide
which candy bar would serve him best that morning. He
watched in mild horror as the kid's skinny, dirty fingers
roamed from brand to brand, fondling each as he passed, as
if trying to read some secret psychic message from the
nougat hidden inside.

Finally deciding on one, the kid plunked it on the counter, then went about the laborious process of counting out eighty-five cents in nickels. Baragon rolled his eyes in frustration, shifting his weight from leg to leg.

The transaction finished (finally), the kid grabbed his candy bar and turned for the door. Upon seeing his face for the first time, Baragon stopped dead and stared. Black, unfocused eyes set too close together, the mouth as small and thin as a paper cut. The rest of the face blank and empty and featureless.

My God—it's the kid from Deliverance*!* he thought to himself, almost screaming it aloud and pointing.

Baragon continued to stare at the kid's back as he exited the deli back out onto Broadway. Once he was out of sight, Baragon slowly turned again, still shaken, to face the expectant immigrant behind the counter.

"Christ," he told the cashier, "he must be, what, forty-five, fifty years old by now? And he *still* looks the same."

The cashier, being used to customers saying things that made no sense, only blinked and asked, "Can I help you?"

"Uhh, yeah," Baragon said, glancing quickly over his shoulder again, then back, embarrassed. "I'll, uhh . . . I'll have a large, umm . . ."

He eventually got his coffee and smokes—absentmindedly tossing a copy of the *Sentinel* on the counter with them—then went into the office. He almost never picked up the paper—not even to see how badly his copy had been butchered. Way he saw it, he didn't need any extra aggravation, so why bother? Today, however, he was curious to see how the Campbell story turned out. Lord knows neither Montgomery nor that little pipsqueak had run things past him for his approval before they went to press.

Guessing they didn't have to worry about being scooped on this, they'd held the story for a day, obviously using the time to try to knock Biddle's copy into some sort of shape. Whenever something about the rewrite needed to be discussed, they made a point of moving into Montgomery's office first, well out of earshot.

Baragon turned on the computer, took the lid off his coffee to let it cool, and sat there. Didn't light a smoke, didn't check out the news wires, didn't even look at the paper. Instead, he thought about Alaska.

He was hearing some awful—and possibly related—things about Alaska from two independent sources. That was the old journalist's dictum: get the same story from two independent sources and it becomes a fact, right? Well, here we had the same story ("Sure Is Some Bad News Up in Alaska!") from two independent sources. What was he supposed to think? Granted, both sources probably heard satanic messages coming out of Buffalo Bob's mouth on the old *Howdy Doody Show*. In fact, both of them probably still watched the *Howdy Doody Show*, whether or not either had access to a television set. But that wasn't the issue. Something weird was going on up there. Maybe he'd be finding himself on a plane after all—but instead of Honduras, he'd be on his way to Fairbanks—or maybe Nome—or what was that other place where the first guy was being held? Wherever. And instead of "Jeb," he'd be on the lookout for a mysterious figure named Kula Bocca, who would tell him many things.

Maybe what Alaska was doing was pulling an old Castro trick, Baragon speculated. Sending all their loonies down here. Or maybe—just maybe—they're lobotomizing folks who saw and knew too much and *then* sending them down here, because they knew that nobody would take their ramblings seriously. Baragon didn't know what sort of Freemason stranglehold existed in Alaska, but he could bet that they were involved somehow.

Unless of course it was all part of an ingenious invasion

plan, with the psychos being sent on ahead as a kind of reconnaissance force. Once they reported back that the Lower Forty-eighters were all sufficiently softened up, then the other ten, twelve people who live in Alaska would swarm down like angry hornets in parkas.

It certainly was something to ponder.

Baragon realized he was starting to think like his subjects. Sometimes it worried him.

In the years prior to that, though—man oh man, he'd been on it. Digging through the Dumpsters behind the Pentagon to come up with the first of several rejected schemes for the Star Wars missile defense system. (He'd been especially amused by the one early plan, forwarded by a brigadier general named Sloman, which involved specially trained ducks.) He'd earned the confidence of the most powerful revolutionary communist group in East Berlin shortly before the wall came down. Some people in the business speculated that it may have been the series of articles Baragon had written about the group that prevented the wall from going back up a few weeks later. He was talking to street gang leaders in Miami when he learned about their scheme for a nationwide series of carefully orchestrated riots. That one he kept to himself, just to see what would happen. Kingpins in the Medellin drug cartel showed him the collection of nice Christmas cards they'd received from high-ranking members of the then-current U.S. administration.

Those had been some years. Of course, he was younger then—late twenties, early thirties—and slimmer, and he was doing a lot of speed. Nevertheless, he'd been everywhere at once, it seemed. He was on top of things. There was a point when every paper in the country wanted him. Radio and television, too. The *Sentinel* had offered him complete freedom to write what he wanted. Not a ton of money, but enough. He didn't need much. Health plan, maybe. What it boiled down to was security—which was something he'd never had before and was curious to try out. So he took it.

Not long after he got settled in, though, "security" started taking its toll. Traveling was suddenly a pain in the ass. He no longer felt like digging through other people's Dumpsters or risking his neck for a story that would appear on a Tuesday and be forgotten by Wednesday, no matter how important it was.

Slowly, almost imperceptibly, he'd shifted from the hardest of hard news to human interest stories. They were easy, he could do them from his desk, there was no threat of being murdered in a foreign land. All he had to do was come into the office for a few hours every day, make a few phone calls, do a little typing, then head to the bar. Before he knew it, he was on the Kook Beat. He justified it to himself and anyone who asked by saying he was providing a voice for people who had no voice. Sometimes he even believed that.

Baragon cut his reverie short (*been listening to Them too much*, he thought), then flipped the paper over and looked at the front page for the first time.

ARSONIST CONFESSES TO SENTINEL was the first thing he saw, next to a grainy reproduction of Campbell's mug shot. He was amazed he hadn't seen the headline earlier, on any of the newsstands he passed on the way in. It was in huge block letters, across the top of the front page, the word *Exclusive!* printed in bloodred ink above it.

"Well, I'll be fucked," Baragon whispered to himself, then flipped the paper open to the story. "By Livingston Biddle, *Sentinel* Staff Reporter," read the byline.

And . . . ? thought Baragon bitterly. *And? . . . who else?* On a hunch that made his guts feel wormy, he turned to the jump and looked at the very bottom of the piece. Sure enough. In tiny italics, it read, "Research Assistant: Roscoe Baragon."

Well, I'll be double fucked.

He decided he'd have to have a little talk with Ed when he came in. Perhaps even a small chat with young master Biddle, whenever he decided to show up—though he couldn't blame Biddle too much for this. He knew who was behind it.

Until then, well, he'd do his job.

He dropped the paper into the garbage can beside his desk—*Lord knows I'm not going to find any news in there*—turned to the computer, and began skimming the news wires.

Twenty minutes later, after racing through the AP, UPI and Reuters wires—even a few of the European services—he thought, *That's odd.* Then he began reading through them again.

While all three wire services had follow-up stories on the various earthquakes that had struck around the globe in the previous days, there was nothing at all about the Ukrainian nuclear plant. Not a peep anywhere.

Granted, the news had been pretty spotty and slow-coming, but still—the previous day, it had been everybody's top story everywhere—usurping the news of the quakes themselves. It made sense, of course—whenever you're dealing with a Ukrainian nuclear facility, you're dealing with bad news. But today it seemed as if it had simply been swallowed up or had never been a problem at all. Now there was only a great, empty, echoed buzzing where the story used to be.

He knew the reasoning on the part of editors across the country—readers get bored—especially with things that take place in foreign countries and don't involve Americans in any direct fashion.

Still, though—Chernobyl, Bhopal—those stories had received nearly round-the-clock coverage for a month each—and with Chernobyl, there'd been regular follow-ups for years afterward. Even if it was nothing this time, you'd think they could drop in a little squib somewhere along the way: "Oh, and by the Way . . ."

As he went through the headlines a third time, he could see that there were, in reality, plenty of breaking stories big enough to shove some piddly little nuclear meltdown in a faraway land out of the way, at least for the moment.

RELEASED HOSTAGES GIVEN PIE, read one headline.

And it's about damn time, thought Baragon, considering, momentarily, slipping his own snack preferences into the next piece. He'd try to do it in a slightly more subtle fashion.

Then something caught his eye—something he hadn't noticed before.

DEATH TOLL RISES TO 5 IN ALASKA QUAKE.

For the first time, Baragon stopped to notice the dateline. *Barrow.*

That wasn't it, was it? He opened the top drawer to his right and began rifling through the collection of audiotapes of old interviews, wishing he'd done a better job of labeling and cataloging these things. He pulled out a handful and began popping them into the tape player, rewinding to the beginning, listening for that strangled voice coming to him from all the way up in . . . ?

When the third tape offered up nothing, he began hoping he hadn't taped over it. He knew you were supposed to keep these things around for at least three years, to stave off potential libel suits—but the recording he made in that case was an illegal one anyway—he hadn't told the guy he was taping. Maybe he rewound? Christ.

Or maybe—

He went across the room to Biddle's desk. It was clean as a whistle. Not only was it free of clutter—it looked like he polished the damn thing. *Wiener*, Baragon thought.

He began yanking drawers open. Files in file folders, stacks of plastic spoons—

"Jeez, hey—what are you *doing*?" Biddle asked when he walked into the office to find Baragon rifling through his desk. Baragon didn't look up. He didn't much care to look at these people. He could barely tell them apart anyway. "Looking for that tape," he said.

"Hey, if this is about the—"

"We'll talk about that dumbass move of yours later," he threatened vaguely. "Right now I need that tape."

Biddle ran from the room just as Baragon opened the drawer that held dozens of neatly arranged and labeled cassette tapes. All of them, it seemed, contained the recorded minutes of zoning committee meetings. All of them, that is, except for the last one. He yanked it from the drawer and turned back toward his own desk just as Biddle returned with Montgomery.

"There he is," Biddle said, pointing, almost hiding behind his portly editor.

"Just what the hell are you doing—well, *this* time— Roscoe?"

"I needed to check something out."

"Biddle says you're going to destroy the Campbell tape over the byline thing."

"Like I told Mr. Biddle, we'll talk about 'the byline thing,' as you call it, later. Now I just need to hear something." He popped the tape in and pressed play.

". . . *Creedmoor and*—" Baragon hit stop, flipped the tape over, and hit rewind.

A moment later, Baragon's own voice was coming out of the tape.

"—*Barrow . . . that in Alaska?*"

"*Yeah—way north,*" Nick Carter replied. "*Look—you gotta get me outta here—They're—*" Baragon snapped the tape off and popped it out of the machine.

"What the hell's that?" Montgomery asked. "That's not Campbell."

"No, it was somebody I got a call from a few days before the Campbell interview. He was up in Alaska."

"So?"

"He was in *Barrow*, Alaska."

"And I said, 'So?'"

"Ed, have you been following the *news* lately?" Baragon let his eyes drift up toward the ceiling. "The rash of earthquakes? Did we happen to report on those? Well, one of them just happened to be in Barrow, Alaska. Shortly before the quake, this guy calls to tell me that something weird is going on in *Barrow*, Alaska? What are the chances of that, huh?"

"Let me ask you a better question—what are the chances that I give a damn?" Montgomery said, then made a move as if to leave.

"Don't you think it's worth a follow-up, Mr. Montgomery?" Biddle asked.

Montgomery looked at Baragon, then to Biddle. "No, Livingston, I really don't. There are things happening in this city right now that are more important—like your follow-up to the Campbell story."

"I don't know, sir," Biddle said, a touch too enthusiastic. There was something desperate in his eyes—something that rested halfway between hope and fear. "I think that—"

Baragon raised a hand to cut him off. He could tell that the kid was trying to make amends (of some sort) for the Campbell affair, but Baragon wanted no part of it. "That's okay, really. Don't trouble yourself—it's not worth anything, anyway."

As Ed left the newsroom and Biddle went quietly over to his desk, Baragon slipped the tape back into its case and the case into his breast pocket, wondering if he should bother telling Biddle that no one much likes a tattletale.

. . .

Later that afternoon, Baragon picked up the phone and dialed Eel O'Neill's number. The phone rang twice before O'Neill picked it up. Eel was probably one of the last half-dozen people in New York who didn't screen all his calls, and one of the last two or three people in New York Baragon still liked.

"*O'Neill!*" Baragon barked, much too loudly.

"Hey, Bear," O'Neill said. "What's shakin'?"

O'Neill was about four years Baragon's senior, a tall, bespectacled man with a head full of explosive dark hair. He was also an unapologetic misanthrope who had spent well over half his life writing, producing, and directing low-budget horror films. Three or four a year, on average. Most of them never found any sort of theatrical release, but none of them had ever lost a dime. Eel didn't seem to understand it himself—but he kept churning them out.

They'd met shortly after Baragon started at the *Sentinel*. At the time, he was still doing serious investigative work and had published a series of pieces on a Long Island–based serial killer who, in taunting letters to the police, was calling himself "John Q. Square," which Baragon always sort of liked.

O'Neill wanted to do a quickie based on the case and wanted Baragon to help on the script, to make it more "authentic." Baragon had declined, but O'Neill had been shocked and impressed (and a little disturbed) by the fact that Roscoe could name all of O'Neill's films—from *Hell-Beast in Retardville* to *Head on a Stake* to *Bullet for a Bald Freak*—in chronological order. They'd stayed in contact ever since.

"Got something I'd like to bounce off you," Baragon began.

"Wait—what, we don't talk in a month and you don't have a hello or a how's it goin' or a wha'cha working on?"

Baragon sighed. "Okay. Hello."

"Hello!" O'Neill said.

"How's it goin'?"

"Swell."

"And what are you working on?"

"*Cannibal Boogaloo 3.*"

"Christ, you got someone to back you after the first two? Or even the first *one*?"

"Laugh while you can, monkey boy, but that first one netted close to nine hundred grand."

"Christ—and it cost you how much to make?"

"'Bout a tenth of that. And once the investors heard that Brando was attached to this one, they basically lined up around the block to hand over a mountain of giant novelty checks. I felt like Jerry Lewis."

"Brando, huh?" Baragon asked, knowing full well how Eel worked. "Let me guess—you signed Mort Brando."

"Manny Brando, actually, so you were close. Nice kid from Jersey City. I know his folks. But, y'know, the money people don't need to know that."

"Uh-huh. Say—now, all that out of the way, can I bounce something off you?"

"Shoot."

For the next several minutes, Baragon laid out what he knew—the phone call, the crazy man in the deli, the earthquake. Given that O'Neill's stock in trade was improbability, Baragon figured he'd ask him first. When he was finished, there was silence on the other end.

"Well?" Baragon prodded. O'Neill was usually faster on the draw than this.

"Hang on, I'm jotting all this down. I might be able to use it at some point."

Baragon waited patiently for a moment.

"Okay, here's my question," O'Neill said, finally. Even with his questions, he sounded confident, as if he knew the answer long before he asked. Baragon figured that was how he got rich people to pony up money for a disco cannibal film.

"Yeah?"

"Now, are you sure all these people weren't just talking about some guy? Some guy named 'Alaska,' who's running around doing terrible things?"

Baragon sighed again and cut his eyes to the right. "You might want to take one more look at your notes."

"That's what I'm doing. Sounds right to me."

"Perhaps I should explain all this to you one more time. Or perhaps I should go home and explain it to my *sink*."

On the other side of the office, Biddle was greeting an almost endless line of well-wishers from around the office—from other reporters to ad reps—stopping by to shake his hand and congratulate him for his top-notch work on the Campbell story. Baragon slowly spun his chair around so he wouldn't have to see any of it.

"I call for insight and this is what I get? 'Maybe it's some guy named Alaska?'"

"Hey, I try."

"Yeah, well—"

"Hey, Bear," O'Neill said, more serious now. "*You*, of all people, especially after all this time, should know the basic flaw of all conspiracy theories."

"Yeah, I know—good ol' Occam."

"*Exactly*. Simplest answer's probably the right one. When you're inside these things, it's impossible to see out. So don't get too deep into it or you're trapped. Take a step back and there's usually a perfectly obvious, logical explanation waiting."

"Some guy named Alaska."

"Or something like that, yeah. You'll find it. Just keep your head up."

"I know, Eel. Thanks. And good luck with *Cannibal Jamboree.*"

"*Boogaloo.*"

"Whatever. When do you start shooting?"

"Next week, if all goes well. Most of the principal photography's gonna be done at a disco over in Seaside Heights. It's perfect—the joint never bothered to become anything else. They've still got all the original fixtures—mirrored balls, colored lights in the floor, everything."

"Do they know you're coming this time? Or are you trying to get that whole cinema verité thing going again?"

"I'll decide that once I finish the script."

Baragon smirked. Sounds like another Eel O'Neill production. "Hey," he said. "You know that Seaside Heights is where they have the big clown convention every year? September or October, I think. I covered that once, and it was scary as all hell. You might want to consider that for the future."

"Thanks, Bear—maybe I will. In fact, I *probably* will."

O'Neill was right, as usual, about conspiracy theories, and it was something Baragon struggled to keep in mind. All these people he'd spoken with—every week, every month for the past however many years—people who had written to him or called or stopped him on the street—they all wanted to let Roscoe Baragon in on a secret.

They were never small, quiet secrets, either—they were inevitably huge and sinister and potentially deadly to everyone involved. Ignoring, of course, that the people sharing the secrets were usually the only ones involved. The secrets themselves always varied somewhat, but the conclusion they reached was always the same—that the United States government is using electronic weapons, or a disease, or radio waves, or mind control, or something even more insidious to do something really awful to a large section of the population. The reasons differed. In fact, the reasons behind these horrible plots, Baragon had discovered over time, were usually pretty vague. Like in an Italian zombie movie— no one really knows why or how the zombies came about, but there they are. And in the case of these conspiracy nuts, for whatever reason and to whatever end, it's always a concerted effort on the part of "the Government."

Baragon had received a letter about a week before Mr. Carter called him from Barrow. The letter came from somewhere in the Pacific Northwest—someone had written to tell him about a rare and incurable neuromuscular disease. The note seemed innocent enough—so innocent that Baragon wondered why it had been sent to him at all—until about halfway down the second page, when the phrase "government genocide program" first cropped up.

Yes, well, he thought, as he slid the letter back into its envelope and filed it away with all the others. At least this time the concerned citizen waited until the second page to spring it on him—usually you can count on the zinger popping up by the second paragraph, third at the latest.

At the bar that night, Baragon told Emily about the letter. He told her everything, shared with her the details of every paranoid he encountered, but thought she'd find this one particularly interesting, given her medical background.

When he told her, she smiled her glorious smile and shook her head.

"If you had a dime for every government plot someone brought to your attention—"

"—I wouldn't have to worry about sitting in that fucking office every day, waiting for another one of them to call me."

"Government conspiracy seems to be the really happening thing right now, huh?" she said. "UFOs, messianic complexes, and spirit mediums are all out—and when was the last time you heard from one of the free energy people? It's almost like there are fads in delusional psychosis."

She was right, come to think of it. Baragon had dealt with UFO people and various messiahs in the past—even knew a medium, and there was a point when the free energy types were everywhere—but there hadn't been a peep from any of them in quite some time. Over the past two years or so, it had been nothing but evil government schemes, one right after the other. People had contacted him to blame the government for their eviction, or their disappearing neighbors, or the fact that they couldn't find a public rest room in Manhattan when they needed one, or their unholy feminine odor, or a disease, or the spraying of insecticides. That guy who was convinced that the Japanese were out to get him didn't seem to have too many problems beyond his plumbing and his linen service. Another recent letter writer didn't even seem to have much of a problem at all herself—seemed perfectly fine and happy, in fact. She just wanted to tell Baragon about the government's widespread use of electronic mind control devices even though the idea didn't seem to bother her too much. She just thought he'd like to know that it was going on.

The thing that captivated Baragon about these people— the reason why he continued to talk to them and publish their stories when he could—was that these people weren't talking about the Kennedy assassination, Area 51, or a faked moon landing. The horrors these people dealt with every single day were all very personal attacks on the part of the government. The United States government—or some branch thereof—had singled these people out for some reason, targeted them, cruelly victimized them, and destroyed their lives.

While Baragon didn't exactly believe their tales of conspiracy, he was fascinated by the thought processes and complex but delusional reasoning that went into them.

After all, if it takes the government twelve years to pass a bill to install a goddamned stoplight at a dangerous intersection, how and why would they toss the money and the manpower around all willy-nilly in order to annoy and confuse some poor slob with no money and a personal hygiene problem? And why spend millions torturing these schmucks for years when they could simply, if it was important to do so, make them disappear for twenty bucks or so?

It made no sense at all. Which was part of the reason he stayed interested.

"Here's the problem all the JFK assassination nuts never deal with," Eel had told him once. "They never factor this in at all. *People are stupid.* And what's more, people are blabbermouths. You know how many people it would take to pull something like that off—*and then* keep it quiet for forty years? Impossible."

"You ever see *Executive Action*?" Baragon asked him.

"Burt Lancaster, Will Geer, and the great Robert Ryan's final performance."

"Right. So what happens there? After the fact, just kill off everyone who knows. Made for a great ad campaign." Baragon didn't really believe it himself. Liked the movie, though.

"Something to think about, I guess."

Just once, Baragon thought—just once, he'd like to get a letter in which someone outlines in obsessive detail how they'd been horribly wronged by evil forces over a period of many years, then goes on to explain that their problems are actually the result of foul machinations on the part of Bigfoot. Or possibly Bigfeet.

Bigfoot—from what Baragon remembered from all the Sunn Classics films he saw as a kid (and so far as he was aware, he had seen them all)—was always a pretty secretive character, being spotted only a handful of times while tromping through the woods of Northern California. But when was the last time anyone heard of a Bigfoot sighting? And working alone, as he seemed to, it was much more likely that he could not only keep a secret better than a governmental cabal but that he would be the type who could hold a personal grudge better, too, choosing to torment a single unlucky soul over a period of years without remorse. That seems much more likely than, say, a multilayered government agency getting involved in such monkeyshines.

Baragon also noted that quite a few of the stories that came his way involved unwholesome odors of one kind or another, whether inflicted upon the victim from within or without. If he remembered his Bigfoot mythology at all, the creature was known, among other things, for its ungodly stench.

In the end, Baragon reasoned, Bigfoot seemed a lot scarier and a lot smarter than the government.

So there you have it.

It was a notion Baragon never, ever suggested to any of the kooks he dealt with, out of fear they might actually buy it.

Two hours after talking to Eel, Baragon's phone rang. He sighed, then picked it up. "Yeah?"

"Hel-lo . . . Roscoe?" the voice on the phone said. "It is Natacia."

She never really had to tell him—he always recognized her broken falsetto immediately. For all the paranoids and conspiracy nuts Baragon had dealt with over the years—and there must've been hundreds of them by now—the only one he still maintained any sort of willing professional contact with was Natacia Ranzigava. He had a rare soft spot for her.

Baragon liked her, he thought, because she not only carried within her nearly every single personal conspiracy theory he'd ever heard but was more than eager to pick up new ones along the way and weave them in with the others she already held dear. He made a special point not to share his Bigfoot theory with her.

"Hey, Natacia—how are you doing today?" He knew that was always the wrong thing to ask her—but on the bright side, he also never knew what sort of reply he would get.

"Ohh . . . I am very sick . . . many infections," she said. "How is . . . your leg?"

She always asked him that. He wasn't exactly sure why. At some point during their first meeting, she had become convinced that there was something wrong with Baragon's leg and now, two years later, would still not let it go.

"My leg is just fine, Natacia. Much better now, thank you—how is your, uhhh . . . ?"

Baragon was hardly the most delicate of men, but still, there were a few things he was hesitant to bring up in front of elderly women, insane or not.

"My wagina?" she asked, as innocently as if she was asking him about his cat.

One afternoon two years earlier, Natacia had stopped by the office unannounced, wearing a tattered pink bathrobe and slippers, dragging behind her a small hand truck that held several hundred pages of court documents, which she wanted Baragon to take a look at.

Her story didn't strike him as all that interesting at first. She'd fled the Soviet Union when she was in her fifties, moved to the States, had trouble finding work, started selling paintings and political pamphlets on the sidewalk outside her Harlem apartment building, got busted for it—and spent the next twenty years trying—and failing—to sue the

NYPD. A quick little human interest story, he figured at the time. Another tale of a little person trying to crawl through a maelstrom of red tape in search of "justice." He could slam that thing out in an hour and head home and forget about it.

The more he looked through the legal documents she'd left him, though, the more intrigued he became.

Since she had no money, she was trying to act as her own attorney. Despite her broken English, the story outlined in her amended complaint to the courts became increasingly peculiar the further he read.

After her arrest for selling pamphlets on the sidewalk and a subsequent two-week-long hunger strike, the case against her was thrown out, and she returned to her apartment in Harlem.

> *Three policemen, upon my landlady's request, broke my door and threatened me with guns. They said there was a "hole in my sink" and it was emergency.*

Fearing for her life, she fled the apartment and never returned. For ninety dollars a month, she took a room in an SRO hotel in the East Twenties. Yet not long after she moved in, there was another knock on her door.

> *He was demanding to be let in because "there is a hole in your sink." He said he was a new superintendent. He did not want me to take his picture. I called 911. Detectives came, and told me I must never in the future call police. They would not come no matter what. "Never call us!" said a detective. Police refuse to investigate crimes in this building. There is a lot of harassment to force old tenants out. And probably murder. Police do not investigate why old tenants disappear.*

Her health continued to deteriorate and her problems at the SRO continued to mount. She was beaten, she told Baragon, and raped, and threatened with murder. As the police still refused to investigate, she decided to sue the mayor. That's when she first showed up at the *Sentinel*'s offices.

"No one will tell me how to sue him," she had pleaded. "I go to City Hall and they say to go here, to go there, and each place I go, they tell me something else."

Out of simple curiosity, Baragon flipped through a copy of the *New York Law Journal* and found that most *everyone* was suing the mayor, all the time. Must be simple, he figured, so he got on the phone and called the Mayor's Corporate Counsel Office, explaining who he was and asking them how a regular joe might go about serving papers on the mayor of New York City.

"I really can't answer these kinds of questions," he was told by the clearly coke-addled woman on the other end. "Those are questions for the plaintiff's lawyer—I . . . I *can't* give legal advice—you *can't* serve papers at City Hall—"

As her voice grew more panicky and shrill, Baragon shh'ed her gently and told her to take a deep breath. She did.

"Look, here's the problem," she told him, her voice a little calmer. "I'm a lawyer, and I'm not sure exactly *where* you'd serve the mayor. I'm just not sure where you'd do it. It's a legal question. It's a question of *jurisdiction*. If you don't do it correctly, you're thrown out of court. . . . I don't want to be in the position of giving out legal advice, because I don't *know*." Her voice started picking up momentum again. "It involves *research*, and we don't *do* that for the press. Call the Legal Aid Society—call the ACLU and try to get a lawyer over *there* to tell you what the proper way to serve process on the mayor is. God, I *can't* do this—I just *can't* do this!" She let out a strangled cry and slammed the phone down.

Well, that was curious, he thought as he put the receiver down.

At that point two years ago, Baragon still wasn't all that interested in the story—"Old Woman Battles City Hall and Loses." That wasn't much of a story. But then, on page six of her original complaint, he hit paydirt:

"Cause of Action Against the FBI."

Suddenly the faux-legalese vanished. It was just Natacia's brain in open free fall. It almost became a form of poetry.

> *There are some clear signs that people constantly search through my things.*
>
> *If I forget to put on my watch when I go out and it is left on the table, I find it always broken, and have to buy a new one. I saw a movie,* The House on Ninety-second Street, *a spy had information in his watch.*
>
> *I could not close a lock on a suitcase no matter how I tried. Then one day, I found the lock closed and in working order.*
>
> *Strange files appeared on my hard disk in computer. I do not have Internet, so nobody can store his files on my hard disk, unless he has physical access to the machine.*
>
> *For several months a Russian woman was always meeting me in front of elevators. Always! She knew that I have a computer and my cats are all very different, though I never invited her into my room and told nobody about my computer.*
>
> *I buy a lot of canned food. Recently, I found that my stock of canned sardines had disappeared from the closet.*
>
> *A neighbor told me she was watched and they do it from above the door. A man did install wires. He said it was for the cable TV.*

There are a lot of guests from Russia and Japan in this hotel.

For thorough search it was necessary to drug me. Sometimes I was unconscious for 48 hours. Anesthesia without consent is battery. My health was injured. I could walk with difficulty just one block.

The whole population of elderly has disappeared from single room occupancy hotels in New York.

Well, there's something, Baragon thought when he finished reading. She didn't have a phone, but she promised that she would call him in a day or two, as soon as she could find a phone she was certain wasn't bugged.

The next day, the phone rang. It was Natacia, and Baragon asked her if she could stop by the office again.

When she arrived, he pulled up a chair for her, got her a glass of water, and turned his tape recorder on.

"The people in the SRO are disappearing," she whispered. "What happens with the people who disappear? Nobody knows, nobody cares. . . . There was a story in the paper about why people become homeless. None of them say they were in SROs before they were homeless. There's a lot of furniture broken, a lot of personal things in the garbage. When people leave, they usually take their things with them. . . . Yes?"

"Yeah," Baragon said. "—I saw that in your brief. But I'm not exactly sure how that ties in with the FBI." He was trying to be gentle with her.

"One day," Natacia explained, her head bobbing slowly as she spoke, "I was walking along the street. Suddenly the sole from one of my old shoes—comfortable old shoes—fell off. Very soon another sole fell off. So I had soleless shoes for my feet!" She opened her mouth wide and laughed a weak, wheezing laugh, and her foul breath nearly made his eyes water. "This has never happened to me before in my life! I think the FBI men were looking inside. There was a crevice in the sole. They were looking in there, and they took it apart and they put it back together. They had been into my apartment."

"I guess that's the logical conclusion," Baragon said, asking himself already why he'd invited her to stop by. "But let me tell you a story. That sort of thing happened to me once. I was on my way to the office, and *flop*—the sole of my shoe just separated, just like that. So what I did, see, was stop at the next deli I passed. I bought a pack of gum, chewed up a bunch of pieces, and stuck the sole back together with that. Isn't that something? It really works, too. You might want to try that in the future, if it happens again. Only problem then is when it rains. The gum doesn't stick when it rains."

Then he remembered she was toothless and that chewing gum might be out of the question. She went on as if he hadn't said a word. They always did. In fact, everybody did, insane or not.

After that shoe incident, Natacia knew something was going on—though she wasn't exactly sure what it was or why it was happening until she started to put the pieces together.

"They certainly know when I go out. I meet with people who want to talk with me. I see the man who raped me. I meet him in the street. He always knows where I am going and what I am saying, because he always wants to know if I am complaining about him. He meets me in the elevator and he threatens me. How does he know that I'm going out on a certain day? He waits for me in the street. They can know what you type on your computer from the outside. With *technology*."

As she became aware that something strange was going on around her, the reasons for it began to make themselves clear. At first she thought perhaps the FBI—which has been known to train cadets by having them "practice spy" on innocent civilians in Virginia—had brought the technique north, to spy—again, just for practice—on the residents of her SRO. She soon realized, however, that what was going on was much more sinister.

"Why me?" she asked, and again she answered her own question, sort of. "Sometimes when I come home, I will see something that is out of place. Recently, I found my computer book under the wardrobe. I always keep it out, so how did it end up under the wardrobe?"

"Well, I'll tell you, Natacia," he offered, just trying to be helpful. "To be honest, I have a big cat at home, and I drink some, I dunno—I've known weirder things to happen. Found a full ashtray shoved into the VCR once. No idea how that happened."

Suddenly her tone changed, and her voice dropped, as if she had something she was afraid to divulge. "I have something else," she told Baragon. "Some hard evidence—"

Baragon leaned in so he could hear her and moved the tape recorder a few inches closer. Some time back, she went to a doctor, she told him. "They checked my infections," she said. "They took sonograms. And they couldn't understand what is in my wagina or in my uterus. They tried to push their fingers in, but they could not—there was something there." The doctors couldn't figure out what it was and couldn't explain how it got there. Neither, obviously, could Natacia.

"Did you mention this in your complaint, uh, Natacia?" asked Baragon. "I don't remember reading about this."

She shook her head. "The agents drugged me; they took me out of the room to the doctor's office. I felt when they were driving me. You know when you are under anesthesia, your body still has some feelings, but the brain is out. So when I was raped, I felt it, but I did not know. When I came to I had this strong feeling. I began to investigate how they got into my room. I was carried away and they put this thing in me. So what is it? They put it into animals and they put it into people, under the skin, so they will always be able to find out where the person or animal is. Navigation, a tracking device. I thought probably they are watching where I was going."

It seems that's how strangers always knew when to meet her on the street and always seemed to know exactly where she was going.

They inserted the device where they did, she told him, because if they were to put it under the skin, as they normally did, it would leave a very noticeable scar. It was just this sort of practice on the part of the FBI, she believed, that had led to the explosion of alien abduction stories. It was an argument that had already been made for some time, in at least a half-dozen books that Baragon knew of.

"Abductees have scars," she said. "They lose track of time. It could be done by people who live here." All you need, she said, is a movie projector and an image of an alien to flash on the wall. Then, while your victims are paralyzed with fear, simply go about your business with the drugs and the implants. "They could not do this to me because I would notice immediately and I'm not a stupid person, not stupid enough to believe in *aliens*."

Well, there's one thing, Baragon thought. Then she began to laugh again, exposing her toothless gums, her sour breath once more catching Baragon like a brick to the head. He subtly shifted his chair back away from her.

This time her laugh was a bitter one—discovering the implant meant that she was still in terrible, terrible danger.

"I read how a woman was killed when poison was put into her pacemaker."

"Oh, yeah," Baragon said. "That's pretty awful."

"You could put some poison into something, put it into

the wagina, and it would look like a natural death. Nobody would find anything. Especially if you're old. They wouldn't even investigate. So I don't know what that is inside."

The thing that bothered Baragon about all this was that, like she herself said, Natacia Ranzigava was not a stupid woman. Not by a long shot.

Certain parts of her story, he would discover in the following days, actually did check out—the old jobs, the place in Harlem, the twenty-plus years' worth of attempted litigation. Weird as it seemed, the "vaginal tracking device" turned out to be a much more common story amongst the tracking device set than Baragon had realized.

Some parts of her story, though, still baffled him. Like that inexplicable canned sardine pilferation.

He spent a lot of time researching Natacia's story, and in the end—much to his surprise—Montgomery actually let him run a three-part series on her travails.

Now, two years after he had first met Natacia and ran his first story about her battle with the city, the mayor, the FBI, and the federal government, he was still in contact with her, still following her case—if from more of a distance.

"How'd the latest hearing go, Natacia?" he asked, once she informed him that the tracking device was still there, that she had a terrible bladder infection because of it, and that she couldn't afford the operation to have it removed.

Sometimes I wonder, Baragon thought to himself, *if she just accidentally got something jammed up there one day, by accident.*

"Not so good," she said. "The judge throw out my new case. Again."

"Again? Well, that's a pisser, I must say. . . . How are things at the SRO?"

"Not good either." Natacia sighed, sounding discouraged. "We have new owner. Strange men. They wear sheets."

"Sheets?"

"Yes, like wrapped around their bodies."

"You mean the *Klan* bought your building?" There's some news.

"*No,*" she corrected him sharply. "Wrapped, like . . . old Greeks."

"So . . . you're saying there was a big toga party at the SRO?"

"I do not know this word."

"Don't worry about it—I mean, that's really weird. Are they American? Are they fat?"

"No—not American. Hard to tell where they are from. They are like Asian, like Chinese, but not really."

"And they wear togas. Now, this is the same place that you've had all this trouble, right?"

She started to say yes, but another line started ringing on Baragon's phone. "Natacia—I'm very sorry—I want to hear this—but could you hold on for just a moment please?"

"Ah . . . yes?"

Baragon went to put her on hold and in the process—he really was a moron when it came to these modern gizmos—hit the wrong button and hung up on her. *Shit.* He punched in the line that was ringing.

"Baragon," he mumbled, still worried about Natacia.

"Hey there, grumpy," a sweet voice said. "How are things going?"

"Hey, Em—*ahh!*—" he grunted. "I just hit the wrong fucking button here and ended up hanging up on Natacia."

Emily knew what that meant.

"Oh, I'm sorry—so now, let me guess—she's either convinced that the FBI's got your line tapped, too—or she's convinced that you're One of Them."

"Exactly. And I don't have a number where I can call her back."

"That's too bad—but you know, I think she'll understand. . . . You've done more for her than anyone else ever has. Anyway—the reason why I'm calling—"

"Yeah, it's odd to hear from you during the day. Is everything all right?"

"Yeah . . . yeah . . ." she said almost absently, as if she were looking over her shoulder as she spoke, "but I think I might have something for you."

"Yeah?" His curiosity was piqued. "Something from the morgue? Does it come in a jar?"

"*No*—now—shut up a second. I'm not kidding. But I can't talk about it over the phone. Or shouldn't, at least."

"Look at what just happened to Natacia."

"That's just my point. I'd rather not talk about it at the bar, either—could I swing by your place?"

"Sure," said Baragon, confused by all the sudden secrecy. He'd never heard her like this before. "I got booze."

"Great. I'll see you after work then."

"Yeah," he said, still a little puzzled. "I'll see you then."

Chapter Six

"Well now," he said as he set the beer down in front of Emily and took the seat across the small Formica-topped kitchen table from her, "to quote too many bad screenplays, 'What's this all about, anyway? What goes on?'" He had no idea what to expect.

Although he'd never asked her to, she'd helped him out on a few stories when she could. He didn't want her to think their friendship was based upon the kind of inside information he could get out of her concerning some recent murder victim or dead celebrity. With Emily, he found it perfectly easy to draw the line between the personal and the professional.

That surprised the hell out of him.

What also surprised the hell out of him was the look on Emily's face as she sat across the kitchen table. He'd never before seen her so agitated about something that had happened at the morgue.

She reached over into his breast pocket and fumbled for a smoke. She'd quit smoking cold turkey a year after they met and now lit up only when under extreme stress. She flicked the lighter and inhaled as Baragon took a pull from his bottle, waiting patiently, knowing this wasn't the time to prod. It'd come out, whatever it was.

"I don't know what you can do with this," she said, "or even if you *should* do anything with it. I probably shouldn't even be telling you—but it was just too fucking weird."

"Uh-huh?" He didn't dare start making wild guesses or stupid jokes.

She took a swallow from her beer. "So okay, about ten-thirty this morning, EMS shows up with a John Doe they'd just found in Tompkins Square Park."

"Wait—" Baragon interrupted. "They found this body and just brought him to the morgue? Aren't they supposed to, you know—bring people to the hospital or something first?"

"Well, yeah. Usually. But I guess this guy was pretty dead."

"Okay."

"As they're wheeling him in through the doors, suddenly all these alarms start going off."

"Like what? Metal detectors? Fire alarms? I'm not sure I get you."

"*Like* them, yes, sort of," she said. "But not exactly. It turns out the body set off the radiation detector."

Baragon had been reaching for the bottle but stopped. "Pardon?"

"Yeah," she said, and nodded.

"Did he have a pocketful of uranium or something?"

"That's the thing—nobody knew—so they rushed him into isolation, then called the fire department."

"Hazardous Materials?" Baragon had dealt with them before. They'd been assholes, at least the ones he'd dealt with, but he figured they'd earned the right to be.

"Uh-huh. The next thing I know, people from the mayor's

office are there, too—along with DOH and EPA—telling us to all stay calm, that there's no danger, typical bullshit."

Baragon's eyebrows were crawling toward his hairline. "Jesus—and where were you while all this was going on?"

"Well, my lab is in the basement, just down the hall from the isolation room, so I pretty much got to hear everyone as they were coming and going."

"And . . . ?"

"*And*—what do you expect? Suits from the mayor's office are trying to keep it quiet, telling people there's nothing to worry about, they've seen this sort of thing before, there's no public health risk. This is all before anyone has even checked out the body."

"You mean the mayor's people got there *before* the fire department? How did they know?"

She nodded. "That was weird, too—I hadn't even thought of that. When the Haz Mat team got there, they put on space suits and pulled out their Geiger counters and, from what I could tell, couldn't find any traces of radiation in the EMS van or anywhere else in the complex."

"But what about the body?"

"That's the really scary thing—Haz Mat went into the isolation room but were out again about a minute later, talking about how 'hot' it was in there—and I doubt very much that they meant it was stuffy."

"Sure," he nodded, astonished by what he was hearing.

"Then the mayor's people—there must've been a dozen of them—tell the chief ME—or so I was told later, at least—that, while there's no danger, they should still get rid of the body as quickly as possible. This isn't EPA or DOH saying this—these were lawyers or Secret Service or something. Maybe emergency management people? I'm not absolutely sure. Fucking guys in suits."

Baragon lit a cigarette and tried to make sense of all

this. This wasn't something he was getting from some guy wrapped in a dirty blanket holding a cardboard sign—this was Emily. One of the sanest people he'd ever met. He couldn't simply laugh this off or file it away in his over-stuffed desk drawer.

He got them two more beers and thought some more.

"We have no idea who this guy is yet?" he asked.

She shook her head. "He's still a John Doe. All I heard was that he was a homeless guy found in the park, dead of unknown causes. No ID, no anything on him."

"Uh-huh."

She could see that bad look creep into his eyes.

"Rosk, no—don't even think it. Look, I thought someone should know—but if anyone there finds out that I told you, it'll be my ass, understand? And I can't afford to lose this job right now."

"That happens, you know I'd help you out," he offered.

"You don't make enough money. Please—just don't do anything stupid, and don't let it slip that I told you *any* of this."

"Oh, you shouldn't worry about that—you know I always protect my sources." She saw the look escalate a notch.

"And *no*—I will *not* sneak you into the morgue so you can steal the body."

The evil light in his eyes dimmed slightly. "Aw, c'mon . . ."

"No."

"Em, it's been so long since I've had a chance, really, to do anything like that."

"Steal a corpse?"

"You know what I mean. I've been doing virtually nothing but phone interviews with insane people for the past five years. Look where that's got me. This is something real."

She sighed. "Look, you want to go in there and steal a body, then get it past three levels of security, be my guest.

What are you going to do? Take it on the subway with you? Hail a cab? And where are you going to take it? Here? What would you do with it?"

She had a point there. "Yeah, I guess you're right," he admitted, a little disappointed. "But will you do me a favor?"

"What?" she asked, more than a touch suspicious and fast coming to the conclusion that she should never have told him. Nobody from the ME's office, so far as she was aware, knew that she knew Baragon. They thought she might be seeing someone—the whispered phone calls gave them that idea, which kept the passes from coworkers to a minimum—but they had no idea who it was, let alone that it was a newspaperman. She never brought him along to the annual Christmas party. Like Baragon, she found it easier and more comfortable to keep work and life separate. She'd passed a few things along to Roscoe before, but never anything potentially quite this big, and now she was doubting her own judgment.

"I don't want you to steal anything or do anything foolish for me," he said, raising a hand to dismiss the very thought.

"Okay. But?"

"Just keep your ears open. And your eyes, too, should anything happen to come across your desk."

She sighed. "You know, if we're connected in any way . . ."

"Hey, Em, remember," he told her with a smirk he saved just for her, "I'm a trained professional."

That worried her even more.

They had one more beer, then she decided she should get back home. It was Tuesday night, and Wednesdays were usually pretty busy for some reason. She also had the suspicion that tomorrow would be busier than usual.

"Hey," he said as he held her coat for her. "You know I trust you too much to fuck things up in any way."

"I sure hope so," she said as she slipped into the coat.

"—And I can't thank you enough for telling me about this."

"Yeah," she said. "No problem—as long as you don't blow it."

He saw her to the building's front door, locked it behind her, then went back upstairs, where he made a cheese sandwich, opened another beer, and popped in *H-Man* again.

Halfway through the sandwich, he stopped chewing.

Why are there radiation detectors at the city morgue?

Forty-five minutes after leaving Baragon's apartment, Emily was unlocking her own front door, still kicking herself for telling him.

It's probably going to come to nothing, she was thinking. *Nothing at all.* But still . . . even if it did come to nothing, she had a sinking feeling that Roscoe wouldn't leave it at that— that he'd turn it into something anyway.

If only there was somebody I could talk to who wasn't a journalist with a paranoid streak.

But there wasn't.

Emily's one-bedroom on West Ninth Street was larger than Baragon's and much cozier. She, at least, had a few comfortable chairs and a couch that seemed safe to sit on. The apartment was filled with plants, and the walls held several framed photographs. Landscapes, mostly. Nature scenes. Every day at work, she was confronted with the unbelievable savagery human beings are capable of inflicting upon each other. At least at home, she could try to remind herself that there was another world out there. One in which things lived.

She checked her answering machine (nothing) while thinking she should get some sort of dinner together. That could wait for a bit, though. She went over to her record collection—packed into the bookshelves along one wall—and began running her index finger idly along the spines of the old vinyl albums. When she found what she was looking for, she pulled it from the shelf, carefully slid the disc from the sleeve, and placed it on the turntable.

A moment later, Cliff Edwards began fingerpicking "St. Louis Blues" on his uke with a plaintive delicacy no one had ever been able to match.

Then, alone in the middle of her living room floor, much as she did almost every night, Ms. Emily Roschen, very quietly and very slowly, began to dance.

The next morning, Baragon got into the office shortly after seven, skipped the news wires, gulped his coffee, and started typing. By the time Montgomery showed up at nine, he was ready for him.

"Hey, Ed," he said, rapping on the open door as Montgomery was unpacking his breakfast from a white paper bag. "Got something for you."

Montgomery scowled. Baragon was the last thing he needed first thing in the morning. Especially before the coffee took hold. "Great. Super. I can't wait. What you got this time, Roscoe—giant crocodiles in the reservoir? Aliens setting up camp in the Chrysler Building?"

Baragon let it slide, if only because he expected it and perhaps even deserved it a little. He still made a mental note to keep those two in mind for the future. He was sure he'd be able to find somebody to confirm them as easily as he got someone (well, Eel) to confirm the existence of real live CHUDs in the sewer system.

"Better, Ed. The real deal—EMS finds a stiff in Tompkins

yesterday, right? Homeless guy. Brings him to the morgue. And when they get him there, they find out that he's—get this—*radioactive*." He paused expectantly.

"Uh-huh. And where'd you dig this one up, Kolchak— some movie you watched last night?"

"I wish you'd stop calling me that, especially around the youngsters—and anyway, in answer to your question, *no*. Someone who's actually close to the case."

"Let me guess—another one of your friends? One who just happened to be walking past the morgue yesterday and peeked in the windows to watch the autopsy?"

Baragon shook his head. "Can't do that, Ed—autopsy rooms are upstairs, and the windows are frosted. C'mon, just look at the fucking story. It's all there, it's all solid. Trust me. No schizos, no crazies."

"Tell you what, Roscoe," Montgomery said as he peeled the plastic lid off his coffee, trying not to spill any on his shirt this morning. "Would it be okay if I had some coffee first? To be honest, I'm a little hung and not in any condition for this yet."

"Yeah. Sure," Baragon said, "I understand completely," before exhaling slowly and returning to his desk. *Picnic boy.*

None of the youngsters were in yet, so Baragon dialed the number of Emily's direct line at the lab.

"Lab," she said when she picked up the receiver.

"Hey—" he said. "You alone?"

"For the moment, yeah." She sounded tired.

"You okay?" he asked.

"Didn't sleep so hot. But I got some coffee; that should help."

"Good. Look—I'm real sorry to bother you at work again, but I thought I'd let you know I did a little something about our guy this morning, but I don't think Ed's buying it. I think he pretty much killed it before seeing it."

"That's too bad, Rosk," she said. "I'm sorry. Really. But you might want to tell him something."

"What's that?"

Her voice dropped to a whisper. "Someone else leaked the story. To the *Times*. The reporter was here already this morning and talked to the chief."

"You're shittin' me," Baragon said, his left hand tightening around the arm of his chair. "Those energetic bastards."

"It's true. Because of it, the chief's going to release a statement. He's not too happy about it, though."

"God-*damn*. Well, at least maybe it'll help Ed reconsider. If we can't get it out there before they do, at least we can get it out around the same time. Any idea who the leak is? You know—just in case I need to point some fingers myself?"

"No idea. I'm not even sure it's anyone here—it could've been EMS—even one of those guys from the mayor's office, but I doubt—look, I should go."

"I understand. Thanks a ton."

"No problem—see you tonight?"

"My treat tonight."

He hung up the phone and went back to Ed's office.

"Hey, Ed—still working on that muffin, I see."

"Yeah," Ed mumbled, his mouth full. "I can see why you became a reporter, Roscoe—it's that eagle eye of yours."

"Aww, Ed, no reason to be cranky. I was just making conversation," Baragon said. "But I got something—I just talked to my source on this radioactive man case. Seems the *Times* caught wind of it, and the chief ME went on the record and is releasing an official statement later today. If you go with my story now, we might beat them to press."

"Hey, there's an idea." Montgomery didn't sound terribly enthusiastic and continued tearing at his muffin.

Baragon stayed where he was in the doorway.

"You aren't going to con me, Roscoe," Montgomery said,

finally, leaning back in his chair, fresh coffee stains dribbling down the front of his shirt. "I can see those rusty little gears grinding away—'Tell him the *Times* has got the same story and he'll jump all over it.' Right? But it's not going to work that way. To be honest, I don't care whether or not the *Times* has this story."

"Why not? This is *news*." He dragged out the word *neewwws* in a way that always made Montgomery's fingernails curl.

"Because there are other things going on in the world— things that actually affect people, Baragon. Did you know that there were three more major earthquakes yesterday?"

Yesterday you didn't know about the first quakes, dumbass.

"—Did you know that some half-finished space station has slipped out of orbit and may well land in a populated area sometime in the next few days? Did you *know* that the economy's a mess, that there are riots in Miami because the cops shot some kid, and that the president hasn't been seen in public in almost a week?"

"Oh, Christ, Ed—how's *that* going to affect anybody? Reporting that the president is missing is like reporting that hostages got pie—what's the point?" sniped Baragon. He admittedly hadn't been aware of some of these things—but he liked that killer space junk story. Must've just broken this morning.

"Right now, believe me, nobody's much worried about some fictional dead homeless guy who glows in the dark."

Baragon pursed his lips. "Okay. But answer me a question, will you?"

Montgomery looked at him but said nothing.

"Why d'you hate me so much?"

"Oh, hell, I don't *hate* you, Roscoe," Montgomery said, wiping his hands with a napkin and sounding almost paternal (if put upon). "I really, really don't. Honestly. But I remember how good you were—"

Oh, here we go again.

"—But you've gotten lazy. You're not trying anymore. And I guess that pisses me off."

"Okay then, answer me this—why does *God* hate me?"

"Roscoe, I'm also being straight when I say that God doesn't hate you. Quite the opposite, in fact. God *laughs* at you. When he's aware of you at all."

"Thanks, Ed," Baragon said, wincing at the obvious truth of it. "That helps a lot."

"Look . . . Roscoe—there are things about you I do like. You scare the kids and keep them in line back there. That I like. You're clever. You have a reputation. It's fading fast, I'll tell you that much—but to some people, it's still there. But it's been a long time since you've really given me anything I could run with a clear conscience."

Baragon thought a second. "Okay. Fine. Screw the radioactive man story. At least until I get hold of the ME's statement. What's the deal with this space station? You got anybody on that?"

"No," Montgomery said. "Not yet. But I got a better idea—though lord knows why. Something you can't screw up too badly. Consider it a chance to redeem yourself— because, in spite of everything, I do like the way you scare those kids back there."

"Uh-huh?"

"You interviewed a geologist once, didn't you? Sometime last year? Back when they had that volcano in California?"

"You're almost there, Ed—he was a geophysicist. And it was about the quake that flattened half of downtown San Diego."

"Right—so this guy knows earthquakes. Get on the horn,

ask him what the fuck is going on. Talk to a few other people if you can—people with *jobs*, Roscoe—people with *professions* and things to say—not psychics predicting the next one, not crazy men who live with their mothers—and give me a story with facts. No monsters or government plots. Do you think you can do that?"

Baragon gave him the same look he used to scare the youngsters sometimes and returned to his desk.

By now, Biddle was settled in, still giddy from his big front page debut.

"Hi, Roscoe!" he said.

Baragon stopped and glared at him.

Ten minutes later, he found the number he was looking for—Dr. Carl Stevenson, who, as of a year ago at least, was some big shot with the government's Geophysical Survey Team.

At least it's not a drought or a flood or a wildfire, Baragon figured. *Those are the worst. Nobody wants to read about those.*

Before calling him, he gleaned what he could from the wire stories. Another one in Hawaii. Another one in northern Alaska. And a monster quake in Chile, which had apparently killed hundreds and left thousands homeless. Trying to get help to all the stricken areas had left the Red Cross and United Nations disaster relief spread paper thin.

Figuring he had at least a fair grasp of the situation—especially given that he was going to be asking this guy more generalized questions—global plate shifts, "what does this all mean," that sort of dusty bullshit, he picked up the phone and started punching buttons.

"Mr. Baragon?"

Confused, Baragon looked to his right to find Biddle

standing there. He stopped punching numbers but left the phone against his ear. *Where do they get these kids?*

"Mr. Baragon—I'd—I'd just like to say—about the story—"

"Biddle, look. Take a close look at me. I'm on the telephone. Or I'm *trying* to get on the telephone. You do not try to talk to anyone while they're on the phone. It's just plain rude. Go sit down. Do something else."

"I just wanted to say I'm sorry things turned out the way they did—but it wasn't my fault—Mr. Montgom—"

"No," Baragon cut him off. "It's never your fault. And it never *will* be your fault. Don't worry, son—you'll do just fine in this business."

"You think so?" Biddle asked, a smile creeping onto his face. "Well, did—did you like the Campbell story?"

Baragon controlled the urge to carom a stapler off young Mr. Biddle's skull, returned to the telephone, and began dialing the Washington number again.

"No, I'm sorry," the woman on the other end told him. "Dr. Stevenson is in the field right now."

"Of course, that's understandable," Baragon purred at her. He'd always been pretty good at purring things out of secretaries, so long as they couldn't actually see him. Usually, if they saw what he looked like, the game was up, and they immediately lost all desire to help him out. "Uh—do you know where he is and how I might reach him? It's quite imperative that I talk to him as soon as possible."

"I'm very sorry, sir," she said. "But as you may know we're in a bit of a crisis situation right now, and Dr. Stevenson is quite busy." From the sound of her voice, it sounded like a lot of people had been trying to reach Stevenson these days.

"Of course, I understand, and I'm sorry," he told her.

"But I'm in a bit of a crisis situation myself. Let me explain what this is about." *Oldest trick in the book.* "My name is Nat Romanoff, and I'm with the Arcata Insurance Company, up here in Fairbanks."

"Yes?"

"You're obviously aware of the situation we're in up here. Up in Barrow, I mean."

"Of course."

"See, a number of our policyholders have lost *so very much* as a result of the recent earthquakes. . . ." He tried to sound earnest, even a little pathetic. "It's just awful what these people have been through. The claims are coming in left and right already—but before we can start to process any of them, see, I need to talk to Dr. Stevenson to check out a few minor but very important details. And well, we'd just like to start helping these poor folks out as quickly as possible. Help 'em get back on their feet and start rebuilding right away."

There was a pause on the other end of the phone. "I've never heard of such a thing before," the secretary said. She sounded suspicious, and Baragon bit his lower lip. "And I've certainly never heard of an insurance company that was eager to process a claim."

"Well, ma'am," he said, his voice smoother than ever, "I guess we're not your typical insurance company. We're actually here to *help* people." It was a bit much, he knew, but maybe she wouldn't notice.

There was another long pause. "Imagine that," the secretary said, finally. He could tell immediately from her tone that she'd bought it. He relaxed again. "Now let me see. Dr. Stevenson is with the Gamma Team, and Gamma Team is, I believe"—she was obviously checking through some files—"yes, he's in Alaska now, too, as it happens—near the site of last week's tremor."

"Really," Baragon said. "Up in Barrow himself then? That'll certainly cut down on my phone bills, won't it?" He forced a small chuckle. "Any idea how I might reach him there?"

Before he hung up, he thanked her profusely, not only on his own behalf, but on behalf of all the citizens of Alaska.

Roscoe was leaning on the wrought-iron fence, watching half a dozen dogs of all different sizes romp about on a muddy patch of earth.

Shortly before he'd left the office, Emily had called, suggesting that it was such a nice day, maybe they could meet up someplace outside.

"Wha'd you have in mind?" he asked. When she suggested meeting by the dog run at Tompkins Square Park, he'd replied conspiratorially, "Ahh, the scene of the crime."

"No, not that. I just thought it would be nice to get some fresh air for once, and that seemed an easy place to meet."

So here he was. He was working on his third smoke, watching in fascination as a Chihuahua made a persistent and noble effort to mount a bulldog. Baragon liked most dogs. Didn't care much for most dog owners, though.

"Safety is a cootie-wootie," a low voice whispered behind his left ear.

He turned, startled, ready for almost anything (especially in a park like Tompkins), only to find Emily smiling at him. "Sorry about that," she said. "But it seemed appropriate. You been waiting long?"

"Just three smokes," he shrugged. "It's good to see you— you know, in the daylight."

She assumed a spot next to him along the fence. "It's good to see you, too." She looked up at the trees and the sky. "This is nice." They still had some light left, and the air was cool but not too chilly. "So . . . you said on the phone that things went well with that geologist?"

"Yeah," he nodded. "It took me four operators, but I got through. Thank God I'm a trained professional. And fortunately, he didn't remember me from that last time we spoke."

"Did you call him something awful back then?" she asked.

"No—"

"Ask him if aliens were behind it?" She was smiling.

"*No*—I'm just always a little relieved when people don't remember me."

"Uh-huh. I can understand that." She was still smiling.

"Anyway, he gives me all the facts and figures. Epicenter coordinates. Original magnitude, number of aftershocks. Tells me that it's atypical, but just a coincidence, that all these quakes, of this force, are clustered together."

"Uh-huh?"

"*Then* he tells me something weird." Baragon was clearly excited. He turned away from the desperate Chihuahua to face her.

Oh, please, Rosk. Just let it be a regular story. It's just a fucking earthquake.

"Yes?" she asked hesitantly.

"Well. It seems that there's something else happening on the seafloor up there. Maybe a new volcano, they aren't sure yet—though it might explain the second quake—and they won't know for sure until they send a camera down there. But the fact is, something is happening up there that's heating the water. And as a result, the ice pack off the northern coast of Alaska is starting to break up."

"Couldn't it just be a result of the quake? Or global warming?"

"That's what they thought at first—but the source of the increased water temperature is coming from below, not above."

"That is weird. Did he have any theories?"

"Oh, just what I said—that it's a volcano."

She heard the doubt in his voice, which led to her next question—the question she was afraid to ask.

"And, uh—do *you* have any theories?" She steeled herself for the worst.

He shook his head. "Not really. I could go nuts with it, you know—but this time, I won't. I'll just let the scientists do the talking."

She relaxed.

"The other thing he told me was that this is the big whale-hunting season for the Eskimos up there."

"Uh-huh?"

"Problem is, all the whales seem to have vamoosed."

"Really."

"Yeah, not a one's been seen so far this year. They're all gone. Or they've gotten smarter."

"Headed toward colder waters, is that it? Or maybe there just aren't that many left?"

"Probably. Not our problem, really—though I guess I'll make a mention of it."

"Well, I'm glad that turned out okay." She clearly had something else on her mind. She stepped away from the fence. "C'mon, let's take a walk, maybe sit down somewhere."

There weren't too many people left in the park, and those who were looked like they never left. Emily and Baragon strolled past the public bathrooms (where the junkies actually lined up in an orderly fashion and waited their turn), then followed a curving path that led them away from the dog run.

Baragon dropped himself on the first empty bench they passed, crossed his legs, and reached for a cigarette. Nobody was sitting near them. "Have a seat," he said, patting the peeling green wood. As she did, a smile tugged at the corner of his mouth. "Coming here has nothing to do with getting some fresh air, does it?"

"Not exactly," she confessed.

"Didn't think so," he said. "What happened with our guy today? You find out something new?"

"Well . . . as a matter of fact, yes." She opened the bag on her lap and pulled out some sheets of paper. "For one, a fingerprint check gave us a name pretty quickly."

"Yeah?" he asked, leaning closer, forgetting about earthquakes for the time being. "John Doe no more?"

"Raymond Martin," she said, glancing at the top page. She kept her voice low. "Thirty-seven years old. Long rap sheet as a petty burglar. Served a little time, but not too much. Never got into anything too heavy. Some drug possession, that sort of thing."

Just as Emily, over the past three years, had taught Roscoe a few things about the death business he never could have imagined otherwise, he'd taught her a few things, as well—like how to interpret a rap sheet.

"Uh-huh?"

"Last known address was in an SRO over on Third."

"Really. I thought he was homeless."

"Well, maybe he was—that's what EMS said—all I'm saying is the fingerprint file gave us an address that was about a year old. I don't know if he still lived there or not."

"You didn't happen to—?" he began.

"Don't know why, but here." She handed him one of the sheets she was holding.

"You're the best," he said as he looked it over. "And I'll tell you another thing there, Ethel—you sure know how to handle things in proper spy movie fashion."

"I try my best, Julius."

"Nothing on here about being radioactive, is there?" he

asked, still scanning the page. "Did he live in the Ukraine for a long time?"

"Not that his rap sheet tells us."

"Damn."

"The other thing that we all got today was this—along with strict instructions that anything any of us says to the press is to come directly from this sheet of paper. Though we're discouraged from talking to the press at all."

"That's very wise," he told her. "Vultures, every last one of 'em." Baragon took the other sheet of paper she was holding and began reading through the chief medical examiner's official statement concerning the radioactive man.

"You're kidding," he said a minute later as his eyes snaked down the page again.

"Nope."

"But—"

"I know. Let's maybe not talk about this right now, okay?" She nodded at the small cluster of people headed down the path in their direction. The one in front was bouncing a basketball.

"Gotcha." He reached over and gave her a light sock on the shoulder. "Thanks, there, you."

"You're very welcome."

"Say—" he said, slipping the papers into his bag, "we don't happen to know where in the park here those EMS guys found him, do we?"

"No idea, I'm afraid. This is as specific as they got." She wrapped her arms around herself. "I'm getting chilly, are you?"

"Sure," he said, even though he wasn't particularly chilly. He looked up at the sky, though, and noticed that it was starting to get dark. If they didn't leave the park soon, they'd have to fight their way out—like *The Warriors*, but on a much smaller scale. "Hey, what say we go over and visit Jack? I miss him."

New York Times, Thursday, March 15
DEAD MAN DISCOVERED TO BE RADIOACTIVE

When the body of a homeless man found in Tompkins Square Park Tuesday morning was delivered to the city morgue, nobody expected him to set off the radiation detectors, but that's what happened. That prompted officials at the medical examiner's office to immediately phone for assistance, and soon the city's Hazardous Materials Unit and officials from the Mayor's Office were on their way to the scene, unsure what they might find.

No traces of radiation were detected in the ambulance that had carried the body from the park, near Avenue B and Tenth Street, or on the paramedics who had come into contact with it, city officials said. Radiation was only detected within the body of the unidentified man.

The man had probably become radioactive as the result of a medical test not long before he died, said Theo von Hohenheim, a spokesman for the medical examiner's office. Such tests—which may involve radioactive materials such as barium—could have easily left enough residue in the body to trigger the sensors.

"The levels of radiation we discovered here were very weak," said Fire Battalion Chief Jack Grimace. "They posed absolutely no risk to anyone who came in contact with the man, and there is no danger to the public at large."

The new radiation detectors were installed last year during renovations that were made at the medical examiner's office. The office also received new state-of-the-art laboratories and additional equipment. Mr. von Hohenheim said officials decided to install radioactivity detectors after a company hired to dispose of biohazardous waste uncovered low levels of radiation in materials being removed from the offices.

Yesterday, while the morgue itself was declared safe from radioactivity, little was known about the man. Mr. von Hohenheim said they hoped to determine the cause of death during an autopsy that would be performed within the week.

Baragon dropped the paper on Ed's desk.

"Funny thing about this story, Ed," he said with feigned confusion.

"Yes, Roscoe? And what's that?" Ed didn't bother to feign enthusiasm.

"Well, Ed, I tell you—it seems most every damn thing in this story is *wrong*. And I have the evidence right here to prove it." He held up the two sheets of paper Emily had given him, trying to hide that the second one was just the official press release.

"Uh-huh? Nice work. But I thought we were dropping this thing—where the hell's my earthquake story?"

Baragon frowned. He should've expected this. "Ed, Christ, this is local news. This is happening right here, right now."

"Sure it's a local story," Ed replied, scratching the back of his neck. "But it's a *stupid* local story, even for you. I asked you for an earthquake story, and that's what I expect."

Baragon's frown deepened, and his shoulders sagged. "You'll have it in an hour," he said, half-deflated, then returned to his desk.

Three days later, there had been no further mention of the radioactive man in the *Times* or any other news source that

Baragon could find. He'd been looking. It seemed to have vanished as quickly and silently as the Ukrainian nuclear plant that, only a few weeks earlier, had been melting into the earth.

Yet according to Emily, radioactive man was still the focus of intense—sometimes furious—interest and debate around the morgue. What's more, he was still there, locked away in isolation.

Emily had been kind enough to smuggle out a copy of the final autopsy report (not a hard thing to do, given that she worked on it) and had gone over it with Baragon in order to explain some of the anomalies and technical details. She'd called him on the nineteenth, the day the report was finished, and asked if she could meet him at his place again that night. She didn't say why over the phone, but he knew.

"They were right, initially, when they said that the source of the radioactivity was internal," she said as they sat at the kitchen table again, working on their third beer. "But it wasn't the result of any sort of medical treatment."

"Yeah, I'd been wondering about that," Baragon said. "After all—how could a homeless guy afford radiation treatment? Y'know—have New York's bums set up a union for themselves, with a really good benefits package? Lord knows I haven't heard of any clinics in the area performing free cancer treatments out of the goodness of their hearts."

"Yeah," she said. "It wasn't that. And it wasn't localized in any way."

He blinked at her. "I'm not sure what you mean."

"I mean, it wasn't like pellets had been implanted, and it wasn't like he'd been given a barium solution to drink—that's the stuff they use to make soft-tissue X rays clearer."

"I know, but I'm still not sure what you're saying."

"What I'm *saying* is—is that it was as if every cell in his body had become infused with something. Every fucking cell. His whole *body* was radioactive. I've never heard of anything like that before. He must've been exposed to something unbelievable."

Baragon was even more confused now. "Any idea at all what might've caused something like that? Could he have been working in a nuclear plant for ten years or something?"

"I dunno—maybe—but I seriously doubt it," she said. "There are two problems with that theory." She went to the fridge for another beer. "You need another?"

"Sure, yes, always," he said as he drained what was left in the bottle. "And those problems are?"

"Well, three, actually," she corrected herself as she returned to the table. "Radiation poisoning to this extent would have killed him in a matter of hours—if not minutes."

"Uh-huh?" he said. Hedora, who'd wandered into the kitchen a while ago and had been slinking around their legs to no effect, leaped into Baragon's ample lap with a tiny yelp.

". . . And given his criminal record—along with his being homeless or living in an SRO at the time of his death—it's doubtful that he had any sort of job working in a nuclear reactor."

"That makes sense," he nodded.

"There's one more thing," she said. "Which makes this whole thing that much more confusing."

Great, thought Baragon. "And what's that?"

"Well," she said, "apparently, it wasn't the radiation that killed him. I mean, it would have—and could have—and *might* have—but our Mr. Martin here died from asphyxiation."

"Pardon?"

"You know—choking, or strangulation."

He grunted slightly. "I *know* what asphyxiation means. I mean—what the hell? Was he strangled, or did he choke on his own vomit, or what?"

"There were clear abrasions on his neck."

"Aww, Jesus—this is all getting way beyond me now." He went for a cigarette, and Hedora, knowing what was coming next, hopped to the floor and returned to his basket in the other room. "So someone killed him. . . . Why didn't Mr. Smarty Pants from the *Times* report that? Huh? And why wasn't that in the press release?"

"They didn't know yet," she said—though she sounded doubtful.

"You said the marks were clear."

"All those things happened *before* the autopsy. Until then, he'd been in isolation, remember?"

Baragon puffed his cheeks as he exhaled. "So—is the NYPD going to get involved now? They seem to be the only city agency that hasn't touched this thing yet."

Emily shrugged. "I don't know. I really don't." She took a drink. "It's out of my hands. I just look through the microscopes, you know?"

"Yeah," Baragon said, looking down toward his shoes. "I know." He reached for the autopsy report, which had been sitting on the table between them, and flipped idly through it. "Emily," he said. "You're amazing. But let me ask you— what can I do with this?"

She squinted at him. "I brought it to you, didn't I?" She smiled slightly. "Dummy. You're dumb and stupid."

He smiled. It was an old joke between them. "I know, but I mean—"

"What you can do with it is up to you. What you can do for me is make sure that I am not connected with it at all. . . . And buy me a few beers."

"Need another?" he asked, gesturing toward the refrigerator.

"Sure. Always."

He stood to get some more. "Let me ask you," he said,

not looking at her. "How many people have access to this thing? I mean—if I were to make its contents public, how many people could this report be traced back to?"

"Oh, they're pretty much considered public information, should you know where to look," she said. "Except in rare cases when they're sealed . . . and, to be honest, this may be one of those rare cases."

"That's what I was afraid of." He bit his lower lip and nodded, mostly to himself. "Thanks."

Backed by the evidence of the official coroner's report, Baragon returned to Montgomery's office the next morning. Much to his surprise, Montgomery relented. Reluctantly, to be sure, but he relented.

"With luck we'll reach the point again where I won't have to say this—but nothing crazy, Roscoe, you hear me?" he said, almost amiably. "Do for me the same thing you did with the earthquakes. It was a good piece, ashamed as I am to admit it—facts, data, a dash of human interest. A little 'ain't this odd?' with the whales. It was fine. Do the same thing this time—but no more than that, got it? It's a human interest story, that's all. No monsters, no aliens, no government plots. Keep it around five hundred, no longer."

Baragon nodded. *You got the Hazardous Materials Unit, the EPA, the DOH, and the fucking mayor's emergency management team involved, a homicide in which the NYPD is not involved, and you're saying no government plots. Righto, Chief. You're a born newspaperman all right.*

"You realize, of course," Montgomery said, "that the only reason I'm letting you do this is so we can show up those smug bastards at the *Times*."

Yeah, sure, now it hits you, Baragon thought. "Whatever you say."

"They think they're so fucking smart—but that's why you need to keep this one blunt and direct—and under control. Got it?"

"Got it."

"Good. Get to work."

Chapter Seven

For a sunny late March afternoon, it was still strangely cool outside. Even on the warmest days, the temperature had yet to rise much above sixty this spring.

That was fine with Baragon. He liked the chill, and more than that, he liked wearing his trench coat. The trench coat, he thought, gave him that "Douglas Kennedy in *Dark Passage*" air and helped him feel like less of a joke.

As he approached the scarred, crumbling hotel on Third Avenue between Second and Third Streets, he could see there was a group of men—residents, he figured—gathered around the front steps, smoking. Unless they were all waiting for the hipster boutique next door to open. Baragon could also tell as he approached that he wasn't going to fit in here very well. But that had never stopped him before—he didn't fit in much of anyplace.

"Hey," he said, raising a hand in greeting as he slowed to a stop. "Howzit goin'?"

The four men—all of them in their fifties, he'd guess, battered and weary—eyed him with suspicion but said nothing.

"Look, I'm real sorry to interrupt," Baragon said, pulling

a smoke from his pocket and lighting it, "Ahhh . . . but do any of you guys live here?" He tilted his head toward the building.

There were a couple quick nods, but the suspicious looks seemed to take a turn for the hostile.

"Ah-hah," he said. "Good, good—look—first off, I'm not a cop, okay? Just to get that cleared up." He opened his coat to reveal that he wasn't packing. "My name's Roscoe Baragon—I'm with the *Sentinel*—you know, the newspaper? The bad one? And I was wondering if any of you might know something about a guy who used to live here."

One of them finally spoke. He looked to be the oldest of the four—though that was hard to tell. Deeply lined face, closely cropped dark gray hair. Sad eyes. He was wearing a filthy blue down jacket over a thin yellow shirt. "And whoz-zat?" he asked. It wasn't exactly what you'd call friendly, but it was more than Baragon'd gotten up to this point.

"Guy named Raymond Martin? I'm told he used to live here."

The old man shook his head. "Don't know'm."

"Wait a second, Sammy," another man piped up, maybe a few years younger than the first but looking to be in no better shape. He turned to Baragon. "Maybe he means Ray? Remember Ray?"

"Oh yeah—Ray," the old man said, smiling slightly. "Ain't seen him 'round here in quite a while."

"Like . . . how long?" Baragon asked. He thought he'd feel them out first, see what they remembered.

"Ohh, hell, I dunno," the first man said. "Couple months, maybe?"

"Naah—I seen him over in the park, like three weeks ago," the second man offered. "Did'n' talk to'm, though."

"We should make sure we're talking about the same guy,"

said Baragon. "Skinny guy, mid-thirties. Had a criminal record, but nothing too major. Burglary, drug possession."

"Yeah, that's Ray, all right. All over. Used to live up on the
fourth floor here, I think."

Baragon's eye drifted up the front of the ten-story building, counting out the windows until he reached the fourth
floor. "How long ago was that?"

"Ohh, I'd say—" the first man began, until he was cut off
by a third voice.

"What you want with Ray?" It was a grave, resonant
voice, and there was nothing friendly about it. Baragon
turned to see that the voice belonged to an enormous man
he hadn't seen before. Probably in his forties, wearing a
black knit cap and a brown leather jacket.

Baragon eyed him up and down and decided it would be
best to simply be honest with him.

"Okay, here's the deal." There was no need to pussyfoot
around it anymore, he decided. "Ray's dead. They found
him over in Tompkins about a week ago." None of the men
seemed surprised at all by the news. There was no shock, no
anguish in any of their faces. If anything, there was a collective shrug. "I'm asking after him because I think there was
something weird about it—and because nobody else is asking about it. Cops won't even touch it."

"You expect the cops to care about some dead junkie?"
the big man laughed, but darkly. "I don't think so."

"I know," Baragon said, with what he hoped would seem
like a sympathetic nod.

"So if they don't care—and *we* don't care—why should
you?"

"Just curious, I guess."

"How'd he get it?" another man asked. They didn't seem
to care too much that Raymond had been promoted to

glory—but suddenly they all seemed very interested in how it had happened.

"Looks like he was strangled," Baragon told them, not knowing whether he should be making all this public quite yet. "Nobody knows who did it, or why."

"Well, I'll tell ya," the old man said, settling himself in on the top step. "Ray, he didn't have too mucha anybody who liked him."

"Why's that?"

"Motherfucker was just *peculiar*, know what I mean?" he said. "Just real fuckin' *strange*."

"Yeah?" Roscoe asked. "How so?"

"Well, you say he was a burglar, right?"

"Right. According to his rap sheet."

"But you never say what he stole."

Baragon shrugged, dropped his cigarette to the sidewalk, and ground it out under his shoe. "I guess I don't know what he stole. I didn't see that."

By now most of the men were smiling, and the old man was chuckling. "Well, ol' Raymond, y'see," he said, "he used to steal *toilets*."

"Toilets." *Yeah, Ed's gonna dig that.*

"And not just toilets, Sammy—" the second man who'd spoken added, "sinks, pipes—all that shit."

"He stole . . . plumbing fixtures? Nothing else?"

"Yeah! Hey—Wesley—tellim 'bout the time ol' Ray hit your place!" They were laughing now, relaxed, as if they were reminiscing about an old friend at an impromptu side-walk wake.

"Man," Wesley began, shaking his head, "that mother-fucker—I coulda strangled him myself that day. So—so I go in to take a bath, right? A nice hot fuckin' bath—turn on the water—an' all the fuckin' water goes right the fuck through the drain on the floor. Takes me a second to know what the

fuck's goin' on. I get down an' look under the fuckin' tub—
and there's nothin' there! He took my fuckin' drainpipe!"

"So . . . what you're telling me," Baragon said, thinking
he was due another cigarette right about now, "is that Ray
would break into people's apartments, with what—wrenches
and shit?"

"Yeah."

"And he'd steal the pipes?"

"An' those were from the rooms that had bathrooms. On
th' other floors—the ones with bathrooms in the hall?—you
just learn not to use those. First place he went."

"And he took *nothing* else? Money, TVs, nothing?"

Sammy shook his head, smiling.

"That's really fucking weird," Baragon observed.

"Just ain't it, though."

"Wha'd he do with them? Did he sell them or something?"

"Dunno," the old man shrugged. "Guess so."

"Uh-huh—do you know if there's much money to be
made in reselling used plumbing fixtures?"

"Dunno."

"Man," Baragon said, shaking his head and scratching the
side of his nose, "that is real fucking strange. . . . What
about the manager? Didn't he have anything to say about it?
If Martin lived here and everyone knew he was doing it and
all—"

The men stopped laughing. The old man—Baragon had
finally concluded that his name was, indeed, Sammy—shook
his head. "Don't do nuthin'. They don' care. I been in this
fuckin' place for eleven years now. Used to be okay, right?
Then 'bout a year, maybe year an' a half ago, the place gets
sold. New manager, new everything. Never see 'im. Don't
do nuthin'. Jus' like before."

Baragon almost asked him why he didn't just move out

but caught himself in time. Instead he asked, "Anybody remember when Ray first showed up?"

There were a few shrugs, but Sammy said, "Oh, I'd guess about a year ago."

"So . . . it was a few months after you got the new manager that he moved in?" He had no idea where he was going with this. He was just going.

"No—" Wesley said after a second, "it was about a week later. Week or so after the new manager. I remember 'cause it was right before that you heard people startin' to complain 'bout the pipes an' shit—how nothin' was gettin' fixed no more."

"Yeah, right," Sammy said. "An' that's when we started seein' him around. Skinny guy."

"Great," Baragon said. "You guys have been a huge help. Thanks a lot. Sorry to have kept you so long."

"'Sall right," Sammy said, and nodded.

As Baragon turned to leave, however, he felt a heavy hand upon his shoulder. He turned to find himself facing, not surprisingly, the big man, whose name he never learned.

"Hey there, Columbo—" the word was loaded with contempt. "We helped you out. Now, don't you think it's just fair that you might help us out a little bit?"

Baragon, who had never once paid for an interview in his life, decided that it was only fair that he make an exception this one time and reached into his pocket.

"Oh, one more thing—" he said as he slipped a couple twenties from his wallet, "This might sound a little crazy"— he handed the bills to the big man—"but since the new management took over, have you guys noticed people— other people who live here—disappearing? It's no big deal. I'm just curious."

Wesley shrugged. "No man—people come, people go— wha' chu think?"

"Nothing," Baragon said, replacing his wallet. "Nothing at all. Thanks again for your time."

He turned and headed back to the subway with a little too much to think about along the way. Maybe he'd give Eel a call when he got back to the office, see what he could make of it.

Then he realized that what Eel could make of it would probably be another straight-to-video masterpiece filmed in Jersey.

Half an hour later, Baragon walked through the *Sentinel*'s front doors, where Ruby, the receptionist, flagged him down and handed him a piece of paper.

"I didn't think this guy would ever leave," she said. "He said he really needed to talk to you. I finally convinced him to write you a note."

"Thanks," Baragon said gratefully. He didn't care much for drop-ins. "Sorry about that."

"That's okay," she said. "But I didn't think he was ever gonna leave."

"They rarely do," he told her as he left the reception area. Walking down the hall, he unfolded the piece of paper she'd handed him and started reading.

> *Dear Mr. Roscoe Baragon*
> *I do not have much time to write . . . this is an SOS . . . red alert prayer request . . . I want to make sure that the president gets the letter that I wrote to him and sent to Wash. DC. It is regarding the extortion crime that was committed AGAINST US etc. It was reported to officials all thru the USA and to the whole world. We went and talked with the Va. State Police in Richmond and to a Detective Jeter in Gastonia, NC. I have been over-*

charged for faxes at the 'Computer Shop' and office supply store in Bryson City NC 2.00 a page—not fair—I have taken the car in to be repaired at Mountain Ford and it works worse than it did before we took it in. The owner said to come back tomorrow—that I should have people pray alot—I said he should pray alot. I sensed the Holy One of Israel in prayer this a.m. before the car would not start (again after having been 'repaired') and the Pillar of Fire and the Cloud of Smoke—as in Exodus—I said this is the Second Exodus . . . Jeremiah 16:14–16 . . . Tammy Kirkland (female) at McDonalds said that she was going to tell my wife to not come in anyway today when the car would not start, and she had called in— screwing around with her hours again THIS IS ALL VERY SERIOUS TO OUR AND TO MY SUR-VIVAL. AND WHAT AFFECTS ME AFFECTS MY CHILDREN PLEASE PRAY AND DO BIG SPIRI-TUAL WARFARE—MEDICINE—I HAVE LEFT MESSAGES AT FOX NEWS AND AT MAYOR'S OFFICE IN NY CITY AND AT THE ISRAELI CON-SULATE AND AT CATHOLIC AND PROTES-TANT PRAYER LINES—AND TO XENA THE WARRIOR PRINCESS—AND MANY MORE. SOS—THIS IS VERY SERIOUS THE GAMES THAT PEOPLE ARE PLAYING—GOD HAS HAD ENOUGH.

God's not the only one who's had enough, Baragon thought, scanning ahead to see he wasn't even half-finished yet. *Sounds like you got all your bases covered.* He was folding the paper back up when he heard Montgomery call his name.

Shit.

"Yeah, Chief?"

"Where in the hell have you been?"

Baragon leaned against the door frame. He was tired. He wasn't used to that much walking. "Well, believe it or not, Ed, I was doing a little legwork."

Montgomery looked surprised, if not exactly impressed. "You?"

Baragon moved into the office and lowered himself into a chair. "Yeah," he huffed.

"For what?"

"This radioactive man piece—remember? Just running a little background on Martin."

"Uh-huh."

"He used to steal plumbing fixtures."

"Did he, now."

"Yup."

Montgomery didn't look in the least interested. "Fine. Whatever. Just get it to me soon. And in the meantime—at some point during your illustrious career, you must've met somebody from NASA, right?"

Baragon's eyes narrowed with interest. "Is this about that space station business? The one that's going to destroy—what is it, Tucson?"

"Maybe."

"Look, Ed—I'm kind of swamped right now, really—but I'd be happy to—"

Jesus Christ—up until last week, it'd been nothing but silence. Now I'm being tossed things left and right. I don't get this at all. Maybe it's time I started getting back in shape—

"Well, do you?"

"Shit . . . *do* I?" He had too much on his mind right now—and he was too beat—to think very clearly. "Y'know, I don't think—" Baragon stopped. "No, wait—there *was* one guy."

"Who's that?"

"Gimme a second. He had a funny name. Met him a while ago . . ." Then it came to him. "Slaughter. There you have it. Hoke Slaughter."

"Yeah, that sounds like somebody you'd know. What's he do?"

"'Did' may be more accurate—we're talking a long time ago. He was a NASA copywriter. Press releases and what-have-you. We got into a fistfight at a bar in Houston."

Montgomery rolled his eyes. "Why am I not surprised—though I find it very difficult to imagine you in a fistfight."

"Oh, you didn't know me back then. I was lithe, Ed—lithe like a *puma*."

"Do I dare even ask why you got into a fistfight?"

"You really don't want to know." Though Baragon smiled at the memory.

"Dammit, Roscoe, we've come this far. You might as well just tell me and get it over with. I know you'll do it anyway, so make it quick."

Baragon's smile broadened. "Well, I was in Houston covering mission control during the first post-*Aurora* shuttle flight. This was for the Chicago paper. You remember *Aurora*, Ed? That's the one that didn't quite make it off the launchpad. Went all kablooey."

"Maybe if I scratch my memory. Please—just get on with it."

"—Anyway—I actually used to do things like that back in those days. I figured everybody else would be going to Cape Canaveral, expecting this one to blow, too. But I knew better, see—I knew that *NASA* knew if that happened, the agency would be history. There was too much money at stake to let that happen. So I went to Houston, figuring I'd have mission control all to myself, and I was right. Any-way—this guy—Slaughter—and I got to talking at this bar. Bar at the time contained the world's biggest collection of geeks you've ever seen in your life. All NASA types—short hair, ties, white short-sleeve shirts, pocket protectors, the works."

"Yeah." *Why did he ever ask Baragon questions like this when he knew he would regret it?*

"So Slaughter and I start talking about movies. Most everything NASA does can be traced back to some movie or another—every single project. They're great that way. Anyway, so these guys, obviously, all know their movies, right? So we start talking. An hour and a lot of whiskey later, we're arguing over whether *The Green Slime* or *Godzilla vs. the Smog Monster* contained the greatest movie theme song of all time."

"Jesus Christ," Montgomery exhaled. *Never ask him anything else ever again.*

"Yeah, that's what I thought—there was no question. I mean, 'The Green Slime' versus 'Save the Earth'? C'mon. Next thing you know, glasses are flying, and ashtrays, and fists, we're on the floor, rolling around under the tables."

"Very noble cause, let me say."

"Well, he kicked the shit out of me—those NASA guys are tougher than they look—but I was right and would not concede."

"You were right?"

"About the song—'Green Slime'—amazing song. I could sing it for you if you like. Even the rarely heard second verse."

"That . . . really won't be necessary. Umm, listen—Roscoe—"

"After that we got along just fine. Haven't spoken to him in years and years, though. Don't even know that he's still there."

"S'pose you could try and find his number anyway?"

Baragon shrugged. "Shouldn't be too hard—let me get

down what I have on this radioactive man business, then I'll get on it. When's this thing supposed to come down, anyway?"

"Nobody's really sure—they keep pushing the time back. First it was late last week, then early this week. Now maybe the end of the week."

Baragon started to stand. "Don't you worry none, Chief, you'll have it in time. I'm a trained professional."

"Baragon—no, you haven't—"

Baragon stopped and looked at his editor, puzzled. "What?"

"I'm wondering if you could find that number and pass it along to Biddle." Montgomery almost seemed embarrassed.

"Pardon?" He was even more puzzled now.

"Well," he exhaled through his nose, "I want Biddle to do the story—but he's been having some trouble getting started. He can't find anyone at NASA who'll tell him anything."

Baragon's eyes narrowed—though not out of interest this time—and his teeth slowly came together like a vise. He tried to relax his jaw before he spoke again.

"That's pretty shitty, Ed."

"Roscoe, c'mon, give the kid a break."

Baragon rolled his eyes and felt his jaw snap shut again. He tried to keep his voice low. "Give that little fucker a *break*? You rip a huge story from beneath me, pass it on to him, put the goddamn thing on page one giving him a full byline—and now you're asking me to give him a *break*? Ed, Jesus—"

This is unbelievable. I need to get those notes down before I forget them. I need a drink. What's around here to throw? Baragon scanned Montgomery's desk but found nothing beyond a stray pen and some papers. The coffee mug was out of reach.

"And don't go looking for something to throw, Baragon— I was prepared."

"And if I refuse? Christ—you learned how to do this job on your own. I learned how to do this job on my own. Nobody gave us any fucking breaks—you want something, you go find it. That's what this job is about. He has that god-damn fancy degree and he doesn't know what to do?"

"Roscoe, please—don't be this way—"

"Is this what he learned at goddamn Columbia Fucking Journalism School? How to get everything he needs handed to him? Stories? Sources?"

"Roscoe—what in the hell are you getting so worked up over? Calm down. Take a seat." There was a flash of gen-uine—if brief—concern across Montgomery's face. "Take a deep breath."

Baragon did, inhaled deeply, contemplated for a second using the lungful of air to let loose with another volley, but reconsidered and let the air drain out of him instead. He was tired. Too tired for this.

"Fine," he said finally, defeated again.

"Good. Glad to hear it. I know how you're feeling, Roscoe—and I can understand why you'd be annoyed. But look—"

Why was he suddenly being so "understanding" these days? Not only was it wrong and out of character—it was just plain creepy.

"—You're not going anywhere. You'll always have a place at this paper. So what's so wrong with helping a fellow *Sentinel* reporter out of a minor jam, eh? Especially one who's just getting started?"

Baragon cleared his throat. "I said, 'fine,' Ed—don't make me recant that. That team loyalty crap doesn't work on me."

Much to Baragon's disgust and horror, Montgomery . . . *smiled*. A dirty, crooked-toothed, loathsome smile. Baragon had never seen that before, and it sent a tingle of fear through his thinning scalp. All he wanted now was to get the hell out of this office, back to his desk, and as far away as possible from this obviously fake Ed Montgomery.

"Well . . . uh . . . I should get back, uh—to work now, Ed," he said, rising from his chair and backing slowly out of the room. "I'll get that number for Biddle."

"Glad to hear it," Ed said, then turned back to his computer.

Man, he seemed fine there at first, Baragon thought on his way down the hall, *but then something went all flippy somehow.* He made a note to keep an eye on Ed for the next few days. Maybe he was on some kind of medication. Or maybe he just had a thing for this Biddle kid.

Baragon turned his computer on, opened the file he had created for the Raymond Martin case, and added what he'd learned from Martin's former neighbors earlier that morning.

Just too odd, he thought, scrolling down his notes. *Everything about this Martin story is just too odd. Not adding up at all.*

He lit a cigarette, took a long drag, and blew the smoke out his nostrils, which sent a burning through his sinuses. *Man, gotta stop doing that.* He looked at the screen again. *Okay, here's what you do. Forget the weirdness for now. Give Ed facts. Keep it short, to the point. Even with the solid facts alone, the weirdness will come through. Turn it in, let it run. Then keep looking.*

Over the course of the next two hours, that's what he did. Dead man found. Sets off radiation detectors at morgue. Officials called in. Everything declared safe. In contrast with earlier reports, however . . . not a medical treatment, identity uncovered, criminal record, neighbors say he stole toilets and went missing (sort of) a week or so before he turned up dead. Cause of death: strangulation. Radioactivity still a mystery. No investigation seems to be under way.

Except my own, thought Baragon smugly. *Heh heh heh*.

He looked up at the screen, realized he had actually typed that last line, and deleted it.

Wait a second—why does the morgue have radiation detectors anyway? He'd asked himself that question before—how could he forget?

He remembered the *Times* story had given some sort of cockamamie explanation, so he opened his hard file on the Martin case and pulled out the clipping.

The new radiation detectors were installed last year during renovations which were made at the medical examiner's office. . . . Mr. von Hohenheim said officials decided to install radioactivity detectors after a company hired to dispose of biohazardous waste uncovered low levels of radiation in materials being removed from the offices. . . .

Baragon read the paragraph a second time. *That doesn't make much sense. Radioactive waste at the morgue a year ago?*

He replaced the clipping in the folder and began reaching for the phone to call Emily but stopped. He looked at his watch. It was 3:30. He'd see her soon enough, and he'd ask her then. She wouldn't be able to talk now anyway. He'd give Ed—ol' Smilin' Eddie—the story the way it stood now, which should make him happy—then get to work on the real digging as soon as possible. *It better be soon, too*, he thought—*it's my guess the evidence won't be around for too much longer.*

Finding Hoke Slaughter's number was easy. He kept it in the special list of contact numbers for people with funny names. It was in there with the numbers for Foam Carter,

LeRoy Gerald Biv (or "Roy G. Biv," as he was known), Presley Buckitt, and Bunny Tang.

Just so he wouldn't be accused of trying to screw with the youngster by passing along false information, he decided it would be best to check it out first, make sure Hoke was still there and still doing what he used to do.

So much to do, he began thinking, making a list. As he grew older, Baragon found himself making more lists. He was also shrugging more than he used to.

He punched the numbers on the telephone's keypad and waited. Slaughter actually worked out of the Marshall Space Flight Center in Alabama. NASA was spread out all across the southern United States—Florida, Alabama, Texas, California. Each center had a different job to do on each mission. On the fourth ring, someone picked up.

"Slaughter," a man's voice announced. Baragon recognized the drawl immediately.

He took a deep breath, gave Hoke a chance to wonder just what was going on, then let loose with *"Somethin' scraymin' 'cross yo maiind!"*

"Gre-een Slliiiii-iii-iiime!" Slaughter responded in kind. "Roscoe, you son of a bitch—you caught me at the worst possible time—but it's good to hear from you. Everything okay?"

"More or less. Well, less, actually—but some things time doesn't alter right? You?"

"Agk," he groaned. "Things are crazy here with this Bio-Lab 1 business."

"You planning on destroying Tokyo?"

"Yeah, that's the first time I've heard *that* joke," he said.

"Listen," Baragon continued, quietly disappointed that Slaughter'd already heard that one, "I don't want to keep you, even though that's the reason I was calling. You still doing the press release crap?"

"Still sitting at the same godforsaken desk, aren't I?"

"Yeah, me too—look—" Baragon said, trying to make this as quick and easy as possible. "One of the new kids here at the paper is trying to talk to someone down there about the space station—" Then it struck him. "You're telling me the thing is called 'BioLab 1'? You're joking."

"Don't you watch the news?"

"I'm afraid I don't. That's a *terrible* name—It's like calling it the P-1, or Rocketship XM, or something—anyway—kid here's working on something, looking for someone to talk to—I was wondering if it would be okay if he gave you a call."

He could almost hear Slaughter measuring things out in his head. "Okay, fine—but I won't have much time. Like I said—"

"—I know," Baragon interrupted. "It's understood. Hey—could I ask another favor?" He was about to ask Slaughter to give the kid a break, toss him a fish, give him a little something that wasn't in today's press release. But then he changed his mind. Let the kid get that much for himself. "Oh, never mind—you're busy enough."

"Okay—tell the kid to call me in forty-five minutes or so, okay?"

"Sure thing."

"What's the name I should be listening for, by the way?"

After he glanced around the room to make sure he was more or less alone, Baragon cleared his throat. "Umm . . . Livingston, uh, Biddle."

"Now *you're* joking."

"I'm afraid I'm not. Look—I'll let you go. It was good to talk to you."

"Same here," Slaughter told him. "I'm real sorry to have to run like this—but you understand. Sky falling and all. But tell me—you gonna be home tonight?"

"Should be. I'll probably be drunk, though."

"Don't worry—so will I. Same number?"

"I think so." He thought about it. "Yeah, must be."

"Okay. I'll talk to you later then. Not sure what time I'll get out of here. Give you a little drunken off-the-record. Something a man of your distinct mind-set would appreciate."

Baragon's eyebrows jumped slightly. "Sounds okay, I think. Talk to you later then."

After hanging up the phone, he dropped the phone number on Biddle's desk, then set off to find Biddle himself, who was, conveniently enough, in Montgomery's office. Baragon stuck his head inside and said, "Just talked to Hoke Slaughter at NASA—you're supposed to call him at about four-thirty our time. I just left the number on your desk. He won't have long to talk—but he'll talk to you. You got all your research and questions together?"

Biddle looked up from his chair. "Mr. Montgomery's helping me with that right now," he said, just a shade too cheerily for Baragon's stomach.

"O-kay, then. Super." With effort, he prevented his tongue from saying what he really wanted to. "Hey, Ed—you get the radioactive man piece?"

Montgomery almost looked at him. "Yeah, yeah," he said grimly. "I saw it. It's fine. Decent filler for page sixteen."

"Okay then," Baragon said, noting that Ed was sounding almost normal again. "And don't forget, Biddle—four-thirty. Don't be late."

Biddle shook his head and smiled but didn't thank him for the help.

.   .   .

The phone rang at ten-thirty that night as Baragon dozed, drunkenly and intermittently, in front of *Deranged.*

He shook himself to full consciousness (not the prettiest of sights) and hobbled into the front room, where he sat and listened to the answering machine before he decided whether to pick up.

"Hey, Caulfield—pick up the goddamn phone." It was Slaughter's code—a reference that very few people ever got—especially when it was explained that it had nothing at all to do with J. D. Salinger.

Baragon picked up. "Hey, Kelloway." That was the proper coded response. "What goes on? You home?"

"Yeah . . . I'm here. First time in three days. PR department's gotta be operating round the clock 'til this thing splashes."

"At least you *hope* it splashes. Jesus, huh? I get the impression I should've talked to you much sooner. What's the scoop?" Baragon asked. "Wait a second—before you answer that—I need another beer." He heaved himself up from the table and made his way to the fridge. He supposed he didn't really need another, but here he was. Besides, this was an occasion—talking to an old friend he'd been out of touch with for nearly a decade. Might as well take steps to ensure he wouldn't remember anything about it the next morning.

When he picked up the receiver again, Slaughter was humming to himself. Baragon wasn't sure, but it almost sounded like "Sister Golden Hair." He decided not to ask, for fear of getting it stuck in his own head.

"Hey, you talk to that kid?"

"Yeah, he called," Slaughter sighed, not sounding too pleased about it. "Tell me—where in the hell are you newspapers finding these kids nowadays? You scouting the special schools or what?"

"Yeah, I know—I keep wondering that myself."

"He'd never heard of *Apollo-Soyuz*. Seems he had no idea that there'd been a space program prior to the shuttle."

"Yeah, that sounds about right."

"I had only a few minutes for him, but I gave him the song and dance—'Everything's fine. Nothing to worry about. Everything's under control.'" There was something odd in Slaughter's tone.

"Maybe it's this old reporter's nose of mine there, Hoke," Baragon said, "but I get the distinct impression things over there aren't going quite so smoothly as you'd like everyone to think. What—it's Detroit, isn't it? We're about to lose Detroit. Because if it is, I mean, there's not much of a loss there. Say, are you guys laying down a lot of bets over where it's gonna come down?"

"Naah," Slaughter admitted, "they really did get enough of a handle on that thing to dump it in the drink neat as a pin. Should be no problem. Few hundred miles off the coast of Chile."

"Chile?" Baragon piped up. "Hey—they just had a huge earthquake there—you hear about that?"

"No, uh-uh. Been a little, uh, wrapped up."

"Yeah, but here's an idea—just something to consider— say you miss the ocean, right? Just say it happens. Just by a little bit. And the thing falls on Chile."

"Uh-huh?" He'd been hearing too much talk like this lately to be amused by it anymore.

"Well, so what?"

"Unfortunately, Roscoe, much to everyone's relief and your disappointment, BioLab 1's going down far from land. That much we know."

There was the first tremor of anticipation in Baragon's stomach. When someone from a place like NASA says "that much we know," it's pretty much a given that there's a hell of a lot they don't know.

"So—what *don't* you know?"

The line was quiet for a moment. Baragon could hear that Hoke was having a drink of his own. He caught the light metallic clink of ice cubes. The quick burble of a glass being refilled.

"Okay, Roscoe, from this point on, everything's off the record—agreed? No tape recorders, no notes, no nothing."

Damn. He knew this was coming and should have been better prepared. He'd left his tape recorder at the office.

"I've never turned on you that way, Hoke—and I won't now."

"Good. Hey—you don't happen to have a copy of an Italian job called *Nude for Satan*, do you?"

Baragon closed his eyes. "If you're going to tell me that NASA's current problems—or next mission—have anything to do with *Nude for Satan*, I'm hanging up. Or sending a résumé over, one of the two."

"No, nothing like that. It just came up in conversation."

"Well, yeah, I do. What of it? You want it?" *Christ, I don't talk to the guy for ten years and the first thing he does is ask me to send him a bad Italian horror film with a lot of boobs in it.*

"Maybe. Some nitwit in engineering didn't believe that it existed. But like I said, I'm drunk, and it's beside the point."

Baragon needed a cigarette. It sounded like he was in for a bit of a haul. For a PR guy, Slaughter always had a hard time getting straight to the heart of the matter.

"Say," Baragon said, "before you tell me what's really going on—how's that lovely family of yours? Jenny and the boy?"

"Her name was Natalie, actually, and she packed up Harry and left. That was about four years ago. Haven't seen her since."

"Oh," Baragon said. He had a real knack for asking the wrong questions sometimes. "Sorry about that. I guess it has been too long."

"Don't worry about it. Happens all the time."

"Yeah, I guess. . . . Hey, enough of that—" he tried to sound perky. "—What the hell's up with this thing now?"

The phone was silent again. Then Slaughter asked, "Roscoe—how much do you know about the BioLab?"

"Not much, I have to admit. I didn't even know the name until you told me. I sort of stopped paying attention to NASA there for a while. Not sure why—I obviously shouldn't have. This was the project that was never finished, right?"

"Yeah, right—that's right. Okay, thumbnail," Slaughter said before taking another drink. "BioLab had been in the planning stages for a couple decades, really. Since before the shuttle program got started. A perpetually orbiting biological research facility, right?"

"The thing they planned right after someone there saw *Silent Running*, sure."

"Yeah. Very good. Anyway—work actually got under way after *Aurora* and after the shuttle program got back on track. Ten years later, it was about two-thirds complete. Enough so that a couple experiments were already up and running. Following me?"

"So far," Barragon said, jotting a few quick notes on the back of an envelope anyway.

"Then everything stopped. You got your Mir, you got your International Space Station, you got all those various Mars debacles. Focuses were shifting, attention was drawn away from it, interest was fading. Then the money dried up, after billions had been pumped into it."

"Which may help explain why I knew so little about this. So . . . where do we go from there?"

"Well, essentially backward."

"Pardon?"

"We back up to the halfway point again."

"Wait—wait—so now are you saying that everything you've told me so far is actually *on* the record?"

"I guess so. It's all public knowledge."

"And everything from here on in is now *off* the record."

"Yeah . . . right."

"Just so we have that straight."

"Jesus, Roscoe, don't be an idiot right now, okay? I'm only telling you this because I have to tell someone. And I'm only telling *you* because I think you're smart enough to make some of the necessary connections on your own."

Baragon looked around the room for confirmation of this, but Hedora was offering nothing. "Okay," he said, "shoot."

The first experiments brought aboard BioLab 1, logically enough, involved the simplest life-forms—fungi, bacteria, viruses. The initial team of scientists who actually lived aboard BioLab for any period of time got the experiments up and running, then left the station a week later. Eight months after they left, a second crew arrived. Shortly after the new squad docked the shuttle and entered the BioLab, it was evident that something had gone very, very wrong. There were problems with the electrical circuitry and the air-conditioning system. The computers and life-support systems were behaving erratically. The crew was yanked out of there after a day of hopeless attempts to rectify the trouble. Word of the exact nature of the problem never made it down to the PR department. They didn't need to know.

Still, you hear things. Sometimes crazy things.

One thing that was clear, though, was that the entire program was scrapped then and there, the half-constructed station left in its own orbit, abandoned, untouched, almost completely forgotten. No one ever went back there, and no word about any of this was ever released to the American public. Why bother? If they don't hear that things have gone wrong, they'll assume that it's just smooth sailing. Before long, something else—like the Mir or the ISS—will come along, and they'll forget about BioLab 1 completely.

Until it came crashing back to Earth.

This was one little trick NASA hadn't been counting on. One day, very quietly, almost imperceptibly—maybe something hit it, they don't know for sure—it arced into a lower orbit. It was only a matter of time before the station—and whatever the hell was on board—returned home.

Tricky thing now was, they didn't know what *was* aboard. Whatever it is, or was, it might well be long dead. If it wasn't, there's a ninety-nine percent chance it'll burn up completely in the atmosphere. Or maybe after mutating for a decade in zero gravity, it can live only in space.

In other words, whatever is on the BioLab presents virtually no danger whatsoever to anything on Earth. Virtually.

That's the word people kept using. But the thing is, they weren't sure. And they wouldn't be sure until the thing hit the water and they saw what happened.

"See, the problem with you NASA guys," Baragon explained drunkenly, "is that you never watch your movies all the way through to the end. You see the beginning, you catch the basic plot, you think, 'Cool,' and you run with it, right? You grab your T squares and your compasses and you get to work. But you never see how everything ends."

"Roscoe, please, I'm not—"

"So, you've got *The Green Slime* here for real, right? That's what's going on here. Space station overrun with some sort of mutant space fungus. If I didn't know better, I'd think you were just pulling my leg, seeing if I'd recognize it. Well, Hoke, I do," Baragon told his old friend. "But I also know you're not pulling my leg." He paused a second. "You're, uh . . . *not*, are you?"

"Roscoe, no, shit—I'm too tired to be doing that," Slaughter told him. "This is . . . I dunno . . . I hate to keep repeating myself—but we just don't fucking know what's in there. It's probably nothing at all."

"Look, you wanna be sure?" Baragon offered. "Go back and watch the movie all the way through. What you need to do is this—send a small crew up there to intercept this thing. Once they're inside, have them throw beds at whatever monsters they find. That's what they do in the movie—they throw beds. When those don't work, have them throw Richard Jaeckel. And when *that* doesn't work, have them blow the damn thing up before it gets down here or we're all fucking doomed. I mean, if you have some control of the thing, why not send it out into space? Send it toward the *sun*. But don't, whatever you do, bring it back *here*. That's just stupid."

"It's too late for that, Roscoe. . . . The thing could splash at any time."

"And you really have no idea what sort of things are on board?"

There was a long silence. "No. Probably nothing."

"Probably. Key word, Hoke. You keep using 'probably' and 'virtually,' and you ain't making me feel any better about all this. And you don't want the public to know about it?"

"We can't let it out, Roscoe. You know that. It'd really fuck us. The agency, I mean."

"Well, hot damn," Baragon said with a sort of cynical pride. "Rule number one in action."

"Excuse me?" asked Slaughter, who was, by now, quite sloshed.

"Don't worry about it," Baragon told him. "And good luck with this thing. Be sure to keep me posted as much as you can, won't you?"

"Oh, yeah," Slaughter slurred. Baragon knew he wouldn't last much longer, so he wished him a good night and hung up the phone. Baragon was now wide awake. Why do people keep telling him these things? He pulled open the second drawer of the short file cabinet next to his desk and flipped through the labels until he found what he was looking for. He carried the manila folder over to the kitchen table and sat. Inside the folder was a single small news clipping, not yet old enough to begin yellowing:

MUTANT BACTERIA NEXT THREAT FROM RUSSIA'S MIR

MOSCOW—Heavyweight debris raining down from space isn't the only potential danger when Russia sends the Mir orbiter to a watery grave early next month—the real threat could be mutant fungi, a researcher said Tuesday.

Yuri Karash, an expert on the Russian space program, said there was a possibility that micro-organisms, which have spent the last 15 years mutating in isolation aboard Mir, could present a threat if they survived the fall to Earth.

"A very realistic problem exists," Karash told a news conference. "But I'm not convinced there is any cause for panic."

Karash, who has undergone cosmonaut training and is currently an aerospace advisor, said his conclusions were based on research carried out by Moscow University's Institute of Medical and Biological Problems.

Researchers have said that the fungi could be especially virulent if mixed with earth varieties that attack metal, glass and plastic.

Western health officials have expressed concerns about micro-organisms that could be brought back to earth after a Russian microbiologist 13 years ago discovered the first of many aggressive forms of fungi inhabiting Mir.

Russian space officials have dismissed the threat, but visitors to the orbiter have found numerous types of fungi behind control panels, in air-conditioning units and on dozens of other surfaces.

Though surprisingly destructive, they give off corrosive agents like acetic acid and release toxins into the air.

That last sentence doesn't make much sense, he thought with a sly grin, *but I'll be damned—what Slaughter's describing sounds a hell of a lot worse than this. These space people* really *need to start watching their movies all the way through to the end.* Then he replaced the clipping in the folder, and the folder in the file cabinet, and went to bed.

Chapter Eight

His sinuses were throbbing when he awoke the next morning. So was the rest of his skull. He hadn't slept much, and when he did sleep, he was besieged by exhausting dreams.

Hedora was at the foot of the bed, snoring as loudly as he'd ever heard any animal snore. Outside, cold rain whipped sidelong across his windows, clinging to the screen, distorting his view of the empty Brooklyn street outside.

Why does it always rain when I'm hung? he wondered.

It was a few minutes before six.

He rolled out of bed and went about the slow, painful process of putting himself together. His head hurt worse after he stood. Part of it was the smoke and the hangover, he was sure. Part of it was the lack of sleep and the frenetic dreams. Dreams always left his head aching. Much of the pain, however, was the result of the accumulated events of these past ten days—especially yesterday. Jesus.

An epidemic of earthquakes, radioactive men—and now an old drinking buddy—one who would know—tells him that there's some sort of mutant alien space fungus on its way to Earth. Probably one with tentacles and multiple red eyes.

This is nuts, he thought as he climbed into the shower and bowed his head beneath the spray of hot water. For the past five years or so, insane people had approached him, begging that he make their stories public—that he publish them in all their lurid Technicolor incoherent glory. *Now* he was being approached by perfectly sane and rational people— some of them, at least—who were telling him equally im- plausible, frightening tales but demanding that they *not* be published—which was infinitely more frustrating.

He was tired. Didn't even know what day it was any- more. Thursday? Friday? Baragon didn't keep any calendars around the apartment. Not any current ones, anyway.

He shut off the water and stepped carefully out of the shower. The water had helped ease the pain in his head some, but not enough. He needed some air and coffee. He opened the medicine cabinet, soaked a cotton ball in rub- bing alcohol, and swiped it beneath his nostrils. Sometimes that helped, too—but not this morning.

He put on the same pair of black slacks he'd been wearing every day for the past three weeks, grabbed a fairly clean light blue shirt from the closet, had a piece of toast and a mug of cold coffee, then looked out the window again. It was still coming down hard out there.

"Shit," he sighed, then, after feeding Hedora and check- ing the cigarette situation, put his trench coat on and opened the door.

He pulled the first smoke of the day out of his pocket and headed for the subway.

Stop thinking stop thinking stop thinking stop thinking—

Baragon looked at his watch—it was later than usual. He still wasn't feeling too shipshape and realized then that he'd been staring at a dark patch in front of him—it might've been someone's coat, or leg, or a shadow, or nothing at all—he wasn't paying attention; all he knew was that it was unadorned darkness, and he was staring into it, thinking *stop thinking stop thinking stop thinking.* It would only cause more trouble if he didn't.

The moment he stepped on the train, he'd caught a whiff of it. After a near quarter century of heavy smoking, his sense of smell had been pretty well eradicated, but this was unmistakable, and it drilled right through both nostrils into his subconscious: the musty, vaguely perfumed scent that he'd always associated with his grandmother's old, dark farmhouse in Minnesota. Everything in her house smelled that way, and even after she died, the things his parents removed from the house and brought home held tight to that odor, exuding it like a cloud, an aura, that became attached to anything those objects touched. It couldn't be washed away. Now here it was again. It was the smell of age, of rural decay struggling to maintain a sense of dignity.

Baragon had been running into that smell with greater and greater frequency around New York these days, usually on the train.

This time it was rolling in great waves off the old man in the beige cap seated next to him. As soon as Baragon smelled it, his brain kicked into high gear, pulling up the childhood memories he didn't care to recall—things he was privately embarrassed to think about. Little shows he used to put on in the basement for nobody during empty summer afternoons. Road trips with his family. Visits to restaurants. The creaky, dim staircase in his grandmother's house. The way he used to speak with the other kids in the neighborhood. He always thought he was smarter than they were—but even if he was right about that, he didn't have to be such a damned smarty-pants about it.

He felt himself sinking, and fast. It probably was the

combination of not feeling so well coupled with memory's return to a purer time, a time before everything went south on him.

He searched frantically for something else to let his brain latch on to—a stupid, repetitive song, maybe. A few days beforehand, "In the Hall of the Mountain King" had gotten him through the day without too much fuss.

This morning, however, nothing was coming. He tried breathing through his mouth to avoid the odor, but even with that he could still taste it faintly, at the back of his tongue.

More old memories—junior high cafeterias on the first day of school. The squeaky rubber frog he used to play with in the tub when he was four. The lightly sweaty smell of the first woman (well, girl) he'd tried to date. Seventeen years old, walking the warm, hushed small town streets long after the summer sun had vanished.

Sometimes he'd have to follow a scent for eight or nine blocks before he could place it. Whenever it first struck, he always knew it meant something to him, but what? Whatever the odor was, it was revealing long-forgotten memories of some sort, but he couldn't see or hear them fully until he figured out what that goddamn *smell* was. So he'd follow people much too closely, or stand in grocery store aisles, stock-still, head slightly tilted, for twenty minutes or more. Not the kind of thing most people like to see overweight, middle-aged balding men doing.

This tic of his, yes, could sometimes cause problems. Until he pinpointed the memory, though, there was little he could do about his behavior. If he didn't figure out what it was that odor was dredging up while he was actually smelling it, he'd be fucked up for the rest of the day. Lost, unable to accomplish much of anything. Once the smell was gone, it was gone. He was never able to call it back up on his own.

Yet even as the scent vanished, those half-constructed memories would remain to pester him.

On a morning like this, even thinking about his grandma's farmhouse—the old tree out back, the quiet rooms upstairs that always spooked him—was better than thinking about radioactive men, or crashing space stations full of some evil, conscious disease, or how much his head hurt, or how much he hated sitting this close to people.

As the train pulled into the Thirty-fourth Street station, he caught a final musty whiff off the man next to him and finally recognized it for what it undoubtedly was and always has been—*mothballs*.

This was a tremendous relief.

The story that topped all the news wires that morning concerned BioLab's perfect and harmless return to Earth, splashing down some thirty-five hundred kilometers off the Chilean coast, in the middle of the South Pacific. Nobody was hurt, the various stories assured everyone, and there was no more need to worry.

Well, not yet, Baragon thought. *Though you might want to check back in a couple days.*

He tried to time things backward—time of splashdown, time of official reentry into the atmosphere—at least as they were reported.

Hmmm . . .

Way he was figuring it, Slaughter was telling him the BioLab saga pretty much as it was all happening. But he said he was at home. Sure sounded like he was at home. Why wasn't he at mission control? He was a top man in their press office—he must have known this was happening—this was the Big Moment, after all. So why wasn't he there for it? Granted, he'd said he'd been there for what, three days?

Unless something happened, some mistake of some kind, and it ended up coming down much earlier than they thought it would.

Either way, it struck Baragon as a tad unusual. Maybe he'd give Slaughter a call back in the next day or two, see what he had to say. He could try bribing him with a copy of *Nude for Satan*.

He finished his coffee and was trying to figure out where to go next with this Martin story. Parole officers, maybe. Or maybe that landlord. Find out who really owns the building these days—those records shouldn't be too hard to come by. Maybe check out the plumbing supply companies. Then the phone rang. "Baragon," he answered.

"Hel-lo . . . Ros-coe?" said a thin voice on the other end.

"Well, my goodness, Natacia, it's good to hear from you—how are you?"

"I am fine. . . . How is your leg?"

Thank God some things in this world are constant, he thought. "Leg's just fine, Natacia, just fine," he assured her, for what he was certain would not be the last time. "Thanks for asking. . . . So, what can I do for you? Oh—and by the way—I'm so sorry about accidentally hanging up on you last time. I hit the wrong button."

"Uh . . . yes. Is okay. Uh . . . Ros-coe? I am just reading your story."

"Which one's that? That is—what's it about?" He was never sure with her. Although he had never been there, he had the impression her room was filled with stacks of newspapers, years' and decades' worth, and that she would occasionally pull a random one out and find something he had done twelve years earlier, thinking it was something he'd just written the previous week. He always had to check before he got too far.

"This is of . . . uh . . . the man with . . . the radiation."

Man, I'd completely forgotten I'd turned that one in already. Well, at least it ran. He'd have to go take a look when he got off the phone, see where they put it, see how badly Montgomery had hacked it.

"Okay, yeah—that was really something, wasn't it?" He began to wonder how long it would be before she decided that the tracking device lodged in her snatch was making her radioactive, too.

"They have found . . . another," she said.

That caught him by surprise. Well, there went his hopes for a calmer day.

"Really?" he asked, perhaps a little too eagerly. Of course, he was dealing with Natacia here, so maybe he shouldn't be too eager yet. "Where'd they find it, uh, him?"

"Around in the same place. Close to park."

"Tompkins again?"

"Yes . . . over by park."

He was about ready to accept this, then stopped himself. Okay, Natacia's a crazy woman. And if they'd found another radioactive man, Emily certainly would've let him know. Which of the two are you going to trust, really?

"Is woman this time," she said. She certainly did sound certain about it, he'd give her that much.

Baragon quietly reached out and turned on the tape recorder. No one's tried to sue him yet. "Wait now, Natacia—okay, let me get this straight. You're saying that they found a dead woman and she was radioactive?"

"Ah, yes."

"How do you know this? I haven't heard anything about it."

"She lived here. In building. She knew they were watching."

Yeah, well, crazy woman or not, I suppose I should check it out. He looked at his watch. It was shortly after eight-thirty.

Emily would be in the lab soon. He'd give her a quick call, see if anything had come through.

"Natacia, now, let me ask you this—how do you know this—that she was radioactive, I mean?"

She grunted, as if annoyed or in pain. "I am here when they come."

"When *who* came?" Sometimes it was so damn frustrating to try to get information out of the insane.

"The astronauts."

Aww, Jesus. Why do I even bother? "The astronauts."

"Yes."

"And they came there."

"*Yes.*"

"To your apartment?"

"*No.* You are not listening—they get her here."

"So . . . astronauts came to your building and got this radioactive woman—your neighbor."

"Yes. They get her here."

"But—" There was so little use in arguing. "I thought you said she was in the park."

"*No,*" she insisted, "*here.*"

"And, uh," he began, rolling his eyes, not really having time for this right now, "how do you know that she was radioactive?"

"I am not stupid woman. I see them. With technology."

"Uh-huh." He shook his head at himself and reached for a cigarette. Sure, Natacia was a little weak in the rafters, maybe—but every so often—one time out of five, say—she was right. Maybe one time out of twenty, but still.

Goddamnit. She probably did see something. It might not be a radioactive woman, but it was probably something.

"Natacia," he asked, knowing he'd regret it, "are you going to be there today?"

"Where would I go?"

"Okay, fine. . . . Would you mind if I stopped by so you could show me everything that happened?"

"Hey, Em," he whispered into the phone. "I'll just keep you a second. Got a quickie for you. You alone?"

"Not exactly."

"Okay then—it'll be a simple yes or no."

"What is it?"

"It'll sound crazy, and I'm sure it is, but I got a call from Natacia this morning—"

"Ahh, the lovely Natacia. You know, I'm starting to get a little jealous. What's she come up with this time? Another excuse to stop by the office?"

"Kind of. Another radioactive body," he said quietly. "This time a woman. Hear about anything like that coming through?"

"Nope." Her answer was quick, bordering on the sharp.

"That's what I figured. Thanks. She's out of her fucking mind."

"Is that it?" she asked.

"Pretty much, yeah."

"Okay, then—I should get back to work."

"I understand. Bar tonight?"

"Yeah, fine." She sounded less than enthusiastic.

"You sure?"

"I said fine," she snapped, openly annoyed.

"Ooo-kay then. I guess I'll see you there. Remind me to ask you something."

"Fine. Good-bye."

"Bye then." He hung up the phone, confused. Probably just caught her at a bad time. He had the timing of a crippled ox.

He put his coat on, checked the tape recorder and slipped

it into his coat pocket, made sure that the small notebook and pen were still in his other pocket, once again assessed the cigarette situation, and headed outside.

The rain had stopped, but the clouds still hung heavy and low. Half the people he dodged around on the sidewalk still had their umbrellas out.

Why do people use fucking golf umbrellas in Manhattan? he thought, annoyed, as he ducked beneath one that had clearly been aimed at his head.

The address of Natacia's SRO—confirmed both with her on the telephone and on her legal papers—was written in his notebook, and he checked it again before he went too far.

The Riverview Hotel, over on Twenty-fifth, way east. After realizing the subway wouldn't get him much closer than he already was, he considered just hoofing it. Then he changed his mind and hailed a cab. He didn't much like taking cabs. They were expensive and they usually took three times as long as the subway. This morning, though, it just made sense.

Half an hour later, hands trembling slightly and feeling a bit queasy, he handed the driver a twenty, secretly promising himself he'd never make such a mistake again.

It wasn't a bad neighborhood, not at all—which made the building stand out all the more, like a blackened fingernail.

The Riverview was another ten-story tenement, the name carved into a haphazard cement arch above the doorway. Next to the building was a garbage-filled vacant lot, surrounded by a twelve-foot-high chain-link fence topped with razor wire. Across the street, and along the rest of the block, all the other buildings were comfortable and expensive condos. Baragon wondered how it was the Riverview still stood here.

Granted, the building seemed to be in better shape—at

least on the outside—than the other place he'd visited—Christ, was that just yesterday morning? He thought a second and realized it was—but it weren't no Ritz.

Strange they should call this place the Riverview, he realized, considering the last view of the river—any river—it had would've probably been sometime in the late nineteenth century. Of course, from the looks of it, that might've been when it was built.

He walked up the three broken stone steps and through the dirty glass doorway. It wasn't locked. There was an inside door as well—and he figured he'd have to be buzzed in but then noticed it had been propped open with a wire hanger.

In front of him was a short hallway, walls spattered with graffiti, tile floor looking like it hadn't been cleaned in many years. At the end of the hallway was a registration desk, complete with bulletproof glass. It looked less like a hotel check-in counter than a subway token booth. Behind the glass sat an obese bearded man in a stained wifebeater. He was clearly asleep.

Too perfect, Baragon thought to himself. To the left of the desk was a door, above which a red electric sign read, STAIRWAY.

Baragon looked around for an elevator but saw nothing. He walked quietly past the concierge and turned a corner, where he found himself standing in another short hallway, this one a dead end. To his right, though, much to his relief, he discovered what he was looking for. Then he noticed that someone had had the courtesy to spraypaint OUT OF ORDER in enormous letters across the closed doors. It was clear nobody expected the elevator repairmen to be showing up anytime soon.

He checked Natacia's room number—702—and hit the button anyway, just to make sure. Nothing happened. He then returned to the front desk.

"Excuse me?" he asked. The man didn't stir, and for a

moment, Baragon was afraid he might be dead. That's when he first noticed the snoring. He also, for the first time, noticed the baseball bat and shotgun leaning against the wall of the booth behind him.

"Too perfect," Baragon repeated to himself, aloud this time. He sighed, resigned to the situation, and pushed his way through the door to the staircase. Then he slowly began trudging upward.

I wonder if she mistook that wifebeater for a big fat sheet, he thought idly.

The climb—which was bad enough—was made worse by the almost unbearable stench. Piss, shit, moldering garbage, other smells he didn't recognize and didn't really care to know about.

How does she do this? he wondered as he paused to catch his breath on the third-floor landing. *And why the hell am I?*

On the unpainted and cracked cement walls around him, in and amongst the indecipherable gang tags, someone had written, in small, neat, Magic Marker letters, ONWARD TO THE GALAPAGOS APOCALYPSE!

He continued up the steps.

When he finally reached the seventh floor, he pulled the creaking door open and found himself in another small hallway, hardly lit by two bare forty-watt bulbs hanging from the ceiling. It looked like it had been carpeted once, but now there were more bare spots than carpeting, and the carpeting that was left had been trampled into a drab brown. The smell was as bad up here as it was in the stairwell. He didn't care to think about how this place must reek in the summer. Given the state of his olfactory nerves, he didn't care to think about what this place really smelled like right now, either.

He made his way down the corridor but didn't have to go far before he found himself standing in front of 702.

He knocked.

Silence. In fact, he noted for the first time, the whole building had been silent. No dogs barking, no screaming matches, no gunfire. No televisions or blasting salsa music. No children. He hadn't encountered anyone on the stairs, heard no signs of life as he passed the other floors. Even the concierge downstairs was sleeping.

He waited perhaps twenty seconds, looked at his watch, then knocked again.

"Natacia?" he said, finally, moving closer to the door. "It's Roscoe—you in there?"

No response.

She knew I was coming, he thought. He looked at his watch, then knocked again, louder this time. *Maybe she went out for snacks.*

He tried the door but found it locked. He called her name again, identified himself, and listened. Nothing. Not even the quiet shufflings of someone trying not to be heard.

This is not what I'm in the mood for, he told himself. *Waste a goddamn morning coming to see a crazy woman.*

He considered, for a moment, trying some of the neighbors, then reconsidered. From the sounds of things, none of them were at home, either.

Part of him was tempted to force the door—kick or shoulder it open. He hadn't done anything like that since he was twenty-five, and even then it was a hell of a lot harder than the movies made it seem. He reconsidered, remembering the pain that followed him for days afterward and remembering that given Natacia's history and mind-set, she'd probably greet him with a bullet to the chest.

He was sweating and breathing dangerously hard by the time he reached the ground floor again. He was getting too old for this. Phone calls are so much easier.

The fat man behind the glass was still asleep.

Baragon tried clearing his throat as he waited for his heart to slow down. Nothing. He glanced around in annoyance, then rapped on the reinforced glass.

"Hey!" he shouted.

The fat man started, caught a glimpse of Baragon, and immediately made a move for the bat. Or maybe the gun.

Baragon took a step back and raised his hands. "Hold it a second pal—no need for that," he said.

The man grabbed hold of the bat anyway and pulled it closer, setting it between his enormous legs. "Yeah?" he asked, obviously annoyed at having been awakened.

"Listen—I'm sorry to bother you," Baragon began. "I'm a little worried about one of your tenants here, a friend of mine," he said. "I was just upstairs—she was supposed to be expecting me—but there was no answer. She's an old woman—very frail—I'm just worried that something might be wrong."

"Who is it?" the fat man asked suspiciously. "The people who live here don't have too many . . . 'friends.'"

"Her name's Natacia Ranzigava? Up in 702?"

The man reached a finger up and absentmindedly began picking at a scab on his right cheek, just above where his beard began, and shook his head. "Don't know who you're talkin' about." His voice was unusually soft and high-pitched—a characteristic Baragon had noted in a large percentage of obese men. He wondered how this guy thought he could intimidate people with a voice like that. Then he remembered the bat and the shotgun.

"Oh, c'mon now, you must—" Baragon countered. "Skinny woman? About 80? Russian?"

"We get a lotta people through here, boss—I don't make a point of meeting every one on, y'know, a personal basis."

Baragon continued. "Wears an old pink bathrobe? No

teeth? Crazy as a jaybird?" he asked hopelessly. "She's lived here for a long time. This is ringing no bells at all?"

The man shook his head.

Finally—it usually didn't take this long—but finally, all the movies came back to Baragon. He reached into his wallet and pulled out a twenty and slid it through the change cup at the bottom of the window. *This is twice in two days now. I've got to stop throwing those things around.* "Okay—does *that* help your memory?"

The man took the bill, shifted over onto his right haunch, shoved it in his pocket, then shook his head again. "I have no fucking idea who you're talking about."

Baragon clucked his tongue, almost amused. He'd seen that in too many movies, too. "Look," he started again, calmly. "I'm just very worried about her. I talked to her," he looked at his watch again, "about an hour, hour and a half ago. She knew I was coming. Her health's real bad." *You probably don't want to tell him why, though.* "And I know it's not your responsibility—but I just figured before I pick up a phone and call the cops or an ambulance or something, that you might be able to help me."

The fat man glared at him as if he were being threatened in some way. He obviously didn't care for the phrase "call the cops."

"What room did you say she was in?" he asked, finally.

"702?"

He flipped through the stained sheets on a clipboard in front of him unenthusiastically. "Naaah," he said, stopping on a page, "there's your trouble, buddy—ain't been nobody in that room for weeks."

"Pardon?"

"Here, wanna see?" The man pulled the page from the clipboard and slapped it up against the window. It was a chart of each room—names, dates, rent paid. There was a name next to 702, but it had been scratched out with a ball-point. Still, he could read enough of it to tell that it wasn't hers. The date next to it was January twentieth. Whoever it was still owed thirty-five bucks.

"See, now, *that* guy I remember," the man said after Baragon indicated he was finished. "He O.D.'d up there. We're still trying to air the place out."

Oh, why does it always have to be like this? "You mean, you don't know of anyone fitting that description? No old crazy Russian ladies?"

"Buddy, listen to me—you wake me up, I'm trying to help you out, I'm telling you what I know."

"Gotcha," Baragon said. "Sorry for the inconvenience."

"Yeah," the man grunted, though his meaning was unclear. "Maybe you got the wrong hotel."

"This the Riverview, for some reason?"

"Yeah."

"Then this ain't the wrong hotel," Baragon said. "Guess I'll just put it down to her being nuts. Save us all a lot of trouble."

The man was clearly waiting for Baragon to shut up and leave so he could get back to sleep.

"Well, I'll let you go then," Baragon told him. "And thanks for your help."

"Uh-huh," the man said. Baragon turned to leave, then stopped and turned back.

"One more thing," he said, approaching the booth. The man's hefty arms were folded now, the bat still balanced between his thighs. "Are you the manager?"

The man shook his head.

"Do you know where I can find him?"

The man shook his head again.

"Okay, fair enough. But tell me—and then I'll leave, I promise—what's the name of the company that owns this building?"

The man said nothing.

"This isn't about you, don't worry about that—you were very helpful."

The man reached down and gripped the handle of the bat with both hands, unsure whether he was being made sport of.

"Right," said Baragon. He pulled out his last twenty and slid it through the coin slot. The man snatched that one, too.

"SVA," he said. "That's all I know. That's all I can tell you."

"All you need to. Thanks a ton," Baragon said, nodding. Then he turned and walked out the front door, knowing full well that he'd never be getting another phone call from Natacia, that she'd never again ask him how his leg was.

Without any money left, he decided to walk back to the office. His legs were still a little shaky after the trip up and down the stairs, but the clouds were breaking up some, and it would give him more of a chance to think. Besides, he could stop at a bank, then grab a sandwich on the way. Before he forgot, though, he pulled out his notepad and jotted down "SVA."

Baragon remembered how much he hated walking across Manhattan. Most of the sidewalks are too narrow, most of the foot traffic too heavy, unpredictable, and slothful. He was moving slow today as it was, but not as slow as some of these people.

To keep things simple, he figured he'd stay on Twenty-fifth until he hit Broadway, then turn north for the last eight blocks. But after crossing Madison, he found himself once again on a too-narrow sidewalk, trapped behind a sluggish woman fresh from a plant store who was toting what appeared to be a massive bundle of pointy dry weeds under her left arm. It was like walking a few short feet behind a mobile tiger pit. Apart from that, all he had to deal with was the regular convergence of strollers, double strollers, over-loaded delivery carts, and hand trucks. Then the gauntlet of sidewalk clothing hucksters, all screaming encouragements that Baragon could never understand.

"Get in the store! Go inside!" one of them shouted at him frantically. At first, Baragon figured an out-of-control truck was barreling down upon him, so he whirled, to find nothing. The man was just trying to sell him some socks, it turned out, and maybe a new pair of Bermuda shorts.

A middle-aged woman, green kerchief knotted about her hair, stood nervously outside another clothing wholesaler's door, repeating the enticing *"socks . . . shirts . . . jeans"* in an endless, droning loop as she attempted to hand a glossy flyer to everyone who passed. Only as he stepped around her and looked down did Baragon notice that the flyers she was handing out were for a used-appliance store.

He held his breath in a cheap attempt to make himself more nimble and keep the growing panic at moderate levels. There were people everywhere, on every side of him, heading in every direction. He tried to pause a moment to look at a knife display in the front window of a pawnshop, but the crowds wouldn't let him. They darted out of doorways and off the backs of trucks, zipping in front of him, making deliveries or returning from having made deliveries, forcing Baragon to stop short every few yards.

Why did I ever come here? he thought.

The sun was high and bright now, the morning's clouds finally dissolving, and the day was growing progressively warm. He'd been sweating bad when he left the Riverview, and now, four blocks later, he was soaked.

When you got right down to it, Baragon simply didn't enjoy being around people very much. He was convinced that most of them had been placed on this planet for the sole purpose of getting in his way.

At the next corner, Christ, whatever intersection it was, he stopped and breathed again, relieved that the light was against him, giving him a chance to stand still for a moment, worry-free, allowing the sounds of the trucks, the Checkers, the sirens, the newsboys, and the harrowing screams of the fruit vendors to wash over him.

The light changed, and he crossed. There was scaffolding waiting for him on the other side. Scaffolding, for Baragon, was never anything but bad news.

As he reached the far corner, a vision of horribleness emerged from the darkness.

Six feet tall and probably approaching three hundred pounds. Some sort of hideous man/woman creature, all dolled up in a shocking white bob wig, enormous wraparound sunglasses, and pancake makeup so thick it was cracking and flaking under the direct sunlight. Around its mouth was a horrifying smear of clown lipstick, thick and drippy and blood red, drawing its mouth into an eternal grimace. Baragon had seen better makeup jobs in the madhouse. Whatever this was, it put the fear into him. The creature stood there in a tight chartreuse dress like a sentinel before the gates of the fifth circle.

Christ, this is all worse than usual, he thought. He didn't even have the time to think about what might have happened to Natacia. Instead, he quickly averted his eyes and put his head down, his steps picking up in a way they would be better to avoid.

"Hey, buddy! You!" a voice shouted behind him, but he ignored it.

Halfway down the block, quick glances over his shoulder convincing him at last that the beast wasn't following him, he began to breathe easier—until he looked straight ahead again to see that at the end of the scaffold tunnel, blocking his exit like an obstacle in some sadistic miniature golf course, a man in a wheelchair was spinning in circles— circles just wide enough to prevent any easy passage.

A doorman stood in front of a nearby building, clearly amused by the paralyzed man's zany frolics.

Baragon stopped, gauged the roving opening offered him, and darted when the time seemed right.

Clear on the other side, almost to the point of, if not screaming, at least whimpering, he finally saw that the corner of Broadway was less than half a block away.

He breathed easier again, and when he reached the corner, he stopped, remembering something. Something else. Something similar. Not to the wheelchair, but to Natacia's story. One of them at least.

Crazy guy, trouble with an SRO. Funny name.

He couldn't quite put his finger on it, so he stopped before turning north and pulled the notepad out again.

Mr. Funny name SRO, he wrote beneath "SVA"—which itself was beneath Natacia's address. Then he started looking for a bank. And maybe a place to sit for a minute before going too much farther.

Shortly before two that afternoon, he emptied his coat pockets onto the desk, removed the coat, and lowered himself heavily into his chair. There were no phone messages waiting, which was a tremendous relief. He was in no mood for any more news at this point.

After his heartbeat returned to something resembling normal, he picked up the notepad and glanced at it. *SVA. Mr. Funny name SRO.*

Funny name should be no trouble, he thought. He pulled open the overstuffed drawer and, within a surprisingly few seconds, was able to retrieve the fax he'd been thinking of. Col. Hans Heg, Retired. Greenwood Hotel. He was even kind enough to provide a phone number.

Before he called, though, Baragon created a new file on his computer, which he entitled simply "SRO."

He quickly typed up what he'd heard from Natacia, her address, what he'd learned from the fat man. Then he scanned through the fax in front of him and typed in everything that seemed relevant. And beneath that, he added, "Raymond Martin?"

At the four desks around him, one reporter was talking to his girlfriend ("And like, everyone was just totally laughing? And so I guess I was like totally laughing too, or whatever. . . ."), one to his boyfriend, and one was eating lunch. Biddle—ah, Biddle—was on the telephone with his mother, telling her all about how bright his future was looking ever since he got that big cover scoop.

Baragon shook his head, not as annoyed as he probably should have been. He had things to do. He went through the fax again and got what he believed to be a reasonably firm grasp on the story. Then he dialed Col. Hans Heg's number.

A recording informed him that it had been disconnected.

"Dammit," he hissed as he hung up the phone. He was in no mood to go out and try to track this guy down, too. Maybe he should have called him right after he got the fax. Chalk up another one for Baragon's timing.

Then he noticed the second telephone number on the fax. This one didn't seem to be identified in any way. *What the hell?* Baragon picked up the phone again and dialed.

"Gree'woo' Hotel," a man with what sounded to be an Asian accent answered.

"Uhh, hello there," Baragon said. "I'm wondering if you can help me—" Before giving the man the chance to refuse, he rolled on. "I'm trying to reach a tenant there with some urgent family news—it's imperative that I talk to him—but I just tried his number, and it's been disconnected. I'm wondering if you could tell me whether he's still living there?"

"Who you look fo'?" the man asked abruptly.

I've seen this movie, too, Baragon thought.

"Uhh—his name is Hans Heg. Colonel Hans Heg." He enunciated each syllable. "Retired."

"Han Lay?" the man asked.

"No, sir—*Hans . . . Heg.* H-E-G."

"Oh! Hanheg! Yah, he no here."

Why am I not surprised?

"Okay—um . . . do you know when he might be back?"

"He no come back. Go far away. He bad tenant. Very bad."

At the top of the fax, Baragon used his pen to absently scratch the word *Yipe!* "Ummm . . . do you know where he went?"

"No! And don' want to know. Very bad. Ruin ev'ything! Loud. Always complain."

"Okay, I understand," Baragon said. "I guess I'll try elsewhere—but before I go—can I ask you a quick question?" Again, before giving the man a chance to refuse, "Is this Mr. Fukuda?" He glanced at the fax to make sure he had got that one right.

"Yah, this Mist' Fukuda."

"Very good," Baragon said. "Now—you're the manager of that fine establishment, are you not?"

"Huh?"

"Are . . . you . . . the . . . man-a-ger?"

"Yah, I manager."

"Great. That's great. I hear you're doing wonderful things with the Greenwood and I congratulate you. One more thing, then I'll let you go—could you, uh, Mr., Fukuda—could you please tell me who owns the building? The Greenwood?"

"Who own Gree'wood Hotel?"

"If you please."

"That SVA, they own. I just manager."

Baragon's eyes widened. He should get out of this while he still could. "Oh, Mr. Fukuda, I would never say '*just* the manager.' You are making everyone proud, I'm sure. Right now, I'm sure you're very busy, so I'll let you go." He hung up the phone before Mr. Fukuda had a chance to respond.

"*Shit*," he said aloud, then began to giggle until he was wracked with thick coughs.

Half an hour later, after tracking down the office's only telephone book, he had a number and an address for SVA Realty. He'd even called the number to make sure there was someone there and to confirm the Brooklyn Heights address. He'd go out there himself, but it could wait until tomorrow. He'd have to be at the top of his form, and right now he was just too damned exhausted. Besides, he'd done plenty today, he thought. Very productive day. He hadn't a clue as to what any of it meant, but it sure felt like he had done something. Walked all that way. Up and down stairs.

In the meantime, he checked the wires to see if anything from the BioLab had made it to the surface yet.

Turned out to be a slow day, news-wise. Economy was still limping, gas prices were going up, some country he'd never heard of was at war with some other country he'd never heard of.

Oh. Here's something, he thought as he saw the headline "Navy Copters Collide in Hawaii; 16 Dead."

Unfortunately, the headline said it all, and there were no surprising details to be found in the body of the item. There was no tension, no reason to read it—after the headline, it was all letdown. He could've handled it better, even without knowing any of the facts. Worst of all, there were no photographs. He shrugged again and went on.

One thing became clear very quickly—if Natacia was right and there *had* been another radioactive person found, nobody was reporting it. Just as well—he'd find out tonight.

Unless, of course, those "astronauts" Natacia was talking about simply took her away and didn't bother with the morgue. Mayor's people, after all, were telling the ME's people to get rid of it, right?

He didn't even want to get started with that sort of thinking.

—And Natacia, too. And everyone else in that place—

Shut up.

—And Hans Heg—

Will you please—?

It could happen.

Shut up.

That's all I'm saying.

Goddamnit—

They're all disappearing—can't you see that?

Enough.

Baragon stopped and looked around the room. None of the others were staring at him. That's good. It meant he wasn't saying anything aloud. Unless they were just ignoring him out of simple courtesy—or fear.

He figured the thing to do was get out, get some air, get a drink. Jack's would be open now, and he'd gladly wait a couple hours for Emily. Though the way he was feeling, chances were good he might well pass out before she showed up. He wouldn't want to do that—especially the way she was sounding this morning. Last thing she needed to deal with after a rough day at the morgue was a fat drunk bald guy who needed to be hauled home again.

He'd take it easy until she got there. He stood and reached for his coat. If Ed caught him on the way out, he'd—as usual—explain that he was going to interview a very important source.

Shortly before six, the door to the bar opened and Emily walked in. Seeing her come through that door brightened him up a notch.

"Hey, doll." He sat, patting the stool next to him. "Let me get you a beer."

"Thanks," she said as she sat down heavily. "I need it." She looked bedraggled.

"You sound tired," he said. "Rough one? It sounded like things weren't going so hot when I called this morning. Sorry if I caught you at a bad time."

"No, that's okay, don't worry about it," she said. "Let me get this beer first before I get into it."

"Understood." He decided to wait awhile before telling her about his visit to the Riverview. He sat quietly as Jack brought the pint over and noticed that Roscoe needed a fresh one.

She took a swallow. "Your story wasn't exactly a big hit with the boss," she said.

"Ohh, shit," he said. "Did I say something I shouldn't have?"

She took another swallow, set the glass down, and shook her head. "Well, let me put it this way—there was nothing in your story that wasn't *true*. But the problem was, very little of it was on the official press release. In fact, you made fun of the press release."

"I know—sorry about that—but that was kind of the point, wasn't it?"

"I know—I know. I'm not saying that. It's just that everyone who had any access to the final report got called on the carpet because of it. He wanted to know who was responsible for leaking it out. This wasn't something that could be blamed on EMS. It had to come from inside."

"Shit—" he said again. "Anything come out? I mean—have they connected us yet?"

"I don't think so—we were all let off with a collective warning about talking to the press."

"Uh-huh. That's understandable. We can be a pretty mercenary lot."

Baragon always worried she'd be tagged one of these days, and he didn't want that to happen, but dammit, the stuff she got him was so *good*—

This radioactive man story was the first time she'd heard anything at all at the ME's office concerning something she'd slipped to Roscoe. She was smart, devious when she needed to be, and beyond suspicion. It sounded to Baragon as if things had gone fine this time, too. She wasn't singled out, after all—merely scolded as part of a group. He was certain nobody suspected a thing.

Weird thing was, though—to most everyone—everyone except Baragon, that is—this seemed like such an insignificant story. Couple tiny paragraphs in the *Times* and nothing anywhere else. Press release that seemed to snuff it right there as nothing.

Emily had certainly passed along much more sensitive material to him in the past—what about those post-autopsy shots of Eddie the Pinhead? The *Sentinel* ran them on the cover, and there wasn't a peep (except from the surviving members of Eddie's family). What was the big deal with this?

"It'll blow over," she said. "All he wants now is for the story to die."

"I'm sure it will," he told her, quietly biting his lip. "And in the end, who could possibly suspect you of anything? I mean, look at you." He squeezed her shoulders.

They both drank in silence.

"So how was your day?" she asked, finally.

"Oh, I guess I've had worse," he said. "Spent the day trying to track a couple people down without any luck. Natacia called this morning—"

"I'm surprised she called back after you hung up on her."

"Yeah, well, so was I. She saw the radioactive man story and was calling to tell me that there'd been another one found."

"That's what you were asking about this morning."

"Right, sorry about that again."

"Nah, it's nothing. It's over. And no, for the record, no more radioactive bodies came through."

"I kind of figured that."

"Just Natacia being Natacia?"

"Sounds like it." Baragon agreed. "She said some guys in space suits showed up and took one of her neighbors away."

"I'm surprised she didn't think they were actual spacemen."

"Yeah, that's not really her game, though. Weird thing is—she was one of the people I was trying to track down today. Went over to her hotel, but nobody was there. Talked to her an hour earlier, told her I would stop by, then she was gone."

"Well," she said, after considering a moment. "I wouldn't worry about it too much. She was probably just taking a nap or something. You'll hear from her in the next day or two, I bet."

"Yeah, probably," he said, wanting to believe it but not sure that he did. They were quiet again.

"Oh—here's something interesting, though," Baragon said before finishing his beer. "Did I ever tell you about Hoke Slaughter, this NASA guy I knew from a while back?"

"You mentioned him yesterday."

"Well, he called me late last night. He was drunk. He was involved in this whole BioLab thing, right?"

"Uh-huh," she said.

"We were both drunk at the time, actually. Anyway, so he calls to tell me that he thinks there's some kind of mutant on board. Some biological experiment gone all catywhompus."

"Uh-huh," she said, though she suddenly didn't sound too interested. "You believe him?"

"Oh, who knows. You know me—I'd kind of like to. Good story. But I guess we'll have to wait and see what swims to the surface."

"Ah."

This was clearly not the time to ask her why radiation detectors had been installed at the morgue. Or it was the perfect time. Maybe if he tried to edge his way around.

"So . . ." he began, "apart from the dressing-down, how was the rest of your day?"

"I need another drink," she said. Jack, one of those rare bartenders who was blessed with precognitive skills, was already on his way with two more.

"That bad, huh?"

She tipped the new pint back, then set it down. "Oh, not really—just long."

"I'm sorry."

"It's okay. Don't be sorry. I'll get over it. I just need a decent night's rest."

They were quiet again, for a long time.

"So . . ." Baragon ventured, "how's our guy doing?"

She turned to glare at him, then looked away again. "You can be such a shit," she muttered.

"Pardon?"

"I can't believe you—that's all that's really on your mind right now, isn't it?"

Awww, jeez.

"Just making conversation," he said. "You didn't seem too interested in my day, so I was asking about yours, that's all. It's no big deal. Sorry if I said something wrong."

"But you weren't asking about my day—you were asking about that fucking corpse. That corpse is *your* guy now, he's not mine. . . . I regret ever telling you anything about this. *Shit*, I'm an idiot."

Baragon was getting the impression that it was going to be a short night here at Jack's.

"Hey," he began, "you're not an idiot. You've had a long day. So have I, I guess—and I'm probably just going to keep saying the wrong damn thing. You want to maybe cut it short after this one, before, you know, the glasses start flying? We could both get some rest."

She took a breath and looked at her half-empty glass.

"No," she said. "I'm fine. I'm sorry I snapped like that."

"It's okay," Baragon said. "I understand."

"It's just that fucking corpse has turned the place upside down. It's like we're all under surveillance there, ever since he showed up." Baragon's ears pricked up, but he tried to give no indication of that. "Everyone's on edge, everyone's snapping at each other. Those bastards from the mayor's office are still around—and I don't even know where they're keeping that fucking corpse anymore."

"You mean it's not in the isolation area?"

"No," she said, shaking her head.

"I'm sorry—" he said, "but I don't follow. Did they move

him? Or do they think someone took him? Mayor's office wanted you to get rid of it, right?"

"I don't know what happened," she said.

"Do they think he just got up and walked away?"

"I said I *don't know!*" Her anger was returning.

"Do they—"

"Jesus *Christ*, Roscoe, aren't you listening? Can't you just shut up for once?"

He did.

"I'm sorry," he said eventually, touching her leg lightly. "It's just real peculiar is what it is."

"I know it is, Rosk. I'm sorry I yelled." She looked up. "Sorry to you, too, Jack."

Jack was there, with two full pints. "'Sokay," he said. "These are on the house."

They both raised the new beers to him. "Thanks, Jack." He nodded, waved a hand in dismissal, and retreated.

"I'm sorry I kept pressing," he said once Jack was out of earshot. "You know how I get with these things sometimes."

"Yeah, I know," she said. "Like a fucking conspiracy-nut bulldog. Now just drink your damn beer and keep your big yap shut."

"Deal," he said, and drank. "Then I'll get back in the cave." But at the same time, his mind was swirling with possibilities, none of them good. He'd ask her about that detector business some other night. "I must say, we're living in very strange times."

"Cheers to that," she said, raising her glass again and clinking it lightly against his.

Chapter Nine

It was eleven o'clock Friday morning, and Baragon was still half asleep. These past two weeks had taken their toll on him, and he looked it. The heavy flesh of his face had slipped toward an undead gray, and the bags beneath his yellow, red-rimmed eyes were even more pronounced than usual. Still, much to his amazement, he was at it again, standing outside the address he'd found—and confirmed—for SVA Realty, on Hicks, just off Montague Street in Brooklyn Heights.

Weird fucking place to find a Realtor who specializes in flophouses, he thought as he looked around. Brooklyn Heights was the swankiest neighborhood in Brooklyn—one of the swankiest in all of New York—full of doctors, lawyers, famous writers, celebrities, and a well-maintained collection of historic brownstones. Montague Street was the neighborhood's central commercial strip, its neatly trimmed sidewalks lined with banks, salons, upscale restaurants, expensive coffee bars, and bookstores. Baragon generally tried to avoid places like this. They made him uncomfortable. It was clear to him as well that the residents of places like this wished he would continue to avoid them. But here he was. Sometimes the job required it.

To his right in the morning sun, if he squinted (which he was usually doing anyway), he could see the courthouse building across the way. To his left, if he really, really squinted, down past the end of Montague and across the promenade (where the wealthy walked their children and tiny dogs on quiet summer evenings), he could catch the light glinting off the East River, the Manhattan skyline beyond.

The streets were busy with affluent types clucking their harried way around him where he stood at the corner, taking up a good portion of the sidewalk.

"Yeah, yeah," he said to a few of the more vocal ones. He was doing his job.

The building he was standing before didn't strike him as looking much like a realty office—just another expensive, well-kept brownstone at the end of a long row of nearly identical brownstones. There was a small garden out front, though nothing seemed to be growing there right now. He slipped the notepad out of his coat pocket and checked the address to make sure.

When he approached the front door and looked at the short row of buzzers, he found what he wanted at the very bottom: SVA. He pressed the button and waited.

He heard a click and a hum, and an echoed voice asked, "Yes?"

"Hello—uh, my name is Baragon—I called yesterday?" It struck him as a rather pointless thing to say, as he'd never given his name when he called. Just checked the address and hours of operation before hanging up.

A moment later the door in front of him began buzzing, and he pushed it open. The inside door was buzzing as well, and that one he pulled. It's always a race with those damn things. No one ever gives you enough time to get through both of them.

Well, now where? There was a flight of wooden stairs in front of him and a door to the left. Next to the door was a small black plastic nameplate with SVA Realty etched in white. He opened the door to find himself at the top of another flight of stairs—shorter than the other—leading downward. A warm, humid breeze caught his face.

All these stairs, he thought. *Jesus.* He grabbed the handrail and headed toward the basement.

At the bottom of the stairs—there were only five of them this time, he noted with some relief—there was yet another door, this one with a translucent window. The company name was stenciled in black across the glass. Nothing too fancy about it. Baragon wasn't expecting too much by way of "fancy."

He knocked once, then turned the handle. The air was thick down here, and moist, and smelled vaguely of mold and—he sniffed quickly before pushing the door open—was that . . . fish?

Least it's not mothballs again.

When he stepped into the office, he stopped. There was thin navy blue carpeting on the floor, a couple of molded plastic chairs to the right, a large, dark wooden desk in front of him. What stopped him, however—together with the almost unbearable humidity in the room—was the immense aquarium behind the reception desk. It nearly filled the wall—it might have been built right into the wall, for all he could tell—well stocked with species of fish he had never seen before. Small, squidlike creatures with what seemed to be transparent wings of some sort danced through the vegetation sprouting from the aquarium bed. Aquatic frogs with spiny dorsal fins floated peacefully in the mild current, and brightly spotted eels with fanned tails darted from corner to corner, their bodies undulating.

"Wow, that's really something," he said, realizing how profusely he seemed to be sweating all of a sudden.

"May I help you?" asked the Asian woman sitting at the desk. She was wearing a white turban wrapped high atop her head and a simple white dress that shimmered with silver light when she moved.

"Yeah—I, uh—" he was having a hard time diverting his eyes from the aquarium. It seemed to glow with its own inner, ethereal blue light. He'd been to the damn zoo, but he had never seen—or even heard of—creatures like these before.

"Yeah—I'm sorry"—he finally snapped his eyes away—"but that really is something."

"Yes, indeed it is," she said in crisp, exacting English. She didn't smile. "Now, sir, how may I help you?"

"Well," he said, "first of all, you mind if I take my coat off? You sure do like it warm in here, huh?"

"Be my guest," she said, slightly less patient.

He began to pull his sleeves from his trench coat, stopping to try to grab the notepad and tape recorder from his pockets before they fell to the floor. As he twisted his stout body in an effort to do this, he noticed for the first time that her simple white dress was, in reality, a kind of toga, made from some sheer material he didn't recognize, wrapped around her slim body and fastened with an elaborate golden pin.

"My name is Roscoe Baragon, and, uh, I'm with the *Sentinel*," he began, "and I know I don't have an appointment or anything, but I was wondering if I might possibly be able to have a quick word with the, uh—"

"Oh yes, Mr. Baragon," she said, much to his surprise, "Mr. Dunham is expecting you. We just weren't sure what time you'd be here."

"Oh," he said.

"I'll go let him know you're here." She stood and disappeared through a door to the right of the aquarium.

"Yes . . ." Baragon said after her, confused, "That's very kind. Thank you." *What in the hell was* that *all about?*

A moment later she was back, holding the door open. "Mr. Bargaon, if you will follow me, please?" He did as she asked, still trying to wrap his brain around everything, including how unbelievably humid this place was. The fishy smell he understood now, but the heat? Maybe it was for the fish.

As he followed her down a short hallway, he noticed that her pale feet were wrapped in sandals made of golden twine.

The walls of the corridor were the same shade of blue as the carpeting and were adorned with paintings of various unrecognizable fish—all of them apparently rendered by the same artist. Strange fish. Fish with nearly human faces.

She stopped at a doorway at the very end of the hall and knocked twice before turning the handle and opening the door.

A resonant male voice from inside the room beckoned, "Come in please, Mr. Baragon." The woman bowed slightly at him as he passed, then returned to the reception area.

The office was small, the air even more rank and stifling than it had been out front (*Why isn't there mildew everywhere?* Baragon wondered), and featured a nearly identical wall-size aquarium behind the desk.

The man behind the desk had kinky, graying hair and a thin mustache. When he stood and extended a hand toward Baragon, it was clear that he was dressed in a toga as well—this one very short, cut well above the knee. He wore a wide belt with a bejeweled golden buckle around his waist. It was hard to read any certain ethnicity into his features. He wasn't distinctly European, or Asian, or Indian. Maybe

Malaysian, with a touch of Eskimo? It didn't matter. His English was perfect, although a touch ceremonious. *Maybe he's Dutch*, thought Baragon as he leaned across the desk and shook his hand, which was clammy and oddly cool, but strong. "Please take a seat," the man in the toga said.

"Thanks, Mr. . . . uh . . ."

"Dunham," he said. "Antonio Dunham. I'm the vice president of SVA Realty."

"Well, nice to meet you, Mr. Dunham," said Baragon as he lowered himself, gratefully, into the soft leather chair. *Man, I'm gonna stick to this*, he thought. His shirt was soaked.

"And what might we be able to do for you? You don't strike me as a man who's looking for a place to live."

"Yeah . . . no," Baragon said, shifting himself around in the chair, draping his coat over one of the arms and quickly wiping the sweat from his nose. "Jesus, okay," he added as he tried to get himself organized. Finally settled, he began in earnest. "Two quick things to begin with. First—um, forgive me for asking here—but is it Roman Day or something? I mean—what's with the togas?"

Dunham laughed gently. "Oh, no, no—unless you wanted to say that *every* day is Roman Day here at SVA."

"Uh-huh. Oh—by the way—do you mind if I turn on this tape recorder here?" Baragon asked, pulling it out and setting it on the desk. "It's no big deal, but I like to make sure I get my quotes right. It protects both of us that way." It was a line he always used, and one that usually worked.

"Please," Dunham said with a short sweep of his arm.

"Great," Baragon said, hitting the record button and making sure things were rolling. "Now. Really. What's the deal with the togas?"

"Well, as you can clearly feel for yourself, this office is a trifle . . . stuffy. The heating system in this building is older than the gods, and the air circulation—especially being a windowless basement office—leaves something to be desired. It took us some time to figure out that it wasn't going to get any better, even during the wintertime, so we decided the best way to manage would be to dress as comfortably as possible while we were here. Does that make sense? Otherwise we'd spend our days being irritable and itchy. It simply makes for a more pleasant working environment."

That almost makes sense. "Fair enough," Baragon nodded. "That was just to satisfy my own curiosity. Second thing I'm wondering—also for my own curiosity—ahh, how, exactly, did you know I was coming today?"

"Ohh," Dunham said, still smiling—though, Baragon noted, the smile seemed distant and well rehearsed. "We have our spies."

"Excuse me?" Baragon asked, startled.

"I'm only joking," Dunham said with a dismissive shake of the head. "You called here yesterday, isn't that correct?"

"Yes, I did—but I never left a name or said that I'd be coming by."

Dunham pointed at a small white box next to the dolphin-shaped telephone on his desk. "Caller ID," he declared. "Amazing technology. When your call came through, it told us you were calling from the *Sentinel*. Now, you get a telephone call from someone at a major metropolitan newspaper, checking your address and asking when you're open, you reason you might well be expecting someone to stop by in the near future."

"It might've just been a fact checker."

"Yes, it might've been. But here you are, aren't you?"

Baragon shrugged. "I guess I am. And I guess that's fair enough, too. I could be an ad salesman, though."

"*Could* be—but you're not. It's all fairly simple reasoning. Now then," Dunham went on, his smile fading slightly, "those two important questions out of the way, what can I really do for you, considering that you're not selling ads or checking facts?"

Baragon leaned back in his chair and crossed his legs. He was beginning to wish he'd thought this whole thing through a little better. "Well, let's begin at the beginning," he said, casting a quick eye on the tape recorder to make sure the red light was still glowing. Unexpectedly dead batteries had cost him more than one interview in the past. "You said that you're the vice president—who's the president?"

"Ahh," Dunham said, his smile back in full force. "That would be Mr. Simon Vaneigm—Simon Vaneigm and Associates, you see? He's a very fine man, indeed. And I'm sure he would have been more than happy to talk to you today himself had he not been on vacation. So, I'm afraid, you're stuck with me."

"I see."

"But, if the gods are with us, I'll be able to answer all of your questions satisfactorily. I've been with SVA almost since the beginning."

What's with all this "gods" crap? "Oh, I'm sure you will," Baragon said. "It's no big deal, actually, like I said. It's just that there seem to have been some strange things happening to the tenants of some of your buildings in recent weeks."

Dunham nodded, looking concerned, but not all that concerned. "Mmm-hmmm? Really. Perhaps if you could explain in a little more detail."

"Sure," Baragon said. Then, over the next ten minutes, as Antonio Dunham listened patiently, he outlined what he had heard from Natacia and read in the fax from Hans Heg—ending with the fact that both people, quite suddenly, seemed to be missing.

"I see," Dunham said when Baragon wrapped up his story. "Now, Mr. Baragon, you're a newspaper reporter. I understand that. And it's your job to uncover the truth and let the public know what is going on in the world around them."

"Yeah, well, y'know, that's sort of the general idea."

"—and I understand that when you hear from people who seem to be sincere and seem to be in some kind of trouble, and then those people mysteriously vanish, your suspicions might become aroused."

"Understandably."

"When it turns out that both of these people lived in dwellings owned by the same company, you figured it would be best to go straight to the one thing that seems to connect them. Any good reporter would do that."

"That's pretty much what I was thinking, yessir."

"That's fine; I certainly can understand that. Now, while we have absolutely nothing to hide here, I was wondering if I may, perhaps, offer you a different perspective on these events?"

"I'm always happy to hear it—shoot." Baragon wiped the sweat from his forehead and upper lip.

"Well then," Dunham said, pushing his chair back from his desk and crossing his legs. (*I really wish he wouldn't do that*, Baragon thought.) "SVA owns nearly two hundred properties in Manhattan, Brooklyn, and the Bronx."

"Okay." Baragon nodded.

"In those properties, we house several thousand tenants."

"Right."

"Now, I'll be honest with you—not all of our present properties are the nicest or most desirable buildings in the city of New York. In fact, several dozen of them are designed to offer low-income housing to people who cannot afford very much."

"Umm—flophouses?"

"—And many of those are of the single-room occupancy variety, yes, what you call 'flophouses,' in which we offer inexpensive, temporary housing for those who might need it. A haven, if you will, until they get back on their feet."

"Right?" Baragon nodded.

"As I said, some of these buildings are not in the best condition—but many of them are also structures we acquired only within the past year or two. Over the years, under previous ownership, many had fallen into various states of disrepair. We are presently making improvements on them as we can—plumbing, heating, electrical wiring. Even cable television in some instances. But it's a very slow, extremely expensive process, requiring the acquisition of various city building and zoning permits as well as the hiring of respectable lawyers and trustworthy contractors. And sometimes, I'm sorry to say, these improvements—despite the effort involved, as well as our good intentions—are not always appreciated by the tenants who may have been living there for some time, like your Mr. . . . ? What was his name again? I'm sorry."

"Colonel Heg."

"Yes, Mr. Heg. Again, however, these were designed to be temporary units."

"Uh-huh?"

"Some of our older tenants—as I'm sure you'll understand—can be very set in their ways. They don't like changes or the disruptions these improvements sometimes entail."

"Yeah, I can understand that." Baragon thought of his own apartment, which hadn't been painted—despite the landlord's valiant efforts—since he moved in.

"Also—let us be frank here. A few of our tenants—especially in the single-room hotels—they are not always, how shall I say? All there. Do you understand? I don't mean to be cruel."

"I understand," Baragon said. "It's not cruel—they can be a little buggy."

"Yes. So you disrupt the life—even if it's with the best intentions in mind—of someone who is perhaps mentally unstable to begin with and there is a fair chance they might suspect it to be the result of some grand conspiracy designed to cause them harm."

"Yeah, I get it," Baragon said, looking at his sweating hands, almost ashamedly.

"You see? There is a very logical explanation to these tales. And given the number of tenants we have, as I mentioned, that you heard two such stories from people who were tenants of separate buildings? Well, Mr. Baragon—" he spread his hands and grinned. "I think the law of probabilities is on SVA's side here."

"That's why I don't go to Vegas anymore," Baragon said. "But still, Mr. Dunham—that two of your tenants—at least two—seem to have vanished right around the same time? Doesn't that strike you as just a little, y'know, bothersome?"

Dunham smiled again, patiently. "Mr. Baragon—those buildings are designed for transients. They come and they go, a day, a week, a month, and we never hear from them again. We don't make an effort to track the comings and goings of our tenants," he said. "We simply provide them with affordable shelter and clean sheets. How they live their lives is none of our concern."

"Sure," said Baragon while thinking, *smooth son of a bitch.* "Well," he said, and reached for the tape recorder. "I think that should about handle it, really. I've taken up enough of your time—and I thank you very kindly for your patience and openness." He shut off the player and stood, gathering his coat.

"My pleasure, Mr. Baragon," Dunham replied, himself standing. "As I said, we have nothing to hide here."

Yeah, the toga business makes that pretty clear.

They shook hands—both of which were clammy now—

and Baragon turned for the door. "Oh—one more thing," he said.

"Certainly."

"Do you suppose it might be possible to get—and if it's not, I understand—but might I be able to get a list, say, of all the properties owned by SVA? That is, if it's no trouble."

Some of the friendly, open kindness blinked out of Dunham's eyes for a moment, then returned just as quickly, his smile never wavering. "Why, of course, that would be no trouble at all—though it may take a moment. Come," he said, gesturing at the door, "I'll have Ms. Hama take care of it right away."

"Yeah, many thanks," Baragon said. The idea of spending any more time in this steam bath wasn't too inviting, but he'd be out of here soon enough.

He followed Dunham down the hall—saw that the aquarium did, indeed, form a window through the wall—and stood by the receptionist's desk as Dunham said, "Ms. Hama—would you be kind enough, when you have a moment, to print out a list of our properties for Mr. Baragon? It would be most appreciated."

"Of course," she said as Dunham shook Baragon's hand once more, then returned to his office.

Baragon sat down in one of the molded plastic chairs, and waited, and sweated.

Baragon was relieved to step back outside into the cool, fresh breeze again. *Got no tolerance for the heat*, he thought as he strolled toward the subway, the list of all the addresses owned by SVA rolled up in his pocket.

He stopped and picked up a salami sandwich before returning to the office. He was beginning to wonder what the hell he was going to do with all this. These past two

days, what had it gotten him? Two possibly missing lunatics—though he wasn't absolutely sure if they were actually "missing"—and a perfectly reasonable explanation. Two
days shot, and none of it had brought him any closer to
uncovering what the deal was with his radioactive, toilet-
thieving, disappearing corpse.

Montgomery called his name as he passed the doorway,
but Baragon ignored it.

He sat at his desk, turned on the computer, unwrapped
the salami and provolone, and began scanning the news to
see what he'd been missing.

Israel and Palestine were at it again. Big deal. Tensions
were increasing between the United States and Guam.
Whoop-de-do. A boat loaded with Chinese slave labor goes
down in a freak typhoon. Another boat—a Japanese fishing
boat—goes down off Hawaii after being split in half by a
U.S. submarine. Floods and drought at the same time in the
Midwest, somehow. Some professional baseball player gets
arrested for smacking a dwarf around in a Denver motel
room.

Something about that Dunham I don't trust, he thought as
the headlines scrolled past him. *And it wasn't just the toga. A
man with all the answers is a man who isn't telling you anything
at all. Nope, nope, nope.*

A few minutes later, the sandwich gone, he crumpled up
the paper and dropped it in the trash can. He retrieved the
tape player, began rewinding the tape, and flopped a hand
around in a desk drawer, looking for his earphone. He found
it, untangled the cord, and plugged it into the machine.
Baragon hated transcribing, but at least it was an effective
way to drown out the jabberings of his office mates.

On the computer screen, he opened the file he'd created
for Natacia, Hans Heg, and their SRO troubles. He'd put
this interview at the bottom, then tried to figure out what the

hell to do with it. The wisest thing, probably, would be to close it up immediately and forget all about it.

"Something just went real fucking weird on me these last weeks," he told Emily at the bar later that night. "There's too much going on—I've been trying to juggle all these different things—but at the same time, nothing's happening with any of them."

"Oh, that just makes sense," she said, setting her glass down. "You've been chasing so many different, disparate things around that you can't concentrate fully on any one of them."

"Yeah, yeah," he muttered, grinding his fourth smoke out. "I know."

"You need to take a break, maybe. Catch your breath."

He shook his head and snorted. "That's the thing—there was a time when I didn't have to. A time when nothing stopped moving, ever. And it was okay—it was the way I liked it. Juggle half a dozen stories at once and have them all come together."

"That's because you were doing a lot of speed back then," she reminded him.

"Yeah, well . . . I think maybe Ed's right and I've gotten lazy. I don't want to think I've gotten old, but maybe I have. All those hundreds of phoners. Who cares? But now here's all this crazy shit. Something—and I don't know what—is starting to tell me that there's something to it all—and I don't really know what to do with it anymore."

"I still think you need to take a break," she insisted, giving Jack a nod to let him know they needed another round. She spun her stool to face Baragon. "I have an idea."

"What's that?" he asked, though he was only really half interested.

"Tomorrow's Saturday. Let's do something. When was the last time we did anything? Other than sit here and drink, I mean."

"Wha'd you have in mind?"

She thought a moment as Jack arrived and took the money off the bar. "How 'bout Coney?" she suggested. "We haven't been down to Coney in a couple years, and that always picks you up. Or we could go shoot some pool someplace. Go to the track. Anything you want."

His mood actually brightened some at the thought. "Yeah, that might be okay," he said. "Help me clear the ol' noggin. Get some sea air, a few beers."

"Spin on the Cyclone, maybe, if we get drunk enough."

"Oh," he shook his head, "I think I might skip the Cyclone this time. I'm too big for the seats these days, and that thing always hurts my neck. I don't want my obit to read 'Fat Guy Dies on Roller Coaster.'"

She reached up and massaged the back of his neck with her left hand. "We'll see."

They drank awhile before he asked, "So . . . any sign of the missing Mr. Martin?" He wasn't sure how she would react after the previous night, but she took it in stride.

"Nope," she said. "Nobody said much of anything about it today. Which, I guess, is kind of strange, come to think about it. But at the same time it was a relief—we had plenty of other work to do. Other people in this town continue to die, damn them, anyhow."

He raised an eyebrow at her. "Yeah? Mayor's thugs still around?"

"Uh-huh, but not as many. Maybe a half dozen? I'm not sure. I talked to a few of them," she said. "And I guess they aren't so bad after all. Just guys doing their jobs."

"Uh-huh," he offered. "Just like the rest of us. . . . So tell me—while we're on the subject, I've been meaning to ask you this ever since this whole thing began—why were those radiation detectors installed in the morgue, anyway? Doesn't that strike you as a little, you know, hinky?"

"I guess so, a little. . . . All I know, really," she said, her voice sounding completely sincere to him, "was that they were put in at the same time they did all those other renovations last year. That's when I got the new lab—remember?"

"Yeah, of course I remember that—and the DNA thingee, right?"

"Yeah."

"But I didn't know until this business came up that they'd installed radiation detectors."

"No, neither did I. And I have no idea why they did it." She took a drink. "There are two of them. See, there are two doors in the garage where they drop the bodies off, each leading down a different corridor to the mortuary area. Both of them have a detector mounted up above the doorway. When the alarm goes off, first thing the guard on duty's supposed to do is call the EPA."

"Uh-huh. But you have no idea why they were put there in the first place?"

"Nope. Nothing more than what I read in that *Times* article."

He wasn't sure if he should push or not but went ahead and did it anyway. "You ever . . . ask anyone? See what other people around there had to say?"

"Of course. But nobody seems to know. I mean, even the guy in the radiography department wasn't sure, exactly. I mean—he's working with radiation with the X-ray machine, sure—but that's no reason to be scanning the bodies as they come in."

"Yeah," Baragon added. "Doesn't make much sense, does it?" He reached behind him and started patting the pockets of his coat, which was draped over the back of his chair.

"What are you looking for?" she asked. This was the last thing she needed tonight. She just wanted a few quiet beers, a couple jokes, a chance to relax and forget about that place until Monday. She missed the days when they both left their jobs behind at the end of the day.

"Fuck, I must've left it at the office," he grumbled to himself in frustration.

"What?" she asked, a little frustrated herself.

"Oh," he said, looking up at her. "Nothing. Just my notebook."

"Rosk, c'mon, calm down. It's no big deal. Just drink your beer. Get some rest tonight. Tomorrow we'll go to Coney, and when you get back in the office Monday, I'm sure everything will work itself out fine."

His arms—which were still rummaging through his clearly empty coat pockets, relaxed. She could see his whole body slump slightly as something seemed to flee from him. "Okay. You're right," he said, smiling sadly and putting his arms back up on the bar. "Sorry about that. I just got a little carried away. For a second. Or almost did."

"It's okay," she told him, reaching over and trying to muss what was left of his hair, "you did. But now drink your damn beer. Have a smoke. Then go home and get some sleep."

"I think that would probably do some good, yeah."

But he couldn't sleep. He lay awake for hours, sweating almost as badly as he had been in those offices earlier that morning, half-phrases circling madly in his head, unable to find a conclusion or any way out.

They met up on a subway platform the next morning at eleven and caught a Coney-bound F train. Baragon was exhausted and more than a little distracted, but he was still determined to put on a happy face for Emily's sake. Apart from his folks when he was younger, he couldn't think of anyone who'd ever really tried to help him the way Emily did. It still confused him sometimes.

Given that it was early spring, none of the rides were open yet. That was a relief to Baragon—it meant he wouldn't have to worry about snapping his neck on the Cyclone.

The rides were secondary at best, anyway. The ocean was still there, and the beach, and a few of the stands along the boardwalk were open—including the bar.

"Wanna grab a beer first?" he asked.

"Sure," she said. "Then can we go down to the beach?"

"You bet."

The sky was clear, and even with the cool breeze off the ocean, the temperatures were climbing toward the seventies. The boardwalk was slowly beginning to fill with men in their shirtsleeves and women carrying bright parasols.

Despite the warmth and the sunshine, Baragon insisted on wearing his trench coat as they walked across the sand toward the surf half an hour later.

"Aren't you dying in that thing?" Emily asked.

"Oh, we're all dying, all the time," he said. It just slipped out.

She socked him lightly on the shoulder. "C'mon, you," she said. "Buck up. We're at Coney. You're not allowed to be grim at Coney."

"Yeah, you're right," he said. "Sorry. If I get too hot, I'll take it off. Promise."

"Okay then."

"It is an awfully nice day, I suppose."

They strolled a quarter-mile up the beach toward Brighton, looking at the few sunbathers who were out this early in the season, stepping gingerly around the broken bottles and the crabs. Baragon had always been wary of crabs.

There was a sound in the air around them—a low whistling or a humming—the kind of sound you'd get if you were to swing a long, flexible plastic tube over your head. They used to sell things like that when Baragon was a kid, but here the source was unclear. Maybe the wind through the Wonder Wheel.

"When was the last time you were down here?" she asked, pausing to look back at the boardwalk.

"Aww, hell," he said, trying to remember. "You mean by myself? I'm guessing it might've been that time I came down to interview a guy who called himself the Amazing Marvini. He was with the sideshow. Do you remember me telling you about that? That was maybe a year and a half ago, I'm guessing."

"I remember the name. Wha'd he do?"

"Oh, he did just about everything, actually. Human block-head, human pincushion, fire-eater, tattooed man . . ."

"Really. To be honest, that sounds kind of bland compared to your normal fare."

"He also claimed he was a werewolf."

"There you go."

"Yeah, he was something all right. And just to prove it, I'm guessing, three weeks after the story ran, he was arrested for sodomizing and killing the hundred-pound rat that was on display next door. Tore its throat out with his teeth."

"That's horrible."

"Ain't it, though? My timing's for shit."

"I mean about the rat."

"Yeah, I always kind of liked that rat. I guess Marvini didn't."

As he talked, Emily could tell that his mind was elsewhere. When she asked him what was wrong, though, he put it down to simple exhaustion, then suggested they go and get another beer.

They were still sitting at the bar shortly after four. Some of Baragon's energy had returned. He seemed more focused. Then he blurted out, "Y'know what really bugs me?"

"What's that?"

"*Rambo 3.*"

Emily rolled her eyes. "And why's that?"

"I'll tell you why. It was the third movie in the series, right? That's obvious enough. But the first one was called *First Blood*. Then the second one they called *Rambo: First Blood Part Two.*"

"Uh-huh?"

"Well then, the third one *isn't Rambo 3*, is it?" He took a swallow and slammed the bottle on the bar more forcefully than he intended. "It's *really First Blood Part 3.*"

"Maybe," she suggested, "they should've called it *Rambo 2: First Blood Part 3.*" If nothing else, this was a Roscoe she was more comfortable with. This Roscoe she knew.

"You see?" he said. "That's thinking. *That* would've made sense. I just can't fucking believe, for all the people who worked on that thing, that nobody noticed. Pisses me off."

She was silent for a moment, watching him stew. Then she asked, "Well, how was it?"

"How was what?"

"The movie."

"Oh," he said, shocked that she would even ask him such a thing. "I never saw it. I mean—I do have *some* taste."

She rolled her eyes again. "I think we need to get you something to eat."

He paused, thought about it, then nodded. "Sure," he said. "That might be a good idea." He began to slide off his stool. "Wha'd you like? Hot dog, corn dog, sausage?" The hot-dog stand was conveniently located on the boardwalk directly outside the bar.

"No, I mean something real. The hot dogs are great—but let's go someplace." She knew they both needed to put more of a bottom on their bellies than hot dogs could offer.

"Okay," he shrugged. "Ummm . . . where'd you like to go?"

"Let's go someplace we've never gone before."

Baragon considered this, briefly chewing his lower lip. "Well . . . there is that one place we've talked about—up on, what, Twenty-eighth? Thirtieth?"

Emily shook her head. "I don't recall."

"Oh—you know it—" The beer had a pretty firm hold on him. "What the hell's that place called?" He wracked his spotty brain looking for the proper door to open. "Barnacle Bill's? Something like that. You know it—the Bilgewater Tap? . . . Washboard Pete's? . . . Slappy Joe's Fruit Cup?"

He was on a roll now, and Emily knew that if she didn't put a stop to it, he could go on like this for the next half hour.

"—The Micronesian Breadbasket? Pork-O-Rama? I'm gettin' close here, I can feel it—a Taste of Canada?"

"You mean the German place?" she finally interrupted.

"Yeah. Zahnpaste—is that it? Wieder Kaput's."

"Gottfried's."

"Yeah, see? I was close."

She took his arm and led him, both weaving slightly, toward the subway that would take them back into Manhattan.

Baragon didn't much like the looks of that neon Families Welcome sign in the front window, but they stepped through the front door into the cool, cavernous, and nearly empty restaurant anyway. For some reason, German cuisine had never caught on in New York the way, say, Burmese and Panamanian cuisine had.

Gottfried's was designed to resemble a modern beer hall, with polka bands on the jukebox and pool tables in the back. The beer came in mighty steins and the staff, though they were clearly ashamed to do so, wore lederhosen. Even the women.

Even though it was late March, both Emily and Baragon ordered the Oktoberfest Platter—which consisted of weisswurst, knockwurst, knabewurst, bratwurst, applesauce, sauerkraut, mashed potatoes, more beer—and, for dessert, apfelküchen. All for one reasonably low price.

"Man," Baragon said, scanning the plate before him after it arrived, "these Germans really know how to live."

As they ate, Baragon's mood lightened. Whenever he tried to bring up work in any form, Emily raised a hand to cut him off, then changed the subject.

When they were finished with their collective sausages, etc., the waitress showed up again holding two plates, each of which contained a monstrous golden brick of apfelküchen, dripping with vanilla sauce.

"Oh no, please," Baragon said. "I'm, uh, pretty much stuffed. All those sausages." He tried to force a smile and patted his belly for emphasis. Emily accepted hers more graciously.

"But it comes with the meal," the waitress said.

"That's okay, really. I think I'll have to pass."

A look of fear flashed across the waitress's eyes as she turned and slowly carried his apfelküchen back toward the kitchen, as if she were marching in a funeral procession.

Moments later, however, the dessert reappeared, this time in the hands of a small, bespectacled, unsmiling bird-faced woman.

"Ziss is *yours*," she said, thrusting it toward him. "Apfel-küchen. Comes viss ze meal."

"No, thank you," he said again. "I'm sure it's quite wonderful, really—but I'm very full." He went for the belly pat again.

"It comes viss ze meal," she repeated. "It is yours."

"It's okay, really—I mean, we'll pay for it—I just don't *want* it—"

"Vant me to wrap it up for you?" she pressed. "Take it home. Enjoy it later."

"No, thanks anyway—"

"*Apfelküchen!*" she barked, and both Emily and Baragon recoiled.

"Maybe you should just get it wrapped up," Emily whispered.

"I don't *want* it wrapped up. The only thing I want is another beer, not any fucking apfelküchen."

"Vat?"

"Nothing."

The small woman thrust the cake toward him again.

Baragon folded his arms and pressed his lips together to prove to her that nothing else was going to get past them that night, and looked away. Eventually, she left, taking the apfelküchen with her.

"Christ," Baragon muttered when she was gone, not sure whether he should laugh.

"You hurt her feelings," Emily said, working on hers. "You should've just taken it. We could've dumped it somewhere."

"By that point it was a matter of principle."

Emily sighed. "Rosk—you're the only man I've ever known who had a sense of principle when it comes to German pastries."

Their original waitress reappeared with a check and an apologetic look.

"I'm very sorry," she said. "I told her you didn't want it, but she insisted. She said, 'I bet I can make them eat it.'"

"That's okay," Baragon said. "She didn't."

"She's the dessert chef here, and I'm afraid you insulted her. Deeply."

"Oh, Jesus." He looked at Emily. "I thought this sort of shit only happened when I was at work."

She gave him a sympathetic look. They paid the bill, then went looking for a bar where they wouldn't have to worry about offending anyone's pride.

On Sunday, he stayed at home, poised nervously in front of the television, watching movie after movie. Emily called in the afternoon to see how he was doing. He was sniffling when he picked up the receiver, his voice rougher than usual.

"My God, what's wrong?" she asked. "Are you crying?"

"Not anymore."

"What's going on?" She was afraid it had something to do with the previous night's dessert. He could sometimes carry scenes like that around with him for days, even months.

"Nothing, really," he confessed sheepishly. "I'm just watching the wrong movies."

Then she understood. "You're watching *Night of the Hunter* again, aren't you?"

There was a long silence before he quietly said, "Maybe." For some people, it was *The Wizard of Oz* or *Casablanca* or *Old Yeller.* For Baragon, it had always been *Night of the Hunter.* Tore him up every goddamn time. Even he couldn't explain why.

"Why do you keep watching that if it makes you cry every time?"

"Oh," he said, clearing his throat, "does 'because I am a

stupid ass' count? Besides, it was the second thing on the pile, and I wasn't in much of a mood for *Kiss Me Deadly*."

Baragon had an e-mail message waiting for him first thing on Monday, March 26. He didn't receive many e-mail messages, if only because he didn't like giving the address out, and was not very good when it came to replying. Every once in a while, though, one would slip through.

> *Roscoe!*
> *What the hell is going on in Hawaii these days? Civilians driving nuclear submarines into Japanese fishing boats, navy helicopters crashing into each other, and now, apparently the whales are getting into it!*
>
> *I heard this morning, that off the coast of Hawaii an enraged humpback whale jumped on the back of a whale-watching boat (à la ORCA), where it broke some woman's knee. Roscoe—is this the beginning of the end? I think that a Pacific-based Lemurian subnautical super-civilization is causing all sorts of mayhem in order to begin their world takeover, ABOVE the water.*
> *Best,*
> *Wade*

Ah, Wade. Dr. Wade Huber. Anyone else reading the message would've assumed he was just another one of Baragon's paranoids, but Baragon himself knew better. Huber was a physicist—a real one—he'd met some eight years ago while doing a piece on fake physicists and their wacky ideas concerning "alternative energy sources." Dr. Huber, who was a tenured professor of theoretical physics at Columbia, was an extremely intelligent and unerringly rational man, not prone to hysterics or wild, unfounded speculations. He was also as big a movie geek as Baragon, and to this day they tried to get together every few months to exchange shopping bags full of videotapes.

He'd have to give him a call one of these days and ask him a few questions about radiation, Baragon thought as he deleted the message. He made a point of deleting every message as soon as he'd read it and deleting every reply as soon as he'd sent it. It seemed safer that way. He didn't care to leave these things lying around.

Baragon lit a cigarette and did a quick check on the wires. Sure enough, there it was—though he had no reason to doubt Huber. Just as he said it had happened. Whale-watching boat about twenty miles off Kaneohe Bay, on the eastern coast of Oahu. "Confused or enraged" humpback—albeit a small one—leaps on the back of the boat and breaks some insipid tourist's knee.

Yeah, those people should've seen Orca *before they went out there*, he thought. Then he stopped. *Wait a second*—he scrolled up to the top of the story again.

Kaneohe Bay. Why did that strike him? Off the coast of Kaneohe Bay, eastern coast of Oahu.

Huh.

Probably something stupid. Probably saw it in a movie once.

Baragon opened the quickly expanding SVA file on his computer, turned away from the screen, snatched up the printout Dunham's secretary had given him on Friday, and started to read through it. It was mostly addresses, but if a property had a specific name, that was on there, too. That was a relief. Made his job easier.

First thing he needed to do was cross-check Natacia and Hans Heg's hotels, just to make sure they were listed.

Yup—Greenwood and Riverview. He put a checkmark next to each name.

I have no idea where I'm going with this. . . . Hey—what was the name of the hotel Martin was staying at? Did he even know? Christ, where was that police file? He fumbled around through the growing pile of papers on his desk and found it. Scanning it, he found nothing. No name at least—but he did have an address, over on Third.

He began working his way down the address list for all the places—

Earthquake.

Was that it?

He closed the file and went back to the news wires. There had been an earthquake in Hawaii not too long ago. That day there were all those quakes. He'd talked to—no—that was it—Stevenson. That Stevenson story he'd done.

He tracked down his original file and opened it. Two-thirds of the way through, he quoted Stevenson as saying, "The recent quakes centered in Barrow and just off Kaneohe Bay . . ."

Well then, that's settled, and he could relax. Brains are funny creatures that way. Always sneaking up on you, like when he'd try to identify a smell. He returned to the SVA list, somehow knowing full well now that he'd find the address of Raymond Martin's final residence on there.

And he did. Even found that it had a name. Homestead. The Homestead Hotel. Very nice.

Wait a second—

He remembered Wade's note. He knew he was stalling at this point, but this was important, too. One more time, he went back to the news wires. That sunken Japanese fishing boat was all over the place. The *Gaira*, it was called, was accidentally split in two by the American nuclear sub USS

Aaron Burr—which, at the time, was being piloted by a group of vacationing golfers who had paid twelve hundred dollars each for a chance to take turns commanding a nuclear sub. It all was part of the vacation package.

The incident had occurred approximately some twenty miles off the coast of . . . *Kaneohe Bay.*

Now that's fucking weird, Baragon thought. He created a new file and began typing as fast as he could. What was a Japanese fishing boat doing off the coast of Oahu, anyway? Hadn't that sort of thing caused enough trouble already?

This was the last thing he needed right now, on top of everything else. But there it was, splayed out in front of him like a gift—he couldn't simply ignore it, could he? It wasn't like it was apfelküchen this time.

Once he got all the facts down, he stopped and took inventory. Okay, he'd found the link between Natacia and Raymond Martin, through the vehicle of SVA. Hans Heg's in there someplace, but he seemed to be worried only about his linen situation and his new bidet.

Aww, shit—and Natacia had all those people coming in to fix that hole in her sink. And Martin was running around . . .

Okay. Okay. That's just crazy. That's just stupid. Think about what Dunham said. They owned all the buildings, yes, and were in the process of renovating them. That makes sense. Perfect sense.

Just like there were renovations at the morgue.

Goddammit, no—

He picked up the SVA list and began reading his way through it again, carefully this time, line by line. He didn't want to jump to any ridiculous conclusions before he knew for sure. But Dunham had told him they owned two hundred properties. Still, they couldn't—

Halfway down page two, he found it: "520 First Ave.—

NYCMEO." Then, as if to prevent any potential misinterpretations, in parentheses next to that it read, "CITY MORGUE!"

Baragon didn't really think the exclamation point was necessary.

He snatched up the phone, dialed the lab, and was relieved when Emily answered.

"Hey, Em?" he said, trying to keep his voice under control. "I don't mean to be alarmist or pushy here—but I think you should quit your job. Right now."

She began laughing. "There are times when I'm tempted."

"No—I mean it—*right now*. You know those slumlord weirdoes I was telling you about? The toga people?"

"How could I forget?"

"*They own that building*. Yours. They're the ones who put the radiation detectors in there."

"Yeah, Roscoe, I know."

He stopped short. "Pardon?"

"I just found out myself, this morning. I was going to tell you tonight. I ran into von Hohenheim and asked him."

"So . . . you *know*? Then why the hell are you still there? Why didn't you run screaming?"

"Roscoe, what the hell are you talking about?"

"They *own* the building, understand? How the hell can that be?" The pitch of his voice was rising.

"But . . . I told you all about it when the city sold the building," she said. "That was a long time ago."

"Yeah, but you never told me that *they* were the ones who bought it."

Emily sighed. He knew damn well that she couldn't get into any of this while she was at work. "I didn't *know* they were the ones who bought it," she whispered firmly. "All I knew was that it was some corporation, and that they were footing the bill for all these renovations. That's all I knew."

Baragon was confused, and furious, and terrified. How could she not have known this? How could this be happening at all?

"I just don't understand," he said, "how the city could sell a city-owned building to a goddamned private corporation. *Especially* the ME's office. Jesus, it makes no sense."

"Roscoe, please. I can't answer that because I don't know the answer. It's a business deal, I guess—and one that doesn't affect me at all. The city didn't sell the morgue itself—just the building."

"So why in the fuck couldn't they have at least sold it to Disney, like everything else? I'd be much happier if you were working in the *Disney* morgue instead of—"

"Rosk, please—" she pleaded. "I'm sorry it turned out to be that very company—but . . . but it's just a coincidence. That's all it is."

"Coincidence?" his voice was different now, almost bitter. "I don't think so. I'm saying there's something weird going on and you're in the middle of it—you could be in tremendous danger—!"

"Oh, Christ, calm down. Please? For me?" This wasn't the time for this. "Take a breath and think a second—you're just talking crazy." She adopted a soothing voice, like one you would use on a hyperventilating child. "Now listen to me. First of all—if I were to leave here, where would I go? Take a job at one of those *other* morgues in town? This isn't a chain operation."

"You'd find something," Baragon said, on the verge of stammering. "Y-you could start your own. I'll help. Put up flyers and stuff."

"Okay, fine, we'll talk about that one later. Second—those

people, no matter how weird they may dress, have no bearing on me, my job, or the workings of the morgue. Not at all, okay? They bought the building, that's all. The city is leasing it from them. It's all part of the deal."

"Yeah, but—the radiation detectors—"

"—were one of a dozen things they improved here. Including my new lab. No, I can't tell you exactly why they're there, but have you thought about one thing? One very important thing?" She'd had about enough of this foolishness. Before she spoke again, she looked around quickly to make sure no one had walked into the lab. "If those detectors hadn't been there, this guy still would've come through. Almost everybody does, eventually. It was because they were there that we knew he was radioactive in the first place." The pitch of her voice was rising. "*Without* those things, you'd have no story. So you should be thanking the gods yourself that the new owners made those renovations."

Baragon was silent but breathing hard. He didn't quite follow the logic of that.

"Look," he said after a moment, "I'm sorry to have bothered you at work. It was my mistake. I got overexcited again."

"It's okay," Emily told him, relieved to hear him say it. "You've been under a lot of strain recently. You haven't been sleeping. I understand that, but Rosk—I really can't be talking about these things while I'm here. I'm alone right now, but . . . you understand, don't you?"

"Yeah," he said quietly.

"Hey, buck up—" she offered, not wanting to leave things on a sour note. "I certainly don't mean to suck all the air out of your balloon—but everything really is okay. Can I make it up to you by buying you a couple tonight?"

He nodded but said nothing, which is pointless when you're on the phone.

"I'll take that as a yes," she said. "I'll see you around six."

"Great," he said. "See you then." He hung up the phone and sat there a moment, slumped back in his chair.

"Thank the gods"?

Chapter Ten

That night, he told himself he wouldn't say a word about SVA, or togas, or radioactive men, or the morgue. Of course, he'd made that promise to himself before. Nor would he complain about his situation at the paper—even though he found it curious that Montgomery hadn't yet called him in to scream at him for not turning in a single scrap of copy in nearly a week. Or had it been more than a week? Either way, it was odd—Baragon could usually be counted on to turn something in to Montgomery—no matter how questionable—nearly every day.

Originally, Baragon was convinced that this was the story that was going to put him right back on top again. The Big One. Pulitzer material. Like so many other potential Pulitzers he'd worked on in the past, however, he could sense that this was turning to dust in his hands, just waiting for someone to come along to blow it all away. Hell, it had probably been dust when he picked it up in the first place. Interestingly configured dust, to be sure, but nothing more than dust when you got down to it.

Montgomery, it was his guess, was leaning back in his

chair, feet up on the desk, fingers interlocked behind his head, waiting for Baragon to either screw himself big time or simply stop coming into the office altogether one day. Either way, Baragon figured, would be just fine with Ed.

She was right, he thought after eating a sandwich around one. As much as he hated to admit it, maybe that freak in the toga was right, too.

He'd been taking the claims of a couple schizophrenics at face value. He should know better than to do that. In fact, if anyone knew as much, he should. So why in the hell start listening to them now?

SVA bought and renovated buildings. That was their business. That's how they made a living. There was a logical explanation for all this shit, at least as far as Natacia and Col. Heg were concerned. And so what if SVA owned the ME's building? He hadn't noticed any change in Emily over the past year. Nothing at all. The explanations she and Dunham had given him were completely logical. Occam strikes again.

Still, though . . . still . . . taking care of those things doesn't get any closer to understanding the radioactive man. Even Em's admitted that. And there was a connection—a clear connection—between Martin and everything else.

He reached for a cigarette.

Maybe I should see if Ed'll send me to Hawaii.

"So I ran into something interesting today," he said after they were both settled in at Jack's.

"Really." Emily's back muscles tensed, expecting the worst. "And what's that?"

"Well, I'll tell you first off that it has nothing to do with togas or radiation."

"Here's to that," she said, raising her glass.

"You heard of this Japanese fishing boat disaster."

"Sure. How many people died in that?"

"Last I heard, it was something like twenty-three," he shot out quickly, trying to get it out of the way, "but I could be wrong. I think they're still looking for some."

"That's terrible."

"Yeah, well, anyway—you also remember that string of earthquakes they had over the past couple of weeks."

Oh, god, here we go, she thought. "Vaguely. You talked to that guy in Alaska."

"Right—Stevenson. Turns out that one of those earthquakes was in Hawaii."

"Uh-huh."

"*And*, I just heard this morning that a humpback whale jumped onto one of those whale-watching boats."

"You're kidding—anyone hurt there?"

Baragon shrugged. "Broke one silly woman's leg, but that was about it. Nobody was killed or anything. It was a small whale."

"Okay, and that was where?" She figured she knew the answer already but decided to humor him.

"That's the kicker—all of those things, it turns out—I looked it up—took place in almost *exactly* the same spot—just off the coast of Kaneohe Bay. That's Oahu."

"I know," she told him. "That's really odd."

"Isn't it, though? Wade—you remember him—Wade Huber? The physicist up at Columbia? Well, he seems to think it's the work of Lemurians."

She raised an eyebrow and shrugged, then reached for her beer.

"It's akin to the Atlantis myth—y'know, a once great and advanced civilization sinks under the sea after a volcano or an earthquake. There's a chance, being as advanced as they were, that they survived and learned how to deal and created for themselves some sort of magical undersea kingdom. The New Agey types are all over it with their crystals and whatnot. They even have maps of the place for sale. And, apparently, now—at least Wade thinks—these peace-loving Lemurians are seeking revenge for something, which accounts for all these weird occurrences."

"I suppose that's one explanation," she said, with no little irony in her voice. "Or maybe the whale was getting his revenge for all the Japanese whale hunting—which might also help explain the fishing boat incident."

He frowned deeply and raised his eyebrows. "I hadn't thought of that."

"You see? I think it's something to consider. It's just as plausible as Wade's theory, I think."

He reached back into his coat pocket and grabbed his notepad—which he had remembered to bring with him tonight—and into his breast pocket for a pen. *Why do I encourage him this way?* she thought as he jotted down "whale hunting" before replacing the notepad.

"Roscoe, I was just joking," she said.

"Maybe so, but that's still a very good point," he told her, the gears grinding. "Because remember—I think I told you this—that Dr. Stevenson had said that all the whales were gone from up in Alaska? That it was the big Eskimo whale-hunting season, but that after the earthquake, for some reason, there were no whales?"

"Yeah, I remember. That is odd. So . . . maybe all the whales went south, is what you're saying?"

"To a point where there had just been another earthquake? Does that make sense? Why *there?*"

"Oh, Rosk, damned if I know." Then she thought a moment. "Where was he again? Stevenson?"

"Oh, yeah—that's another thing. He was up in Barrow—

which is the northernmost point in Alaska." Baragon was always reasonably proud of himself when he could recite obscure facts like that. "And that's where that guy—remember that guy who'd been kidnapped by Alaska?—that's where he was calling from."

"Hmmm," she said.

"What?"

"I may be wrong about this"—she paused and took a drink, wondering why she was about to tell him what she was about to tell him—"but if I'm not mistaken, I think those two are located along the same longitude."

"What, Alaska and Hawaii?"

"No—Barrow and Kaneohe Bay."

He squinted at her. "You're kidding." He wondered how long his heart would hold up if shit like this kept happening.

"I dunno. I could be wrong. I probably am. You'll have to check it out yourself."

"You probably *aren't* wrong, though. You never are when it comes to stuff like this. Christ—how do you *know* that?" He was already reaching for his notepad again.

She shrugged. "I just do, I guess. Picked it up somewhere along the way, some geography class, and it stuck. I was always pretty good in geography. Besides, I might as well ask you how it is you can name every movie and television show Wally Cox has ever appeared in."

"Guess you have a point," he said, flipping the notebook open. "But why can I remember crap like that when I can't remember anything that matters unless I write it down? Not that, y'know, Wally Cox doesn't matter—but you understand what I'm saying." He continued to scribble a few quick notes, praying he'd be able to decipher them the next morning.

"The brain can be cruel," she offered.

Chapter Eleven

First thing Tuesday morning, Baragon scoured the *Sentinel*'s rarely used research library for an atlas. There were plenty of outdated travel guides and outdated restaurant guides and movie guides and record guides, style manuals, dictionaries of foreign tongues—but where the hell was the goddamn atlas?

He eventually found one buried beneath a stack of glossy fashion magazines. He dumped the magazines to the floor (*lousy kids*) and carried the atlas back to his desk, where he cracked it open and began flipping through the wide, smooth pages, looking for Alaska and Hawaii. Even as outdated as it was—many of the African and Eastern European nations, he noted, hadn't been called what this atlas called them in at least a decade—it would still do the trick. The coordinates hadn't been shifted, so far as he was aware.

"I'll be damned," he said quietly to himself five minutes later, using a ruler he'd had in his desk to check and counter-check the numbers he discovered. "Isn't that odd."

He went to the file in which he had jotted the notes about

the Japanese fishing boat and the whale and typed in "K. Bay, Barrow—157 deg. W. Long."

He marked the pages, closed the atlas, and left it on his desk. He might be needing it again.

He was about to add some notes regarding everything else he knew about recent events in Hawaii and Alaska— including Emily's whale-hunting theory—when he noticed Montgomery standing next to him. When seen together, Baragon and Montgomery could actually be a rather frightening pair—like a couple of aging, balding, drunken, and graceless American sumo wrestlers.

"I must say, Baragon," he said, the unmistakably snide vocal pattern of the Old Ed firmly in place again, "it's such a pleasure to see you around the office now and then. You're like a ray of fuckin' sunshine in this place."

Baragon replaced the ruler in his desk drawer. "Been busy, Ed. Working on things. Research. Foot leather. You know—all those outmoded concepts. Why, they may be outmoded to members of *today's* youth, but to *my* gener—"

"Roscoe, please, I don't need it this morning. Just kindly tell me where you've been and what you've been doing."

Baragon sighed and spun his chair to face Montgomery. "I'll be straight with you, Ed. I spent a good deal of time— too much time, admittedly—trying to track down something that wasn't there."

"Another ghost story, maybe? Because you know there's nothing I look forward to more than another patented Roscoe Baragon exclusive about the ghosts of—"

Now it was Baragon's turn to cut Ed off. "Ed—" he said, raising a hand. "Enough. I thought there was a story. There apparently wasn't. I wasted a lot of time on it. And now I'm on something new. You'll have it in the next couple days. And you can thank me for not trying to turn nothing into something and then foisting it off on you."

Montgomery came close to smiling. "You know, Roscoe, you actually have a point there. And I do thank you."

"You're very welcome."

"Now," Montgomery asked, his scowl returning to normal, "did you want to give me a hint as to what to expect, and when to expect it? This isn't a monthly, remember? We're daily. I need to know these things. Or are you planning on surprising me, as usual?"

Baragon pondered the choice, did some calculating, and smacked his lips. "I . . . think I'll surprise you this time, if it's all the same with you."

Montgomery shook his head and let out an annoyed breath but left the room, which was the desired response Baragon was after. He'd ask him about those tickets to Hawaii later.

Then he set to the business of trying to track down Dr. Carl Stevenson once again. Not sure whether the geologist was back from Alaska yet, he began with the Washington number. If the same secretary answered the phone, he decided it would be wise to use a different voice—or at least a different story. She'd probably be on to him by now. Maybe he'd do his Walter Brennan—or better yet, his Doodles Weaver. That'd keep her off balance.

Half an hour later, he'd been patched through to a radio—it was unclear to Baragon exactly how such a thing had been accomplished—at Dr. Stevenson's current base of operations, a campsite near La Higuera, on the coast of Chile, site of one of the most recent quakes.

"Gotta say, there, Doctor," Baragon shouted into the phone in order to be heard over the static, "you sure do get around."

"You can't study these things sitting behind a desk," Stevenson shouted back. "Now please, Mr. Baragon—I don't have much time—we're very busy around here. This place is a mess."

"I realize that, Doctor—and I'm sorry to bother you with this—but something was pointed out to me last night, I thought I'd see what you thought."

"Please make it quick."

"Okay, sir—let me ask you—by chance—" Baragon's throat was getting sore. He wasn't used to this much yelling. He glanced at the office door. *Shoulda closed that first.* "Is there a fault line, a plate juncture, anything—that happens to follow the line of one hundred fifty-seven degrees west longitude?"

The phone crackled as Stevenson pictured it. "No—there isn't. Wouldn't expect one to be, anyway. I mean, your whole Pacific rim is a hot spot—Ring of Fire, we call it . . . but it doesn't work that way . . . following man-made lines. . . . Why do you ask?"

Baragon wished he'd at least gotten himself a glass of water or something first. "I ask, Doctor, because—as you know—two of the simultaneous quakes were—well, one was centered in Barrow, Alaska—and the other was just off Kaneohe Bay, on Oahu."

"That's right."

"Well, sir—those two places happen to lie along the same line of longitude—one-fifty-seven west."

Baragon wasn't sure, but he thought he could hear Stevenson crossing his eyes and sticking his tongue out. "Yes, that's right—" Stevenson shouted back. "But there was also a quake down here in Chile at the same time. And Chile, you'll see, is quite a ways off that longitudinal."

Damn, Baragon thought.

"It certainly is peculiar—" Stevenson continued. "I'll give you that—but believe me—it's just a coincidence. An odd coincidence. Nothing more than that."

"Gotcha!" Baragon shouted into the phone. "I'm sorry to have bothered you again, sir—thanks for your time—and good luck down there."

Stevenson's voice began to break up as he shouted his good-byes. Then the line went dead. Baragon hung up the phone, chastising himself for not asking Stevenson about any unusual whale activity off the coast of South America.

I guess I can ignore Chile, he thought.

For much of the rest of the day, Baragon churned out a short feature, a follow-up to his initial earthquake piece. Something Montgomery couldn't much complain about. By this time, most of the other dailies had dropped the earthquake stories in order to concentrate on the *Gaira* incident—the hopeless search for survivors, the arguments over who was culpable. Doing a quick earthquake follow-up was, Baragon thought, a very responsible bit of journalism on his part.

He had no real new facts to add—he simply juggled around everything that had been in the first story to make it look new. He also—in a way he hoped Montgomery wouldn't notice or pay any attention to—buried a few hints that there was something perhaps a little too weird about that "oddly coincidental" simultaneous chain of earthquakes that had rattled the Pacific—specifically along one-fifty-seven-west longitude.

He turned the story in at three-thirty and made a move to return the atlas to its place beneath the fashion magazines in the research library. He paused, considered it, and slid the oversized book beneath his coat instead. Tonight, maybe, he'd do some more research.

For the rest of the afternoon, he turned his attention back to his collection of SVA notes—specifically that Raymond Martin seemed, before his untimely demise, to have been working for SVA on a freelance basis. At least if what Sammy and the crew out in front of the Homestead had told him was true. Maybe he'd need to ask Dunham a question or two about that.

He knew he shouldn't be doing this. That there was nothing there and he should simply let it be. It all added up to nothing—that's what everyone had told him in the most reasonable of terms—but he couldn't help himself. It still nagged at him. Perhaps he could get a little something out of this anyway—who knows? So all that work (and all those stairs he'd been forced to climb) wouldn't go completely to waste. Something mild and inoffensive—"Tenants Battle SRO Landlord." *Yeah*, thought Baragon, *then disappear, or turn up dead and radioactive.*

Maybe he wouldn't bring up that part of it. Not yet, anyway.

As he was getting himself together to head for the bar, Baragon's phone rang.

No, no, no, he thought, *you aren't getting me this time, you crazy son of a bitch—whoever you are.*

The phone kept ringing, and Baragon felt himself weaken. It might be Emily with a change of plans. He picked it up in the middle of the fourth ring.

"Baragon," he announced, hoping his voice would make it evident to whoever was on the other end that he was in no mood for some psychotic chit-chat.

"Hey," Eel said, "I just thought of something."

"What's that?"

"I just realized how to ruin every single movie we've ever loved. Every one that's ever meant something to us."

"That's great news," Baragon said, his voice flat. "And now you're going to ruin everything for me, too, aren't you?"

"No, hear me out."

Baragon sighed. "Okay, tell me—how can we ruin every single movie we've ever loved?"

"By asking yourself, in the middle of the movie, 'Why didn't they just use their cell phone?'"

One thing Baragon had to give Eel—he had the magic touch. "Yeah, gotta say—that'll do it."

"So what's up with you?" O'Neill asked.

Oh, where to begin? "I guess it's been a while since we've talked, hasn't it?"

"Not all that long. Last I heard, you were concerned about an invasion of Eskimos—though I saw the earthquake story you did last week. . . . Correct me if I'm wrong, Bear, but that was kind of a throwaway, wasn't it?"

"Yeah, I guess—but that seems to be what they want around here these days. How's *Zombie Hootenanny* coming along?"

"We're editing now. Should be done in the next week and a half or so." Baragon didn't know if Eel was ignoring the joke or if he actually had moved on to some new project called *Zombie Hootenanny*.

"How'd Brando work out?"

O'Neill gave a disgusted snort. "Don't get me started with that," he said. "I had to rewrite the entire script after the first day's shooting to make sure he wasn't required to speak any lines."

"That bad, huh?"

"Yeah, well—I think it turned out just fine, regardless. So what are you working on?"

Baragon glanced at his watch and wondered if he should get into it now. Realizing that O'Neill might well be the one man who could possibly understand—or at least not make fun of him too much—he decided to give him the nutshell.

"Well," he said after taking a deep breath, "here's a hypo- thetical. Say a body shows up at the morgue, right?"

Over the next fifteen minutes, he laid it out, trying to

keep his voice low so no eavesdropping youngsters would go blabbing to Montgomery. Through it all, O'Neill was silent.

"So?" Baragon asked when he was finished. "Any ideas?"

"To be honest, chief," Eel told him, sounding vaguely disappointed, "I liked your Alaska story better."

"But you made fun of the Alaska story."

"Doesn't mean it wasn't a good one—look—the Alaska story was a funny, wacky story you got from a paranoid schizophrenic. It was action packed. This here is something I'm hearing from a good friend of mine who seems to be taking it all a little too seriously. In fact, it sounds a bit too much like one of my movies—and not one of the better ones, you hear what I'm saying? More like something I was doing back when various substances were cheaper and more readily available."

"Yeah, but—this here—it's all *real*. This isn't crazy people telling me this. These are real things I'm discovering myself."

"—And that Alaska story, I'm sure, was just as real to the paranoid schizophrenic who called you. I dunno, Roscoe—sometimes I have to wonder if you haven't spent too much time around those people."

Baragon didn't say anything.

"Or maybe—dare I say it? You've seen too many Douglas Cheek movies. Or just that *one*."

Baragon remained silent. It was becoming clear to him that he was alone in this.

O'Neill noticed the silence. "Look, Roscoe, I don't mean to bring you down," he said. "It's just that you're my friend, and you seem to be a tad too earnest about this radiation man deal. . . . Unless you're just angling to write the script for my next film."

"Maybe I am, Eel." Baragon sighed ruefully. "I'll see how this turns out. I may have to be looking for other work in the near future anyway."

O'Neill chuckled, but Baragon didn't. "Look, Eel—I gotta get to the bar. I'm late. But good luck with the edit—be sure and send me a copy when you're done."

"I always do, don't I?"

Baragon got back to his apartment about ten, more sober than he generally preferred being. He dropped the atlas on the table, hung up his coat, and reached for the Wild Turkey bottle on top of the refrigerator. At the bar that night, he hadn't said a word about radiation, or corpses, or SROs, or Alaska—except to let Emily know that she had been absolutely right about the longitude. He was even able to show her in the old atlas he was carrying with him.

Instead of making a sandwich and popping in a videotape, he carried the bottle and a small glass over to his desk.

He picked up the cassette tape that was sitting there and slid it into the small, dying stereo. He didn't know why he still had a stereo, given that he never listened to music, except for what he heard on film soundtracks. Tonight, though, he was glad he hadn't yet gotten around to dumping it on the curb.

He hit the play button and heard Abraham Campbell's unmistakable voice discussing his failure to get a job as a psychiatrist for the state of New York, even though he was fully qualified.

Baragon hit stop, then rewind, then he waited, taking a long sip of his whiskey. When the tape clicked loudly, then stopped, he hit the play button once more, then listened to the leader hissing through the speakers.

Hedora strolled sleepily into the room and stretched.

Suddenly he heard his own voice: "*—we're on the same page here. Why do you think she—your wife, that is—wrote, uh, to me?*"

Baragon sat back in his chair and listened to the rest of what the man in Alaska—Nick Carter—had to say, ears primed for any other clues.

Maybe it was all just a prank, Baragon thought. *Something Eel put one of his buddies up to, to see how far I'd take it. Wouldn't put it past him. That's why he blew off the Alaska story when I first told him and was so interested today. Maybe that's why he was taking notes.*

On the recording, Carter yelped, and that other, incomprehensible voice took over. It wasn't Carter. Wasn't Eel, either. Eel was great with voices and dialects—but Baragon had never heard him do anything like this.

He stopped the tape, rewound for a few seconds, then hit play again.

"—*Yeah—way north. Look—you gotta get me outta here—They're—*"

Then the yelp, then that other voice.

He rewound again.

I wouldn't put it past him. Or anyone. But the fear in Carter's voice sounded too authentic to be a joke. His scream was real, too. There was no giggling afterward. If this were one of Eel's pranks, he'd at least give him a giggle at the end to tip him off.

Baragon focused on the second voice. What the hell was it? Inuit? Some Asian dialect? It sure wasn't anything Western.

He rewound the tape again.

He wished he was more adept with languages. Maybe it was something Middle Eastern. Farsi, maybe, or Urdu. He had no idea. He'd studied German and Latin in school. Knew a couple phrases in Russian and Polish. Even tried to study Mandarin Chinese on his own once, in his early teens, but gave it up as hopeless, coming away having learned only one phrase: "We have not had cauliflower in some time.

Surely there is some to be had." Nowadays, he couldn't even remember how the Chinese went—only the English translation.

He rewound the tape one more time.

No, it was definitely Asian, he thought. But it was garbled. To make it worse, the phone connection wasn't all that great—and there were all those voices behind him.

He rewound the tape again.

Then again.

"Hey, Biddle?"

It was shortly after ten o'clock the next morning, and the room had been mostly silent until Baragon spoke. His eyes were red and he hadn't shaved. His morning coffee had been a pale imitation of the real thing and hadn't done him the slightest bit of good.

"Yes?" Biddle asked, spinning his chair around. He was outwardly chipper and eager to please, but quietly suspicious. Baragon generally never spoke to him unless it was to say something nasty.

"Yeah," Baragaon said, staring at his computer screen as he talked. "Let me ask you—how are you with languages?"

Biddle sat up a little straighter. He'd take what he could get from the old man. "Okay, I guess—I mean, I studied quiet a few in school, plus some linguistics. I guess I thought it might be able to help me out in this business."

"Yeah, whatever," Baragon said. "With luck you might be able to help me out here right now."

"How's that?"

Baragon stopped staring at the screen and deigned to turn his chair slightly toward the young man in the insufferable bow tie who sat across the way. "You remember that Campbell tape?"

"Sure."

"You listen to the whole thing?"

Biddle's face fell slightly. He was sure Baragon was going to yell at him for something. Dammit, though, he'd done a good job—he didn't have to take— "Sure. Why?"

"I mean, did you listen to the *whole* tape? Did you hear the few minutes before the Campbell interview started? The part with the stuff about Alaska?"

Worry spread across Biddle's features. He wasn't sure how he was supposed to answer this. Was there something on that tape he wasn't supposed to hear? Or was this a test of some sort, to see how thorough he'd been? He was innocent—it wasn't his fault. "I . . . guess I rewound the tape to the beginning when I first put it in, so yes. At first, you know, I wasn't sure what Campbell sounded like, so yeah, I guess. Should I—?"

"It's no big deal," said Baragon. "I'm glad you heard it. So enough with the stammering—you can relax now."

Biddle did.

"Now, the question is"—man, but he was tired—"right before the Campbell interview starts, what you're hearing is part of a phone call I received from some poor lunatic who said he'd been kidnapped."

"Uh-huh?"

"—And at the very end of it, you hear him yell and another voice come on the line."

"Yeah, I remember—"

"Could you understand what that other voice was saying?"

Biddle smiled, then caught himself. "Okay, I have to confess—" he was happy and lighthearted again, like some slumber party jackass playing Truth or Dare, "—I listened to that a couple of times, because I . . . thought I *did* understand it. At least part of it. It sounded like Japanese."

"Really. What do you mean, '*like* Japanese'?"

"Well, it was *bad* Japanese somehow. It wasn't really like . . . y'know . . . totally grammatical."

"Uh-huh? Like, perhaps, somebody pretending to be Japanese?"

"Maybe something like that, I don't know. Or maybe it was just some weird dialect I'm not familiar with."

"So you know Japanese?" Baragon woke up a little bit.

Biddle nodded, a touch too proud of himself for Baragon's taste.

"So what was he saying?"

"See, that's the thing—I thought it must have been a joke."

"*Biddle!*" Baragon shouted. "What the *fuck* was he saying?"

Biddle's eyes widened, and he began to stammer. "I . . . I . . . don't—"

Baragon hit his small tape recorder's play button, pointed the speaker toward Biddle, and turned the volume up. They both heard the voice, distorted through the tiny speaker.

"*Kakawarazu koitsu ooserareru! . . . kono aru kaimu! . . . jideiku nitaisuru gojira!*"

"Now," Baragon said, snapping the machine off. "*What . . . did . . . he . . . say?*"

"Like I said," Biddle began, clearly uncomfortable again but no longer stammering. "It doesn't make much sense. It's just . . . words strung together. Like someone opened a Japanese dictionary and made an English sentence out of them without worrying about, like, grammar or anything. Just plugged the words in."

Baragon closed his eyes so he wouldn't catch sight of anything he might throw. "But what . . . *does it* . . . *say?*"

"Well," Biddle finally said, ". . . essentially, what he says—or the best I can figure it, at least—is something like—though I may be wrong here—but it sounds like, 'No matter what he says, this has nothing to do with . . . '" Biddle paused. "Something. There's one word in there, and I don't really know it—it sounds something like . . ." he shrugged, "*gojira*?" Something like that. I suppose I could try to look it up."

Baragon opened his eyes and stared at Biddle.

"*Gojira*," he whispered.

"Something like that."

Baragon rewound the tape and listened one more time. Sure enough, the last word the voice uttered was "*gojira*." Why in the hell hadn't he caught at least that much earlier? If nothing else, Christ, why not *that*?

"Thank you," Baragon said, thinking loudly, *You fucking kids know* nothing! "You won't have to bother looking anything up."

"No problem!" Biddle replied. "Glad to be of service. Do . . . you know if it means anything?"

Baragon shrugged and turned back to his computer screen.

No matter what he says, this has nothing to do with Godzilla.

Baragon put his face in his hands and smiled coldly to himself.

Well, at least that takes care of that part of the story. It had to've been an Eel O'Neill prank. He didn't think Wade Huber would ever do anything like that to him. Send him off in search of nothing that way. Hoke wouldn't do that, either. Besides—when he called him, Hoke had clearly been surprised—plus, he would've been too busy with BioLab to set up something like this.

No, it had to've been Eel. Nothing to do with Godzilla, my ass. He was just waiting for me to come back to him after I figured out the translation, all hopped up. Well, I'm not about to give him the satisfaction.

That earthquake thing is still a little strange, though. But like Stevenson told him—nothing more than a coincidence. Up until now, Baragon had been a firm believer in the occasional odd coincidence.

For a moment he felt like crying, but by God, he was too tired, even for that. All that wasted time.

Maybe he should try to get back to some real work. Let everything slip back to normal. Maybe make a few phone calls, see if anyone else had vanished from any other SVA hotels. Or any of their fancy buildings, for that matter. Or the morgue.

Better still, maybe he should call the fire commissioner instead and ask him why a couple of his men were so rude to Babs Abkemeier last year.

The phone calls he'd made over the course of that afternoon had provided nothing, and Baragon, had he been in a more lucid frame of mind, shouldn't have expected them to. What, a building manager is going to tell him, "Why, yes—any number of our residents have vanished mysteriously over the past several months, come to think of it"?

No, that wouldn't work. He had two options open to him now. Slam out a little something using the three people he had right now—along, maybe, with those guys outside the Homestead again—or get back out there and go to these places himself, try to nab residents on their way out.

Tired as he was, he was leaning toward the former. In fact, come two-thirty, he called Emily and told her he was too bedraggled and thought it might be best if he went straight home tonight and tried to get some sleep.

"You sure everything's okay?" she asked. "This has been happening more often lately."

He thought about it. "Yeah . . . yeah, I'm fine. Sleep'll

definitely help. I'll be my normal, chipper self again in the morning."

"Well, okay then." She sounded less than convinced. "As long as you're sure that's all it is." Then she added, "I'll miss you tonight, Rosk—but you get yourself some rest, okay?"

"That's what I plan on doing."

"Good. You sure you're going to be okay?"

"Yeah, I'm sure," he said. "Oh—" he added, before he hung up, "quick yes-or-no—anyone else happen to disappear over there?"

"Nope."

"Good. That's what I figured. Glad to hear it."

"So am I," she said.

He lit a cigarette and let the afternoon pass, wondering if maybe he shouldn't pick up some more beer on the way home.

Stupid prank or not, Biddle's translation of the tape this morning—even if he didn't know what the hell he was saying—had left Godzilla stuck in Baragon's head. It had been a while—at least a few weeks—since he'd watched any of the Toho masterpieces. Nothing since that bad bootleg of *Gargantuas*. Well, okay, there'd been *H-Man*, too. Put it this way, then: He hadn't seen a real honest-to-goodness bona fide Godzilla movie in far too long. Watching destruction on a mass scale—especially when undertaken by a couple enormous radioactive monsters of some kind (one of whom happens to be Godzilla)—somehow always helped him relax.

After pouring more food into Hedora's dish, making himself a sandwich, and opening a beer, Baragon walked into the front room and blearily scanned the titles in the enormous stack of Toho films atop the television.

He eschewed the classics—*Godzilla, King of the Monsters; Godzilla vs. Mothra; King Kong vs. Godzilla*—choosing instead *Godzilla vs. Megalon*, a feature that was more often than not considered to be one of Toho's worst (at least among those who, sadly, take the time to rate such things). Baragon didn't care to think in terms of "worst" when it came to Toho. He much preferred "least respected" or "grossly underrated" or "most underappreciated." He hadn't seen it since its initial American theatrical release. He had been, embarrassingly enough, fifteen at the time, alone in a theater full of eight-year-olds. He'd felt like a pervert. A pervert and a geek simultaneously. But it was a new Godzilla film, dammit, and there was no question as to whether he'd go. Especially given that it was part of a double bill with *The Giant Spider Invasion.*

He admitted quietly to himself, even back then, that *Godzilla vs. Megalon* perhaps wasn't the most fantastic entry into the series, but it had its moments. When he found it on videotape, he had no choice but to pick it up, if only for completist's sake.

He slid it into the machine, sat down, and took a draw from the beer.

That's right, he thought when the first chase scene rolled around, about ten minutes into the film, *this is the one that was directed by that annoying eight-year-old kid in the short pants and the baseball cap.*

It was doing the trick, though—well, that and the beer. He felt his body shutting down, his eyes slipping out of focus. He'd be surprised if he wasn't asleep before the remote-controlled tanks appeared.

It was only a few minutes later that Baragon had about decided to shut it off for the night and get in the shower. That's when he heard an atrociously dubbed character—one of the baddies—say, "Seatopia! . . . Seatopia!" Then heard another badly dubbed voice reply, "This is Seatopia!"

That almost sounds familiar, he was thinking as he was pushing himself up from the couch. *But it can wait until tomorrow night.*

When he opened his eyes more fully to glance at the screen one last time before shutting it off, he found himself looking at—*Antonio Dunham.*

He shook his head, the way people do in movies when their brains can't register what it is their eyes are seeing. Then he looked again.

"Okay." He sighed aloud. It wasn't Dunham. He was just tired is all, not seeing straight. But, still, it sure was someone who *looked* an awful lot like Dunham. Same mustache, same kinky hair, same fucking *toga* even, for godsakes. Even had the same indeterminate features—though that might have had something to do with the quality of the print. This one was wearing a tiara. He didn't remember Dunham wearing a tiara. Maybe he'd hid it in his desk when Baragon showed up.

This is too weird to let slide.

Instead of shutting the movie off, he hit the rewind button, back to where the baddie was on the radio, and started it again.

"Seatopia! . . . Seatopia!"

That still sounded familiar. And there was the guy impersonating a slumlord again.

Christ. This is too fucking strange.

Then there was an interpretive dance number, featuring a group of Japanese Seatopian women in sheer white dresses and turbans—just like Dunham's secretary, Ms. Hama. Then the Dunham character—turns out he was the king of the Seatopians—an ancient undersea civilization somehow connected with Easter Island—woke up a giant cockroach with drill bits for hands and sent him to the surface to wreak havoc on Tokyo, just like in every other Godz—

Wait.

Seatopians. Isn't that what what's-his-name was talking about? Campbell? The secret war he was involved in was with the Seatopians. That's what he said. Half his family was Soviet, and the other half was—

Baragon wracked his exhausted and only mildly drunken brain. *Shit, why didn't I bring that tape home with me?* Half was Soviet and half was Seatopian something.

South Vietnamese Army—that's what I thought he meant. But he meant Seatopian . . . something . . . Vigilante Army. Not 'Army'—'Action.' That's it—Seatopian Vigilante Action—SVA. S . . . V . . . A.

Baragon felt a shock of recognition and a strange, renewed energy flowing through his body. He wasn't tired anymore. At least he didn't *feel* all that tired. What a fool he'd been! Simon Vaneigm and Associates? They weren't fooling anybody. Not anymore, at least.

And to think he was about to give up on this? When all along the key—the singular, overarching connection he was looking for—was sitting right there, right on top of his fucking television. Thank God something kept bringing him back to this story, whatever it was.

It wasn't just the radioactive man, and Natacia, and SVA. Jesus Christ—this involved Campbell, too? What the fuck was going on?

He hit the rewind button, then went to get the notepad from his coat pocket and a pen from the kitchen table. It looked like it was going to be another long night.

As he settled back down in front of the television, he realized how lucky he'd been. He could have decided to go with *Godzilla vs. the Cosmic Monster* instead.

. . .

He watched the film in its entirety, then rewound it, knowing he'd have to watch it at least one more time, if not more.

There wasn't, he had to admit, very much by way of Seatopian action in the movie. Just that first scene. Most of the rest of the film concerned a tag-team wrestling match involving three giant monsters and one robot (Jet Jaguar) who can become a giant whenever he so chooses. No communists, no SROs, no New York real estate shenanigans, no Alaskans. At the end, even, the leaders of the (surface) world decide to stop undersea nuclear testing in order to allow the Seatopians to live in peace and not send any more havoc-wreaking gigantic cockroaches to Japan. Still, there was no denying that it was a film full of clues.

Shortly before midnight, Baragon had discarded the tiny, useless notepad he'd been using in favor of a legal pad. Hedora had watched him with some curiosity and concern for a while, then curled up in his basket near the window and went to sleep.

By two A.M. here's what Baragon knew for sure:

1. The undersea kingdom of Seatopia rests on the ocean floor just off the eastern coast of Easter Island.
2. Nuclear testing in the South Pacific has really irked the Seatopians.
3. It's also probably left them radioactive, as it has their monsters. (He underlined the word *radioactive* twice.)
4. Abraham Campbell knew of a secret war the United States government fought with Seatopia within the past decade. Talk to him again? Too late?

5. Nick Carter knew of a secret war he himself was fighting with Alaska—one that also apparently involved Seatopians.

6. The second voice on that tape was obviously Seatopian, pretending to be Japanese.

7. Japanese fishing boats are sunk by giant radioactive monsters in virtually every Toho film.

8. Any survivors are left radioactive.

9. Japanese fishing boat sunk off K. Bay by a so-called "submarine." Survivors? Radioactive? Check.

10. Raymond Martin was radioactive.

11. There are earthquakes in virtually every Toho film.

12. Toho's earthquakes almost always portend the arrival of some giant radioactive monster—more often than not, Godzilla.

13. Those simultaneous quakes were unrelated to fault lines.

14. The quakes in Alaska and Hawaii took place along the same longitudinal.

15. The Alaska quake was centered in the very place Nick Carter was calling from—which was obviously under Seatopian control.

16. The whales abandoned Alaska after that first quake. Scared away? By what?

17. The whales in Hawaii—perhaps the whales from Alaska?—are pissed or scared about something and are attacking civilians.

18. Antonio Dunham is the king of the Seatopians.

The list went on for five pages, detailing nearly two hundred known facts (only a couple of them duplicated, and only one involving the need to buy more beer), many of them connected with lines and arrows. The atlas was open on the kitchen table, a ruler marking the page. A pocket calculator lay next to the book, atop a scattered array of sheets torn from the legal pad, each of them covered with numbers; arrows; brief, arcane calculations; and scribblings. The ashtray was overflowing.

All the Seatopians really did in the movie was hijack Jet Jaguar, the robot (in an effort to create an army of robot slave laborers) and unleash Megalon on the surface world—but it was clear there was something else going on. Evidently, whatever accords the governments on the surface had signed with the Seatopians at the end of the picture didn't hold up too long. Baragon added a note in the corner of one of the pages, reminding himself to check on the status of the Nuclear Test Ban Treaty.

Around two-thirty, while Baragon sat at the kitchen table, scribbling furiously, Hedora had clicked into the room. The cat stopped at the foot of the chair in which he was sitting, looked up at him, and asked, "Oahu?" before sliding into a wide yawn.

Baragon stopped writing and glanced curiously down at the cat, who was staring back at him with anxious wide green eyes.

"Yes, of course—" Baragon told the creature. "I'm considering Oahu. It's perhaps the most important geographical focal point here. Everything points toward Oahu. But thank you. I appreciate the help."

The cat, confused, meeped at him and trotted over to the food dish.

Point one-ninety-seven on the pad he was still holding—the final entry, for now—read: *"Despite what some sources may indicate, this does* not *have* nothing *to do with Godzilla. This has* everything *to do with Godzilla."*

. . .

The shrill electronic chirping of a telephone ruptured the darkened silence of the pleasant, inoffensive box of a tract house some seven miles outside of Huntsville, Alabama.

Hoke Slaughter, eyes still closed, rolled toward the nightstand, arm outstretched. He found the water glass and his spectacles before finally slapping against the phone, knocking the receiver loose. Before he got it to his ear, he heard a voice on the other end howling, *"Somethin' scraymin' cross yo' maiiind!"*

He swallowed, tried to open his eyes, but didn't sit up. "Roscoe?" he grunted, "Shit . . . is that you?"

"Greeeeen Sliii-iii-iiime!"

"Yeah, yeah, okay—what, uhh . . . what the hell time is it?" He tried to squint at the clock without bothering with his glasses but—still disoriented—was looking in the wrong direction.

"Good—it *is* you. That would've been real embarrassing if I'd a had a wrong number, huh? Um, I'd guess now it's around four-thirty New York time, whatever time that would make it over by you," Baragon told him. "It doesn't matter. Look—sorry to call so . . . early, late, whatever—but this can't wait—I needed to make sure I caught you away from prying ears. They don't monitor your home phone, do they?"

"Ahh . . . who?"

"*NASA*, ya goof."

What the hell was he talking about?

"No, of course not," Baragon continued before receiving an answer, "—otherwise you never could have called me the other night. Right? Sure."

"Roscoe, are you drunk? 'Cause I'm not—"

"—drunk yet? That's fine. Good. I need you sober right now. Sober as I am. Sharp as a tack. You can get drunk later. Look—I need to know a few things about the BioLab."

"About . . . ?" he mumbled, and nearly hung up the phone. "I'll send you a fucking press release tomorrow, how's that?"

"No—screw that. That won't do. You know as well as I do that those things are for suckers. Nothing but lies. Packs and packs of lies. Look—tell me—I need to know exactly where it went down. *Exactly.*"

Slaughter was in no mood for this. There was a staff meeting the next morning—no, *this* morning—at eight-thirty, and he had to be there.

"The South Pacific, all right?" he said, wanting desperately to get off the line. "Didn't you read the damn—?" then he realized he probably hadn't.

"I need exact coordinates, Hoke. Please. I'm sorry about this—but it's mighty important."

"There are no *exact* coordinates, Roscoe"—he couldn't believe he was doing this—"it broke up on reentry—it was spread out over a, what, two-, three-hundred square kilometer area, if not more."

"As accurate as you *can* then—I mean, *where* in the South Pacific?"

"Jesus, Roscoe—I have a meeting in the morning—" He was beginning to whine.

"Please. I'll owe you."

Slaughter exhaled heavily into the phone, thinking that Baragon already owed him. "Off Chile. A ways. Maybe . . . thirty-five hundred kilometers, roughly. Something like that. There's nothing out there, just empty ocean."

Back in New York, Baragon was scanning a page in the atlas with a magnifying glass. "No, Hoke—" he said, staring at a patch of blue on the page, "that's where you're wrong."

Maybe he couldn't ignore Chile after all.

. . .

"Someone better be dead," Eel O'Neill announced when he picked up the phone at ten after five on Thursday morning. He'd been awake—he just didn't care much for phone calls at this hour. Nothing but bad news.

"Where in the hell is Monster Island?" Baragon demanded without so much as a hello.

"Excuse me?"

"When was the last time you saw *Godzilla vs. Megalon*?"

"It doesn't sound as if anyone's dead," O'Neill surmised, "but someone may well be in the very near future."

"C'mon, Eel—it's important—and there's not much time." There was a desperation and a strain in Baragon's voice O'Neill had never heard before, and he didn't like the sound of it.

"Don't tell me you've been up all night watching *Godzilla vs. Megalon* over and over again." He knew all too well how Baragon operated sometimes.

"That doesn't matter—when was the last time you saw it?"

O'Neill thought back. "Few years at least . . . must've been around the same time I was doing the movie about the man-eating roaches, I'd guess."

"*Creepy-Crawl*? Okay then, that's not too bad. . . . How well do you remember it?"

"I remember that it was pretty fucking awful. Godzilla wins, though, right? Listen, Roscoe," O'Neill adopted a slow, deep, yet nasal voice, "why are you asking me this question?"

Baragon was frustrated. Eel wasn't listening to him. If anyone would understand, Eel would. "Everything I've been telling you about—Alaska, the radioactive guy—the weirdo at the realty office—it's all there—it's *all there* in that movie."

"Like Jet Jaguar?" asked O'Neill. "Is he in your story, too? And do all the monsters in your story communicate via sign language?"

O'Neill waited for the knowing, ironic chuckle that never arrived. He was starting to get worried. Baragon had always been a little off-kilter, but until now he'd always been keenly aware of it. He'd been sounding far too serious about all this crap lately and that was scary. But maybe it was just a joke. Maybe he was just drunk and goofy, toying with him. Trying to set him up.

"You're not listening. Everything just came together. It all makes sense now."

"Yes?" O'Neill asked, deciding to play along. "Continue."

"Barrow, Alaska," Baragon announced, his voice picking up tempo and pitch, "kidnappings, earthquakes, strange whale behavior—one-fifty-seven west longitude."

"Okay?"

"Kaneohe Bay, Oahu. Earthquakes, strange whale behavior. Japanese fishing boat goes down. Helicopters collide. *One-fifty-seven* west longitude. Man in Alaska said it had nothing to do with Godzilla—but why would he say that if it didn't?"

"So . . . you're saying what—that Godzilla sank the boat?"

"Doesn't he always? What the hell else does that sound like?"

"Roscoe—a submarine sunk that boat. An American submarine being piloted by vacationing golfers."

"A submarine being driven by *civilians*, Eel. Get it? They weren't civilians at all—they were SVA. If it really *was* a submarine."

"Roscoe, when was the last time you slept?"

"Listen to me—just listen—Seatopia, according to the movie, is just off the coast of Easter Island."

"And three miles straight down, right? Okay-y . . . ?"

"And where in the fuck do you think the BioLab went

down?" Before giving him a chance to answer, he drove onward. "*Exactly*—just off Easter Island, at one-oh-nine west longitude, twenty-seven south latitude. And what *else* happened there? An earthquake. Same exact time as the others. Are you following me? Are you following the *numbers*?"

"Hey now, Bear—"

"When was the last time you read any Lovecraft? Probably a long time ago, right? It's for geeky teenage boys, right? But did you know that Cthulhu rises from the sea at one-two-six west longitude, forty-seven latitude? It's in there, Eel. In black and white. Add it up—Barrow, Alaska's at seventy-one north latitude. Kaneohe Bay's at twenty-one north latitude—"

"Jesus, Roscoe—stop. I keep waiting for you to laugh—and not a scary, creepy laugh, either."

"The numbers are all there—New York at seventy-three west longitude, forty north latitude. This is why I need to know where Monster Island is."

"I don't *know* where Monster Island is," O'Neill said. "You're obviously the man with the atlas sitting right there—just look in the index under 'M.'"

"This isn't a fucking joke, Eel—it's down there somewhere, you know that. Besides, I already checked, and it's not *in* the atlas. Y'know what was on the BioLab? I ever tell you that?"

"I think, uh. I—"

"*We don't know.* We just don't know. Something alive, though—something that went wrong. An experiment, some sort of virus. Like the Green Slime. And now it's in *their* hands. You wonder why people are disappearing? Becoming radioactive?"

O'Neill finally broke in. "Roscoe, you got yourself another snootful of crank, didn't you? I thought you swore off that stuff ten years ago. You're getting old—and you're fat. I hate to say it, but you are. That shit'll stop your heart—"

"This has nothing to do with drugs, Eel. It's nothing but facts. They've been all around us, they've all been adding up, and no one else has seen it. I didn't really even see it myself until I watched that movie tonight—there's been a covert operation under way that they undertook within the past decade to—"

"Roscoe—" O'Neill broke in again, trying to remain patient. "Roscoe, listen to me—*Godzilla vs. Megalon* is not— I repeat, *not*—a documentary."

"You don't know that. It's been waiting. Or rather, *they've* been waiting."

O'Neill sighed again. "Bear, hey—this is me talking now, okay? If you're going to base some stupid conspiracy theory on a Japanese monster movie, why couldn't you at least choose one with good villains? Like *Monster Zero*, or *King Kong Escapes?* The evil scientist in that one was pretty cool. Not some dork in a tiara."

"This isn't a fucking joke, Eel—I keep telling you that— and besides, there are parallels to *King Kong Escapes*. Don't think I haven't considered it. The whole robot slave labor angle. But it's not the same. This isn't the work of one mad scientist—this is an entire army, working right under our noses."

This had gone far enough. "And nobody knows about it but you, right? Look—" O'Neill said, "I think maybe I should give Em a call, have her come over there. Keep an eye on you, calm you down. . . . You're just not making any sense—"

"*No*—" Baragon snapped, "I'm *fine*. Besides—I don't know if she knows too much or too little. When I met with the king of the Seatopians in his office, he kept saying 'the gods,' you know? Just like that—but which gods? Then Emily was saying it that very night? Coincidence? How likely is *that*, given that the Seatopians own the morgue?"

"Hey, Roscoe, c'mon—you're just not making any sense. You're out of control."

"—Here's another thing—did I mention the earthquake in Chile?"

O'Neill was weary, and what he was hearing saddened him. "Christ, Bear . . ."

"And the plumbing—why the big deal with the plumbing? Martin—the radioactive man?—why was he stealing all the pipes and toilets? Simple—because they're an *aquatic* people. That's why the goddamn office was so humid—they had to arrange to keep the atmosphere as damp as possible. Obviously, that's the only way they can function up here."

"You want me to come over there?"

"*No*—" he barked again. "Why aren't you listening to me? Easter Island is bordered by three volcanoes—it's farther from any continental shore than any other island in the world—and why? Because they want it that way—so they can devise their nefarious plots in secret! Like the Green Slime they've got now!"

"Nefarious—?"

"And one-five-seven also passes through Dehpehk—a tiny island off the coast of Pohnpei—"

"Pompeii?"

"No, but that makes sense, doesn't it? Throw off the unwary? No—it's the capital of Micronesia."

O'Neill sighed heavily. "Roscoe . . . I think I've about had enough for tonight, okay? You need to get some rest. Put the atlas away, go to bed, and stay there for a while. A day or two. And if you have to watch a movie, watch something gentle and quiet. Watch a screwball comedy or something. Maybe *Charlie the Lonesome Cougar.* That's a good one. No more monsters for you. Not until you get hold of yourself."

Baragon shook his head. "Can't afford to. We don't know how much time we have. I've been thinking about this, and it suddenly came to me in a flash about three this morning—"

"Is that when you finished the bag?" O'Neill thought aloud, but Baragon went on as if he hadn't heard him.

"The Seatopians have obviously established a strong foothold in New York. But why? Why does SVA own so much property? All those flophouses and the morgue? They're making room, you see? They created all these diversions on the other side of the world—and it almost worked on me, see? But it's *New York* that they want. Then everyplace else. You take control of New York first and everywhere else'll be a snap. Unless they're everyplace else *already.* Hawaii, Alaska. That guy in Barrow wasn't kidding. They can make people *disappear.* It's a fucking silent invasion. And I have no clue as to how to call Godzilla—or even if I should, or what the hell needs to be done. I mean, sure, if it were Mothra I was after, all I'd need to do is find those two tiny Japanese chicks—the Peanuts—"

"I think I dated them once," O'Neill said quietly, hoping Baragon wouldn't notice. He'd about given up trying to get through to him.

". . . But Godzilla always seems to know where to show up, right? Most of the time. Maybe if I can get it all into the paper, get it all down before they know that I know . . . I mean, why steal a robot, right? Why go to the trouble of stealing a robot to use as a prototype to build more robots for—for *slave* labor when you can get all the radioactive corpses you want right here? People nobody would miss, see? Don't have to worry about keeping spare parts handy—

You don't hear anything about *famous* people disappearing, do you? No rich people or movie stars or musical, umm . . . musician . . . people. And why? I'll *tell* you why—because those people would be missed. People would be out *looking* for them. These people—the bums, these old people, junkies? Nobody cares. They're killed, strangled to death, and the police won't even investigate it—it's a perfect plan—use 'em and throw 'em away like disposable razor blades—"

"*Stop!*" O'Neill erupted. "*The Seatopians—aren't—real. Godzilla—isn't—real.* They are both—are you listening to me?—they are both copyrighted creations whose names and images are owned by Toho Company, Ltd."

Baragon clucked a patronizing tongue. "You, Eel, of all people, should know better than that. We've had this discussion before. How do we know, really, that there aren't supervillains out there, blackmailing world governments left and right, the fate of the world dangling by a thread, until they're thwarted at the last possible minute by some James Bond–like super spy? We'd never know about it. Never read about it in the newspapers. I know that. It could be happening every day."

"And you're the James Bond who's gonna save the world this time? Bear, look, I love you like a brother, but that idea doesn't exactly fill me with comfort."

"That's not what I'm saying, but somebody has to—"

"Roscoe, Jesus—think about what you're saying for a second—if a five-hundred-foot-tall radioactive lizard stomped through Tokyo on a fairly regular basis—or even once?—I think we'd read about it in the papers."

"Don't be a sap—I've told you what the first law of journalism is."

"Sure—but you just made that up after Montgomery killed five of your stories in a row."

"Case in point—why were they killed?"

"Roscoe?" Eel's frustration had finally forced him into brutal honesty. "Maybe some stories don't run because they're wrong and stupid and *untrue*."

Baragon was silent.

Chapter Twelve

Baragon laughed—perhaps a tad maniacally—but wasn't the least surprised when he stumbled across the story during his regular cursory glance through the news wires shortly after arriving at the office.

Thurs., March 29
NO GODZILLA ON JAPANESE TV

TOKYO—a Japanese TV station Tuesday postponed airing a Godzilla movie on fears that scenes of the monster attacking fishing boats could remind people of a U.S. submarine's recent collision with a Japanese trawler off Hawaii.

Tokyo Television Network Corp. (TTV) had planned to broadcast the movie on March 31, a company spokeswoman said Wednesday.

But TTV postponed the airing indefinitely out of sensitivity to victims of the March 23 tragedy, in which the USS *Aaron Burr* nuclear submarine collided with and sank the *Gaira*, a Japanese fishing trawler, leaving nearly 30 people drowned or presumed drowned.

In the opening of the film, the monster Godzilla emerges from the ocean to attack and sink Japanese fishing boats in rough seas.

The accident has strained U.S.-Japanese ties while heaping pressure on already unpopular Prime Minister Hiro Yamamoto for his seemingly nonchalant reaction to the tragedy, adding fuel to rising demands for his resignation.

"Hey, maybe it was Godzilla!" he had chuckled to several reporters when initially presented with the news.

So it really is happening—now the blackout begins, Baragon thought to himself. *I guess we'll have to see about that.*

"Who's wacky now?" he asked aloud, to the otherwise empty office.

Not only had Baragon not slept at all in two days, he hadn't changed his clothes in two days, either, putting the same stained blue shirt and underwear and black pants back on after he'd showered. The stench of mingled sweat and smoke now hovered around him like a pale green aura. He didn't much care. The important question facing him now was, knowing what he knew, how did he put a stop to it?

Even more important than that—did he want to? That's the one thing none of the paranoids he'd interviewed had ever admitted. Oh, all the conspiracies were evil and horrible and terrifying, yes—but where would they be without them? There had to be a certain tingle of superiority in knowing you were the only person in the world who really knew what the score was. Conspiracies, moreover, also help make the normal redundancies of life a little more bearable. More than bearable even—they made things exciting. It was pretty seductive, leaving the world of stubbed toes and clipped coupons and phone bills in order to enter the world of spies and evil scientists and monsters. In short, stepping into the movies. Without their fears, what would these people do all day?

Of course, difference here was, everything he was finding was real.

Baragon was one of those kids who, growing up when he did, always kind of ached for a nuclear war—or, as he thought of it, "the world's greatest fireworks display." He didn't tell too many people about that, though.

Since then, given some of the things he'd witnessed in his travels, he knew better than to hope for such things. But again, this? This was different somehow.

It would be kind of neat to see Godzilla, he thought, leaning back in his chair, weighing his options. *Then again, if I were to kill that sleazy slumlord, thus revealing him to be, in reality, the king of the Seatopians, well—*

The phone rang.

He heaved himself forward with some effort and grabbed the receiver. It wasn't even eight o'clock yet.

"Baragon?" he said hesitantly, unsure who would be calling him at this hour.

"Hey, you," Emily said. She sounded worried.

"Uh-huh." Baragon still wasn't sure what the deal was with her. He wasn't even sure anymore how much he could trust the reports she'd slipped him. Maybe it was all part of some scheme to throw him off the scent—or draw him into a trap he could never escape.

"Rosk—c'mon—what's going on? I didn't hear from you all last night, then I get this call from Eel. He was scared to death—which is something new for him. He said you were out of control."

He shrugged. "Do I sound out of control to you?"

There was a moment of silence. "Well, no—not exactly. But something sounds weird."

"I wouldn't call it weird."

"Well then, Rosk—what *would* you call it? Eel said—"

"—Okay." Baragon cut her off. "Maybe I shouldn't have called Eel when I did. I was in a bit of a state. I didn't really know if I was right or not at the time and was a little excited. But now—now I know I am right. So I'm okay."

"Right? About what? He said you were listing numbers—"

"Coordinates," he corrected.

"Coordinates, whatever—he said you were sounding like one of those crazy flyers you see tacked up around the East Village."

"It was late," he started. "I wasn't able to sleep, so I put in a movie I hadn't seen since I was fifteen. I was excited about it is all. I'm sorry if I scared him—I thought he'd understand." He paused. "But I guess nobody much likes hearing the phone ring at five in the morning."

He could hear her relax. "Yeah, that's true, I guess."

"So don't worry—everything's fine." It was true, too—an inexplicable, eerie calm had settled into him.

"I'm glad to hear that."

"You still at home?" he asked as he quietly began opening files on his computer.

"Yeah," she said. "I'm about to get myself together and go in to the lab—but I thought I'd call you first. After hearing from Eel, I was worried—and you know, if you needed me, I'd be there in a second."

"I know you would," he told her, "and I appreciate that. But I'm doing fine. In fact—I should probably get back to work. I need to catch up here before Ed cans me. These days, I'm guessing I don't need to give him too much more of an excuse."

He lit a cigarette while staring at the screen, not bothering to notice that his ashtray was missing.

Half an hour later, he had combined all the relevant files—Natacia, Col. Heg, SVA, Hawaii, earthquakes, radioactive man, BioLab, Abe Campbell—into one. To those files he added the notes he had written the previous night, reevaluating and editing the What Is Known for Sure list as he went.

Now he was carefully poring over the rather overwhelming avalanche of data, rearranging things into as coherent a form as he could figure right then.

The one question that still kept nagging at him was this: Why was SVA in New York when all these other obviously related events were taking place along a comparatively narrow vertical band almost a third of a world away? He'd been so certain of it a few hours ago, but now, looking through everything he had, he wasn't sure. Was it, as he'd first suspected, nothing more than a diversionary tactic? Or was there something else going on? Maybe their foothold in New York was solid enough already that they could afford to begin establishing their surface presence elsewhere—slowly occupying all that empty space between Easter Island and the city.

Baragon knocked on Montgomery's door and stuck his head in. "Hey, Ed."

"What is it, Baragon?" He was flipping through that morning's edition of the *Sentinel* and didn't look up. His voice was, oddly enough, both harried and bored.

"Just letting you know I'm stepping out—I have to go and do some research in Brooklyn Heights. Talk to a couple people. I should be turning something in to you tomorrow if all goes well."

Unless, he thought, *I'm required to fly off to the South Pacific to save the world.*

"Yeah, whatever . . . whatever, Roscoe," Montgomery replied, voice unchanged.

"Okay then," Baragon said, turning to leave.

"Oh—Roscoe, by the way—" Montgomery stopped him. "That earthquake follow-up? I had to hold it—there wasn't really anything new there."

"Eh, that's okay, Ed," Baragon told him, smiling slightly. "Just chuck it, I don't care. I'll have something new for you tomorrow."

"Something I can use?"

"Oh, yeah—I think you'll be able to use this one." It's not every day a newspaper can warn people beforehand that Godzilla's on his way to save us all from an evil undersea race. Or something.

"And Roscoe?"

"Yeah, Chief." He was getting a little impatient now.

"If you're going to be talking with any real, y'know—human beings today?"

"Uh-huh?"

"You might want to change your shirt."

Baragon looked down at what he was wearing, which didn't seem all that bad to him. He shrugged slightly. "Maybe I'll just keep my coat buttoned."

"Yeah, you do that."

Before descending the stairs to the subway platform, Baragon stopped at the video closeout store two blocks from his office. He tried to make a point of stopping there at least once a week to check on the new inventory and to see if anything he needed had been unearthed. This was one of the few places in New York that recognized Baragon as a good customer. Still made him pay full price, though.

Most all their tapes were priced under six bucks—and while most of the stock consisted of movies released within the last ten years (thus making them useless to him), he rarely walked out of there with fewer than five new tapes. The Sci Fi/Horror section was especially rich.

He wasn't here to simply browse today, though, see what struck his fancy. He was doing research. If the atlas wasn't able to tell him exactly where Monster Island was, and if Eel wasn't able to tell him, either, he knew the exact location had to be in one of the movies, someplace. Buried some-where in one of the few he didn't already have. Maybe *Godzilla on Monster Island*—he didn't have that one. If his guess was right, it would be somewhere along one-five-seven, maybe a bit south of Dehpehk. He gave a small wave to Akhmed and Abdul behind the counter, skipped the new release tables (which, to be honest, hadn't featured anything new in seven months), and headed straight to the horror section. There, when he was in the mood, he could always count on finding a good selection of Toho releases. They even maintained a special Giant Monsters bin.

Today, however, the bin was empty.

That isn't right, Baragon thought, his eyes scanning the nearby bins in panic, wondering if some inconsiderate cus-tomer had merely misplaced them. *This bin is never empty.*

No, there was nothing. Nothing at all. Except for *Gorgo*—but that didn't count. That was nothing but a British rip-off.

This isn't right at all.

"Hey—" said Baragon, returning to the elevated front counter. "Where's all the Godzilla?"

"G'zilla, boss?" Akhmed asked.

"Yeah—you always had a bunch in the monster section."

"G'zilla, g'zilla . . ." he muttered, trying to recall. Then his eyes brightened, and he smiled, straightening his back and putting his arms in front of him. "Oh! You mean—" he rocked back and forth, "*Errrrrrr . . . !*"

Baragon nodded, "Yeah—that's it. Where'd it all go?"

The Iranian proprietor looked over Baragon's shoulder toward the empty bin and said, "Funny man. Funny man come in this week an' buy it all."

Baragon squinted at him. "Funny . . . how so?"

"Dress funny, Chief," he explained. "In a dress, you know what I mean? A white dress."

He was sitting on the Brooklyn-bound train quietly, still stunned. His head was spinning with the horrifying implications, but he kept his eyes on the floor, trying not to look at anyone around him. He heard a woman's voice to his right say, "I know you."

"No you don't," he replied, not bothering to look at her. For his money, anybody who claimed to know him didn't.

"Ja, I sink I do," the voice persisted.

"Trust me on this one," he said, finally looking up, "I'm—"

He found himself staring at a tiny, unsmiling, bird-faced woman.

"Aww, *shit.*"

"You are very inconsiderate," she told him. "Best apfel-küchen in ze whole of New York, and you spit on it. Und me as vell."

"Look, lady, like I said—"

"You owe me an apology."

"Lady, I do *not* owe you an apology—please, this is a very bad time—"

"Vat is wrong vis my apfelküchen for you?"

"If I give you something nice, will you go away?" *Jesus*

Christ, I don't need this. "Please, there's nothing *wrong* with your apfelküchen. Tell you what—I promise that sometime soon, I will come back to Gottfried's, okay? And I will try your glorious apfelküchen. Fair enough? Two pieces, even."

She didn't smile but seemed satisfied by this. Baragon was relieved that she didn't happen to be carrying a piece on her. At the next stop, he pretended to get off the train but only scooted down to the next car, checking to make sure she wasn't following him.

Christ. Maybe we'll all get lucky and the world'll end in a few weeks.

Chapter Thirteen

By the time he reached Brooklyn Heights, a heavy cloud cover had moved in, and a light rain was beginning to fall.

Probably makes it easier for them to function outside, he thought shrewdly, gazing up at the clouds. *Seatopian bastards probably love the rain.*

He punched SVA's buzzer and waited.

"Yes?" Ms. Hama's voice chirped.

"Uhh . . . hello there, Ms. Hama," said Baragon, who spent most of his life on telephones but really hated talking to people through intercoms. "It's Roscoe Baragon again. I . . . uh . . . stopped by earlier this week?"

"Of course, Mr. Baragon—what can I do for you?"

"I was—was wondering if I might be able to speak with Mr. Dunham—very briefly?"

"Oh, I'm sorry," Ms. Hama said. "He's out of town today."

Aha, he thought, *undoubtedly out of town watching my goddamned Godzilla movies.*

"Mr. Vaneigm, then? Is he available?" He was rocking

from foot to foot, hands balled up tight in his deep coat pockets.

"No, I'm sorry—I'm afraid Stanley's out of town, too."

Stanley?

Baragon sniffed. "Hmm—well—might I be able to come in for a second anyway? It's really starting to rain out here." That wasn't exactly true but was worth a shot. He knew they had no windows.

"As you know, Mr. Baragon," the voice replied calmly through the box, "this office is no place to try to dry off."

That I do know, indeed, yes, he thought.

"I won't stay but a minute," he promised. He crossed his fingers and waited for the buzz and click. When it came, he stepped inside, grabbing for the inner door before she could change her mind.

It was all working out surprisingly well, Baragon thought. Receptionists, in general, not only know everything there is to know about the companies they work for—but they also tend to harbor a deep-seated resentment toward said company, which makes them more prone to spilling their guts to strange, overweight, balding newspapermen.

The SVA office was unchanged, which was a relief. Had he stepped through that door to find air-conditioning, hardwood floors, a goldfish bowl, and Ms. Hama wearing a beige pantsuit, Baragon might well have wept. But no—it was still rank and humid, alien fish still drifting in the wall behind the desk, and Ms. Hama still wearing her formal toga.

"Thanks so much for letting me come in," he said, closing the door behind him. "Woo! What a storm outside!"

"You don't look very wet," Ms. Hama noticed.

"Ah, well, I guess the wind is whipping up pretty good, too," he said as he slid out of his coat to reveal the already sweat-stained shirt underneath.

"I see. Now, Mr. Baragon—I'm very sorry neither Mr. Dunham nor Mr. Vaneigm is here to see you today— perhaps if you had called first you could have saved yourself a trip."

"No, no, no—don't worry about it," Baragon told her with a dismissive wave of his hand. "I was in the neighborhood, remembered I had a few follow-up questions and, well—here I am."

"Yes, here you are." She didn't seem tickled to see him.

That's good, he noted. *More likely to slip up that way.*

"In fact," he said, reaching for the notepad, "it really was such a minor few things—you might well be able to answer them for me. That way I won't have to bother any of you again. Did I—y'know—catch you right in the middle of everything?"

"I am expecting—"

"Just a quick second," he said, flashing a smile that, ten years ago, might have been considered charming.

"What." It wasn't a question so much as it was a starter's pistol.

"Okay," he said, flipping through the notepad that, had she looked, she would have seen bore no questions. "When was SVA founded?"

"Here in New York?"

Aha. "Yeah—for starters."

"Seven years ago next month."

"Great." He jotted that down. "Now . . . you seemed to imply there that you have other offices elsewhere?" he asked as nonchalantly as possible.

"Oh," she said, smiling for the first time since his arrival. "This is the home office, but we have other offices all over the world. I am sometimes very amazed by the number of places SVA is operating."

I bet you are. "Like—where else, for instance, if I may ask?"

"Oh my—we have offices in Florida and California and Chicago. . . ." She looked toward the ceiling as she thought. "Rome. Ahh, Hawaii—we have an office in Hawaii. Several in Europe, in South America. . . ."

"Alaska?" Baragon asked—though he hoped it didn't come out as pointed as it was sounding in his head.

"Alaska . . . ?" she seemed unsure. "I don't think so, no—but you know, Mr. Baragon, I wouldn't be surprised if we did." She smiled again.

He smiled back and pretended to make another note. "Yes, very good, uh-huh. And . . . do you know exactly where in South America?"

Her eyes darted to the right as she tried to recall. "Ummm . . . I know we have one in Brazil and . . . in Argentina . . . and—"

"*Chile?*" he erupted. Her eyes snapped forward again. She looked worried, perhaps wondering for the first time how wise it was to let him into the office.

"Sorry," he muttered, trying to cover up. "Um . . . I just had a little muscle spasm there. . . . Those certainly are some funny-lookin' fish."

"Indeed," she said, nodding slightly.

"Now, er, being the receptionist, I bet you hear everything that goes on here, don't you."

She looked puzzled, clearly not much liking where this was headed.

"Do your bosses do a lot of talking about plumbing?"

She shook her head. "Nothing . . . inordinate," she said. "They deal with many contractors."

"Uh-huh? That's very interesting. Contractors, huh? Say . . . among all the contractors they deal with, do you know if any of them happen to specialize in . . . *radiation* detectors?"

Ms. Hama was clearly uncomfortable now, and Baragon

was growing more agitated, pacing around the small office. She glanced over her shoulder, but the fish weren't going to help her. Not yet, anyway. "Mr. Baragon—I believe I should get back to work. I'm sure the rain has let up by now—"

"Yeah," he spat. "I'm sure it has. But you can never tell with rain, can you? Just one more question, Ms. Hama—no, two—aww, hell, maybe more."

"Mr. Baragon, please, really—"

"Does the name Martin mean anything to you? You ever hear them talking about Raymond Martin?"

"I—I don't think—"

"Nick Carter? *Abe Campbell?* Ever hear of them?"

Her mouth opened, but she made only a small noise, trying to keep her eyes on Baragon, calculating his next move as well as her own.

He took a step closer to her desk and gave her another smile. "What does SRO stand for?"

"I'm sorry?"

"You know—SRO hotels. I should know this, and I did at one time—but I just can't seem to find it in my notes." He held up the pad for emphasis.

The fear in her eyes melted into a deeper bewilderment. "Ahh . . . single . . . room . . . occupancy . . . ?" She said it as if she were answering a question on a quiz show.

"Uh-huh." Baragon nodded, jotting something down. "Are you sure it doesn't really stand for *Seatopian Replacement Occupation?*"

"Sea . . ." The fear was back again.

"And SVA—it doesn't *really* stand for Simon or Stanley Vaneigm and Associates, at all, does it? *Does it*—?!"

"Please don't hurt me—" she whimpered, tears beginning to well up in her eyes. "Please—just go away—"

"What do they have in *mind*, Ms. Hama? Your bosses, the *Seatopians?*"

"I . . . I don't know what you're saying—"

"Oh, come off it, Ms. Hama. Even if you aren't one yourself, you know what goes on here—Does one-five-seven west longitude mean anything to you? Huh?"

She was desperately stabbing an index finger at the telephone keypad. The hand that held the receiver was shaking.

"Ahh, I see," Baragon announced, "—calling your Seatopian buddies, eh? I know how you people work." He began slipping his arms into the sleeves of his coat. "That's okay; you can stop. I'll be leaving now. I have all that I need here. But when they get back from Easter Island, or Barrow, or wherever the *fuck* it is they are right now, watching *my movies*—you let them know that Roscoe Baragon is on to them." He reached for the doorknob. "I'm three steps ahead, and there's no stopping me. I just hope I'm around to see the looks on their faces when *Godzilla* shows up!"

He slammed the door behind him and stomped toward the steps. Then he paused a moment, thinking. He looked back over his shoulder at the office door.

Instead of sitting at the bar, Baragon took a small table near the back of Jack's that night. He'd stopped at the library after leaving the SVA offices and was now surrounded by stacks of photocopies. He was in the midst of making a series of tiny, mathematical notations on the borders of one of them when Emily walked through the front door, Eel closely in tow. Eel was a tall, stout man, wearing an expensive black leather jacket over a white T-shirt. From the looks of him, he was either the director of independent horror films or a gynecologist who was slumming it for the night. In Eel's case, it might've been a bit of both.

Baragon looked up when they stopped by the table.

"Oh—hi," he said. "Em, please sit—" he reached out and

squeezed her hand. "Eel, always a pleasure—I thought you were editing all day today."

"I was planning to," he said as he pulled a chair out and sat down. Emily did the same. "But Em thought it might be good if we both came to see you tonight."

"Yes, wonderful, great," Baragon said. "I'm glad you're both here, actually. It's the damnedest thing. Okay—Eel, remember what I was telling you last night?"

Emily and Eel glanced at each other nervously. "Uhh . . . yeah?"

"Well, after paying a little visit to Seatopian headquarters this afternoon, I stopped by the library to do a little more research."

"Seatopian headquarters?" Emily asked.

"Togas," Eel whispered to her.

"In Brooklyn Heights, yes," Baragon continued. "SVA Realty, they're calling themselves. I told you about them. The people in the togas, right—the ones who own the morgue? I was so blind the first time I was there. Anyway— one-five-seven west longitude? Remember that? Well, I'll have you know that line *also* happens to denote the eastern border of groundfishing territory in the Gulf of Alaska."

He looked from one to the other, waiting for their response. They only stared back at him blankly.

"Yeah, I was pretty astonished, too, when I first discovered that. The earthquake? The whales? Makes sense now, right? Now, over here"—he began to shuffle through a stack of photocopied nautical maps—"I'll show you—"

"Roscoe?" Emily said softly, reaching over and placing a hand on his arm. "Please stop."

He froze and looked at her. "Oh. Okay. Wait—you need beers—I'm sorry—"

"I got it," Eel said, standing.

Baragon glanced around at all the papers, wondering

why these two weren't nearly as excited about this as they should be.

"Roscoe, what the hell is going on?"

He looked at Eel, standing by the bar. "How much did he tell you?"

"Enough."

"I don't know what that is—what that means—because I don't know enough yet myself. I know where they are and roughly how they're operating—but I don't have all the details yet. It's got to be something big." He squinted at her. "You might know more than I do. Probably. Disappearing radioactive men, right? Gathering a radioactive slave army? I'm not stupid. I caught that 'the gods' slip. And BioLab—"

Emily glanced quickly toward the bar. Eel, thank the gods, was on his way back with the beers.

"And how do I know that you're not radioactive yourself? I don't have a Geiger counter on me—do you?"

"This is what I was talking about," Eel said as he sat down with three pints.

"You seemed so calm this morning," she told Baragon.

"Oh, and I was—but the more I uncover, the more I realize that time is short. It's looking like I'm going to be up another night as it is. I have to start getting it all into some coherent form."

"Wow, good luck with that." Eel snorted, then turned to Emily. "Do you have any idea where he might have gotten himself a batch of bad crank?"

She shook her head. "He would've told me if he'd done that."

"No need to talk about me in the third person," Baragon interjected. "I'm right here."

"Oh, Rosk," Emily said, slouching. "I'm so sorry I ever told you about that guy. And that I encouraged you the way I did. I thought I was helping, that it would get you out of your slump. All that happened is that I got bawled out, and you got . . ." her voice trailed off.

"What? Crazy?" he asked, his eyes aflame, "I'm not crazy. This is all *real*. That's the difference. I'm not saying I have an FBI tracking device shoved up my ass."

"No," Eel observed, "not yet. All you're saying is that a bunch of people you saw in a monster movie are real and are trying to take over the world. Oh—and that Godzilla's coming to save us all."

"That depends," said Baragon.

"On what?"

"Well, on whether it turns out to be the good Godzilla or the bad Godzilla. You usually don't know until it's almost all over. You should know that."

Eel put his face in his hands and shook his head.

"But Godzilla's . . . a fictional character," Emily said, trying to be understanding here. "It's just some guy in a big rubber suit."

"Don't even get him started on that one," Eel said, his voice muffled, as he hadn't yet moved his hands. "Hey, Roscoe—I'm surprised you haven't connected mosquito spraying to this yet. Maybe the Seatopians are behind that, too—didn't you report once that the spraying was some kind of eugenics experiment funded by the Rockefellers?"

"Someone else said that. I just reported it. Completely unrelated, so far as I know at this point. As things stand, here's the deal. It was all still a blur when I talked to you last night. I'm sorry, but I'm starting to sort it out. Okay, so, a secret treaty was signed with the Seatopians some thirty, thirty-five years ago, right? We apparently broke that treaty. As a result, they're retaliating. Up until now, however, they haven't resorted to using any giant monsters. No, uh-uh— they've been plenty quiet about it—*very* subtle—buying up real estate, making people disappear, screwing with the whales. All those earthquakes may be the result of mining operations, where they're forcing slave labor—like Raymond Martin and Natacia—to do the digging for them. All that exposure to a radioactive race has obviously left these slaves radioactive themselves—*unless* it comes from what they're digging up. Element X, perhaps? Wouldn't surprise me one bit."

"Oh, Christ."

"Then the BioLab gets pulled down. What's on it? Some sort of mutant. That's their next step. Get rid of us that way. My guess is that's where your giant monster is coming from."

"Yeah, I was wondering about that," Eel said. "'Cause to be honest, I can't think of a single instance in which Godzilla shows up just to stop some evil real estate developers."

"Oh, no, no, no," Baragon corrected him. "That's where you're very wrong, my friend. . . ."

They argued, they drank, but Eel and Emily were able to make no headway with Baragon, who maintained his position that, among other things, the Seatopians obviously had made inroads into city government, which allowed them to do things like purchase the medical examiner's office and dozens of other properties, where they would be free to carry out their fiendish experiments on us land dwellers. That would also help explain why the mayor's people—who arrived on the scene first—spent so much time hanging around the morgue after Martin was discovered. And what did we know about the mayor himself, really?

"There's no getting around it," he said after he had laid it all out as neatly as he could. "Everything fits."

"Roscoe," Eel told him, "everything fits because you *decided* that everything would fit. You come across something that doesn't fit, you ignore it."

"Those things had no effect on the things that do fit. They were irrelevant."

It seemed hopeless. "By 'those things,' do you mean logic? You keep talking about the first—well, *your* first—rule of journalism," Eel said as it crept past one A.M., "but what about the second?"

"Everyone's a liar," Baragon recited.

"Exactly."

"What of it? It's still true—that's just the point, can't you see? Nobody told me these things. These are all things I've had to find by myself. Nobody came to me with these connections. I saw them myself. Solid documentation. It's all right here." He patted the stack of photocopies. "And when I told people about them, everyone had a perfectly logical explanation to offer, trying to dissuade me. Telling me that I'm wrong in all this. Neat as can be little answers. *Too* neat, if you ask me."

"Okay then," Eel went on, knowing he could outwit him somehow. "Aren't you the one who also told me a couple years ago that most conspiracies can be dismissed with a perfectly simple, clear, and rational explanation, like—didn't you once say this—'the stupidity and thickheadedness of the conspiracy theorist in question'?"

Baragon started to say something, started to protest—he could, you know, argue that one right away—but as he looked from Emily, to Eel, then back to Emily, he noticed for the first time how very tired they both looked. And sad. Especially Em. He had to admit, she didn't have too much of the Seatopian about her. Good thing, too—given the way he'd been shooting his mouth off tonight. Giving everything away.

"Jesus," he said finally, looking first at Emily, then down at the table. "I know I might've let this get the better of me. But . . . I just can't help thinking that I'm right about all this. That it needs to be revealed. You must understand that."

He waited for an answer, a reaction of any kind, but received none. They weren't buying it.

"Roscoe?" Em finally ventured. "Are you sure . . . that . . . that all this isn't just your way of reacting against the . . . I don't know what to call it . . . the cruel indifference, maybe, of the way you see people treated in this city? Especially the people you deal with? Like Natacia. You've said before that you're giving these people a voice. But Christ—with this—" Her words trailed off for a moment again. "I guess what I'm trying to say is, bad things happen to people in New York, Roscoe. Bad things happen to people *everywhere*. You can't save them all. People are going to disappear, people are going to turn up dead. And coming up with some crazy movie plot to try to explain it all away, it just isn't . . . ?"

There was a long silence.

"You think that's all it is?" he finally shot back. "That I feel *bad* about the homeless and deranged and all those poor 'lost souls' out there? No. Wrong. You're way off on that one, I'm afraid."

"Yeah?" she replied, growing angry herself. "Then how about this one? Real life *isn't* a movie, Roscoe. I'm sorry. No matter how much you want it to be sometimes. There aren't big plots with clean resolutions. Things are sloppy. Things just happen. And sometimes things that shouldn't happen, happen. There's no changing that."

He recalled what he'd been thinking himself (albeit about other people) earlier that morning. Damn it, anyhow. His exhaustion finally began to catch up with him.

"Okay," he said eventually, feeling outnumbered, if not necessarily defeated. He started to gather his (now mostly beer-soaked) papers together, attempting, in vain, to shake them into a neat pile. "Let's make a deal, all right?"

"We're listening," Eel said.

"I'll shut up now. I'll stop trying to convince you."

"Okay, good. Then what?"

"Then we'll all go home, we'll all get some sleep. Tomorrow, I'm going to go into the office early, and I'm going to start typing this up. I'm still going to write this story because I think it's an important one and it needs to be written. I know you don't agree—and I can respect that, that's fine—but I still think it's a major story. I'll get it turned in. Then maybe I'll get some more sleep. When it's done, I won't say another word about it."

"Sounds good to me," Emily said, relieved. She knew he rarely talked about stories after they'd run. He gets obsessed for a while, then purges himself. This case, though, had been more extreme than most. She wasn't sure he'd be able to drop it as easily as he'd dropped all those others. If this is what he was saying he'd do, though, she had no choice but to accept it and hope for the best.

"Sounds good to me, too," agreed Eel.

"And when the Seatopians unleash the Green Slime, and when Godzilla shows up, you both—*both*—owe me a beer."

"Fair enough," Eel said.

"One thing," added Emily. "What if Ed doesn't run it?"

Baragon smiled. "Oh, don't you worry about that. If any story of mine runs, this one will. I'll make sure of that. Now, if you'll excuse me, I think I'm gonna go piss. Then we'll get the hell out of here." He left his papers in a pile on the table and headed toward the back of the bar.

Once the door closed, Eel looked at Emily.

"Man oh man." She sighed.

"Yeah."

"Thanks for your help, Eel—I—"

"No need," he said, shaking his head. "This is what we do, right? You did a great job, by the way."

"Let's hope so."

. . .

At three-seventeen A.M. EST, those New Yorkers who were awake and paying attention might have noticed a slight trembling underfoot. It was gone quickly, and those few who noticed it at all probably put it down to a passing subway train.

At nearly the same time, maybe a few minutes later, NORAD's array of Early Warning Devices—set up across the Arctic Circle to alert military officials to a (then-) Soviet first-strike attempt—began to register a series of unusual signals.

A cursory analysis determined that it wasn't any sort of missile activity—probably just another minor aftershock in the Gulf of Alaska—there had been hundreds of them since the big quake—so they were ignored. There are other people whose job it is to deal with things like that.

They were mostly right about all that, too.

Nearly three hundred and fifty miles north of the Arctic Circle, and several hundred feet straight down, the floor of the Arctic Ocean was rumbling again—just as it had two weeks earlier. Also, as during that previous event, the water temperature began to rise dramatically—much higher, this time, than it ever had before.

The fissure left in the seabed after the first quake began to widen, this new tremor rending a deep wound in the floor of the ocean. From within it came a glow of intense orange light. Unlike a volcano, however, this was not the glow of magma forced up from the earth's interior. This instead was simply . . . *light*. Pulsing, orange light—accompanied by the sound of a bow slowly being drawn back across the untuned strings of a cello.

Baragon allowed himself an hour's sleep that night, if only because he had promised Emily and Eel that he'd sleep.

He never promised for how long. Nor did he promise it wouldn't be fitful. He got up, showered quickly, and put the same blue shirt back on. He drank a mug of cold coffee, packed up a bag with the atlas, his copy of *Godzilla vs. Megalon*, and all the papers he'd photocopied at the library.

He hit the narrow and broken sidewalk outside his apartment shortly before five, took a quick glance up and down the block for the Apfelküchen Lady, then headed for the train. The sky hadn't yet begun to lighten—and from the feeling of the air, chilly and damp as it was, it wouldn't lighten too much for a couple hours.

He paced the brightly lit platform as he waited for the train to arrive. There were only two other figures down there at that hour, but they kept their distance.

He clicked necessary points off in his head, over and over, rearranging them into sensible order, condensing them as much as he could. It had to be straight, it had to be direct—no speculations. Facts, numbers, quotes. That's what Montgomery wanted, and that's what he would get.

The train arrived, and Baragon took a seat next to the door. For the rest of the trip—about half an hour—he scanned the faces of his fellow passengers, looking for any telltale signs in features or dress. None of them was blatantly Seatopian, but who knew? They were devious creatures. If it weren't for the toga, he'd probably look right over Dunham as well—and he was their damned king.

He skipped the coffee and extra smokes that morning, letting himself into the office and heading straight for his desk. He turned on the computer, emptied the papers from his bag, put his phone on "Do Not Disturb," and began typing.

He began with the discovery of Raymond Martin on March thirteenth, then quickly—but coherently, he thought—spiraled outward from there, to Alaska, Hawaii, Easter Island—then back to Brooklyn Heights and Abe Campbell. Then back out again. Structurally, Baragon felt it was as perfect as anything he'd ever done. A veritable nautilus of words and ideas, it was.

His fingers danced across the keys, trying to keep up with his brain. He'd never been much of a typist, especially considering that was how he made his living, but this morning something had changed. Everything else fell away. He didn't even notice when the youngsters arrived and began yapping amongst themselves. Normally, that would've been distraction enough to make working impossible—but this Friday—traditionally the loudest day of the week in the *Sentinel*'s offices—things were different.

Apart from occasional glances at a photocopy or a quick flip through the legal pad in search of a number, Baragon never looked up, never moved from his chair. He had everything he needed up there. When it came time for fact checking, everything would be right there, in the papers, in the atlas, on the tapes.

In the back of his head, a tiny, relieved voice whispered, *Tonight you will be able to sleep.*

At one fifty-seven that afternoon (*How appropriate,* he thought) it was finished. He checked his spelling, checked his numbers, then read it through two more times.

Yes, it was finished. Everything was there. Everything fit. Everything was airtight. It was a bit long—but for a story like this? It was necessary. By the middle of next week, it would be filling newspapers across the country, it would be the top story on the television every night until the crisis was averted and the Seatopians were on their way back to the bottom of the ocean. And it would all start right here. Screw the Pulitzer—he might get a fucking Nobel for this one. Saving humanity and all.

He still needed a title. It was usually out of his hands, but he could at least provide a suggestion. Something quiet and subtle. If he went too nuts in the title, Montgomery wouldn't even bother reading it. Baragon could accept that before, but this was one Ed had to read. Everything depended on it. Not only his own future in this business, but the future of, well, the whole damned world.

He sat back in his chair and thought about it, toyed with a few possibilities, then leaned forward once more, typing a few words at the top of the piece. He saved it, closed it, copied it to a floppy disk (security reasons—he'd hide that disk in a safe place), then zipped the story to Montgomery's computer electronically.

He inhaled deeply and nearly began weeping softly to himself. Only now was he beginning to recognize how numb he had become. Except for his head—his head was pounding. But it had been worth it—and when the story appeared—not this weekend—nobody read the weekend *Sentinel*—Monday would be much better, yes—when the story appeared on Monday morning, well, he'd be ready. He took his phone off "Do Not Disturb," figuring Ed would be calling him soon.

Then he went out and bought a sandwich.

At seven minutes after three, his phone rang.

"Baragon."

"Roscoe, come down here," Montgomery said. "I'd like to discuss this piece with you." He wasn't yelling; there was no sharpness to his voice. *Hell*, Baragon thought as he hung up the phone and headed toward Ed's office, *he sounded almost human.*

"Hey, Ed," he said brightly as he tapped on the open door, then took a seat across the desk from his editor. "So wha'd ya think?" He tried to control the nervous, proud grin he could feel tugging at his mouth.

"Well, Roscoe, I must say, I always knew you had it in you," Montgomery said, leaning back and locking his fingers behind his skull. "Yessir, you finally proved that you could really do it."

Baragon gave up struggling to control it and let the rare, proud smile bloom across his exhausted features. "Thanks, Ed."

"No, Roscoe, I'm the one who should be thanking you."

Baragon sensed a tiny change of tone but put it down to Montgomery's clear excitement.

"Yessir," Montgomery continued, "I always knew the day would arrive when you'd really come through for me."

"Well, thanks again, Ed—but there's really no reason to go on—" he could almost feel himself blushing, something he hadn't done in nearly twenty years. "Is there anything you think needs revising? I mean, I think it's all there, it's airtight, but still, if—"

"Oh no—" Ed said. "I think it's perfect the way it is. Absolutely perfect."

"Well, great then." Baragon knew he was blushing now and was slightly embarrassed for it.

"Let me ask you something, though."

"Sure, Ed."

"Are you aware that you need help? I mean—do you know that? Serious, *serious* help."

He could feel the blood slipping back out of his face. "Uhh—?"

"You're a sick, sick man, Baragon."

"Ed?"

"*Sick.*"

This wasn't right.

"And the *Sentinel* is not in the business of letting our reporters put their illnesses on parade. Other people's maybe, on occasion, but never their own. In fact, I think most people—including our advertisers—would agree that would be a terribly irresponsible thing to do."

Baragon started to stand, but Montgomery waved him back into the chair.

"No, no, no—sit down. Relax. I've been waiting for this for a long time, Roscoe—and I'm going to savor it. Please let me savor it."

"Ed, I'm not—"

"You're not *anything*, Roscoe. Nothing. Not anymore. 'Nightmare Seatopian Plot Unveiled'? That's some doozy right there, I'll tell you that much. What was it again? Six thousand words?"

"Like I said, Ed, I could trim it—" Baragon interrupted, "—if you give me a chance to—"

"No, uh-uh," Montgomery replied flatly, shaking his head. "No, no, no—for some reason that's beyond me, I gave you chance after chance after chance already—but that's it. That's all. You're gone. You're fired."

"Pardon?"

"No more stories, no more *anything*." Montgomery seemed unusually calm about this whole business. "And believe me, everyone will stand by me on this one. I want you to clean out your desk now—right now—and be out of here this afternoon. That's it. Good-bye. Good luck. I'll write you a letter of recommendation."

Baragon stood, not taking his eyes off his now-former editor. There wasn't the wailing and great gnashing of teeth Montgomery had been expecting, even hoping for. From where Ed sat, Baragon seemed almost dangerously relaxed himself, suddenly. His face wasn't ashen, his knees weren't trembling as he stood. He didn't offer to shake Montgomery's hand, but he stopped at the doorway.

"Know what's kind of funny about this whole business here, Ed?"

Montgomery stared back but said nothing.

"Funny thing about it is, well . . . I guess I've always been wondering what it would take, know what I'm saying? How far I would finally have to push you before you did something . . . Now I guess I know." He shrugged at Montgomery one last time, smiled dimly and briefly, turned and left the office, strolling toward his cluttered desk, feeling lighter somehow.

A now-apprehensive Montgomery immediately picked up the phone and dialed the office manager's extension, telling her to get hold of a locksmith. They'd need some work done by the end of the day.

Back in his office, Baragon said nothing. He scanned his desktop, sorting things out in his head. He'd keep the atlas and a few other books, but that was about it. He trashed all the files on his computer. Wouldn't be needing those anymore. He kept the disk with the Seatopian story on it. You never know who might be interested. One of those places in Florida, maybe.

He decided he'd leave the hand-lettered sign up on the wall. Whoever sat at this desk next might get some use out of it.

Had anyone noticed, they wouldn't have understood—but as he packed his things together, a weakened, bitter smile crept across Roscoe Baragon's face, and he quietly began humming to himself. An old song he'd first heard as a young boy—a sweet Malaysian tune once sung by two tiny women. He knew full well it wouldn't help. Still, he figured, it was worth a shot.

ABOUT THE AUTHOR

Jim Knipfel lives in Brooklyn. That much he knows.

ACKNOWLEDGMENTS

I would like to humbly thank the following people for their help, inspiration, direction, and encouragement:

My agent, Melanie Jackson, and my editor, Marty Asher—without whose wise counsel, hard work, and sense of humor, the impossible would never have happened.

For their continued support, I would also like to thank Ken Siman, David Groff, Ken Swezey and Laura Lindgren, Innes Gumnitsky, Chip Kidd, Derek Davis, Mom and Dad, Mary, Bob, McKenzie and Jordan, and the staff of *NY Press*—most notably John Strausbaugh, Russ Smith, Lisa Kearns, and Russell Christian.

Special thanks are also due Gary Hertz, George Higham, Scott Ferguson, John Graz, Linda Hunsaker, Michael Arrington, Homer Flynn, TRP, d.b.a., Ruby's—and the great Akira Ifukube, for his indispensable soundtrack(s).